# A Day For

# A

# Day

Donna Lee Comer

Dedicated to my oldest sister, Gloria,
whom I miss every day.
She is no longer with us, but
she would say, "You can do
anything, if you just try!"

And to my husband, Bob, for all the
times he read through the
pages and found my mistakes.

And finally to Mona Tippins for her
patience and corrections.

# CHAPTER ONE

Maggie struggled to open her eyes, but the pain was so excruciating she couldn't do it. She tried to remember what happened. In her mind she frantically searched for a rational thought she could hold on to, long enough to try to understand. Finally she pried her lids open and concentrated on driving the pain from her mind. The odor of filth and urine filled her senses and she fought to keep from gagging. The bile rose in her throat and mingled with the already bitter taste on her tongue. and she had to fight to keep from vomiting.

"Where am I?" she whispered aloud. A movement in the corner caught her eye. Her skin crawled when she saw a rat run across the floor. She tried to raise her head, but again the blinding pain stopped her attempt. Slowly she tried to raise her arms to rub her forehead but they wouldn't move. The realization that she was lying on a small bed and her arms were bound to the posts at the head of the bed became all too real. She looked down and saw a sheet draped over her, and felt ropes around her ankles. Maggie began to understand that someone must have brought her to this small room against her will.

Maggie tried to quiet the turmoil inside by taking some deep slow breaths. The last thing she remembered was sitting in her back yard in front of the swing set. She asked aloud, "What day is this? How long have I been here?" The sound of her voice echoed in the small room and the horror spooked her and she thrashed on the bed pulling with all her strength against the ropes. Her wrists started to burn and she whimpered a small cry and fell back on the bed exhausted. An overwhelming fear settled in on her. "Think, think, Maggie," she whispered.

Maggie desperately racked her mind for any memory of how she got in this dirty, damp, small room. She looked around and the only other things in the room were a few shelves, a table in the corner and a bucket sitting on the floor. She twisted her body around, and spotted a small window behind her head.

I remember sitting in my yard around 6:00 in the evening and if the sun is rising, I must have been here all night. As a picture of her daughter's face comes in her mind, she remembered what happened to Sarah. I left her alone and that is why I am here. It was my fault and now my Sarah is gone. My fate is to die here all alone, she thought. "Sarah, please forgive Mommy," she murmured. A buzzing in her head and the foul taste in her mouth takes over her thoughts, and she drifted down into a drug-induced stupor.

A short time passed and again Maggie stirred on the bed. She shook her head back and forth to clear the fog. She jumped when she heard a familiar sound and had a little glimmer of hope when she realized that a vehicle had pulled beside the shed. She started to scream as loud as she could to attract the attention of the driver. "Help me, can you hear me? Please, someone has taken me prisoner. I need help," she yelled. Her throat was on fire but she kept screaming, hoping the person was able to hear her.

Suddenly an awful thought popped into her head and she fell silent. The possibility that the person outside was the one that tied her to this bed, and may be coming back, hit her full force. The panic tripled in her heart and she fought the ropes around her wrists violently trying to free her arms. She knew if he had the wherewithal to overpower her and put her here, he would not care that she had no desire to be here and was scared to death.

Maggie braced herself when she heard the person on the other side of the heavy door, and she muffled a scream when the door swung open. A strange man entered the small room. Maggie had never seen him before.

6

She held her breath and tried not to shake as he approached the side of the bed.

He glanced at her, then turned and walked to the small table in the corner. He had a cooler and after he sat it down, he walked over and touched her arm. Maggie flinched and pulled away, she was more afraid than she had ever been.

He smiled at her and said, "Maggie, I am glad to see you are awake. I wanted to get here earlier, but I had to cover for one of the guys at the plant. His wife went into labor and he asked me to take his place for an hour."

Maggie tried to comprehend what he has said. He knows my name, she thought.

"I had to tie you until I could explain why I brought you here. I just couldn't wait to get here to see you. I hope you are not too angry with me. I had to save you from everyone else. I wanted you to be away from the sorrow I saw on your face every time I watched you on TV. Now, you will be safe with me and I will take good care of you."

Maggie blankly stared at him as her mind tried to understand what he said. "You wanted to save me by taking me prisoner and locking me in this tiny filthy room?" she thought.

He said to her, "I helped search for Sarah and I knew I had to bring you here the first time I saw you. I hated watching you in misery after what happened to your daughter. I wanted you to give me a chance to make it all better, and our life together will be wonderful."

He patted her on the arm and returned to the cooler. "I brought you egg sandwiches. My Mother taught me how to mix the eggs with a little milk so they would be light and fluffy. She used to put onions in with them, but I was afraid your stomach might not handle onions right now.

7

I used wheat bread. I guess you stay so slim by eating the right kind of bread.

I make a special sauce I spread on the toast; all the guys at work love it. Sometimes I make extra for them, if they are nice to me. Now, are you ready to eat?" he asked her.

He brought a sandwich to her and she tried not to move a muscle. He saw her hesitation, calmly laughed, and said, "Oh, I guess you can't eat very well without your hands, can you?"

He reached to untie her hands, and rubbed her wrist where the rope burn made them red. He gently laid each one of her hands beside her on the bed. Maggie tried to raise her head but was instantly sick to her stomach. He knew she was having a hard time and asked her what was wrong.

"I am going to throw up, I have to lie still for a few minutes," she told him.

"Here, let me help you sit up. I guess I used too much of the drugs. I keep practicing with the amount, but it will wear off soon. After you eat you will feel better," he told her.

Maggie used all her strength to sit up in the bed, but her head was still spinning. She had no idea what kind of drug he gave her and her fear intensified at the thought. After he was satisfied she was not going to vomit, he took the sheet off her legs. Maggie was relieved to see that she was still fully dressed. Thank goodness, he had not raped her while she was unconscious.

He untied each leg and helped her swing them over the side of the bed. Maggie felt weak, but she fought with all her might to stay calm. She told him that she needed to go to the bathroom and he went to the corner and uncovered a bucket.

"This is all I have so you have to use it for now. I will go out and let you have privacy. Can you get up?" he asks her.

"Yes, I think I can," Maggie said.

He went out and shut the door and she stood on her feet. The room spun, but she knew he would be coming back shortly. She forced herself to walk to the bucket. She finished and hurried to the bed, sat, and waited.

In a few moments, he came back into the room. "I will help you eat if you need me to. I do not have very long to stay, I have to get some sleep so I can work tonight. I brought you some orange juice to drink. I will leave it in the ice chest for you."

Maggie mumbled, "Thank you. I think I can eat by myself."

"I have a few things to take care of outside so I will let you eat and will come back to check on you before I leave. I am so glad I found you Maggie, I can't wait until we get to know each other and start planning our life together," he told her.

Maggie watched as he went out and closed the door. "What am I going to do? Is he going to hurt me? Did he harm Jim or my family? I am a prisoner and no one knows where I am. How can I survive this? I thought I wanted to die but not like this," she thought to herself. The combination of the drug and her terror caused tremendous pain. She doubled over and gripped her stomach. She did not hear the door open and was surprised when she felt a hand on her shoulder.
"Maggie, are you alright?" he asked her.

"No, I need something, my stomach is killing me," she said to him. A thought came to her mind. "Maybe I can get him to leave to get me some medicine so I can have some time to think." She moaned to convince him that she really was in pain.

"What can I do for you?" he asked.

9

"Could you go and get me some medicine, please. I would appreciate it," Maggie said.

"Of course, I will go right now. It will take me 30 minutes. Is there anything else you need?"

"No, I just need something for my stomach."

Walter started toward the door and assured her that he will not be gone long.

Maggie waited until she heard the car leave and sat up trying to collect herself. She wrapped her arms around herself and swayed from side to side. "Oh, Jim, I am so scared. Please, God help me. I don't know how to handle this, I need your strength and peace with me," she prayed.

# CHAPTER TWO

Maggie lay down on the bed and curled up into a ball after the man who kidnapped her left. The fear in her heart caused her pulse to race and her body to shake. She clasped her hands together to keep them still and practiced a yoga exercise she learned from her fitness team. It helped her to calm down, at least for a few minutes.

Her mind was scrambled and she concentrated on figuring out what she should do while she searched her memory for a picture of her captor's face. He told her he helped with the search for her daughter Sarah, but she could not remember seeing him. Those two weeks were a blur and she finally told herself that after what she went through no one would expect her to remember one face out of all the hundreds of volunteers in the park. He was an average looking man. She had noticed a scar on his right cheek. Nothing else about him would stand out in anyone's memory. He sure did not look like a kidnapper to her.

Maggie went through her options. She had to hurry before he got back. She looked around for something she could use as a weapon, but saw nothing. She could not think straight. She knew that he drugged her and hoped that when the effects wore off, she would be able to concentrate. She finally convinced herself that for her own safety she had to watch everything she said to him. Maggie got a picture of Jim in her head and silently tried to hold onto the image as long as she could. She promised herself that she would make it back home.

She heard the car returning. She sat back on the bed and dreaded to see the door open. The man came in and was so happy he was beaming. He brought a bag to the bed and gave her a bottle of Pepto Bismol. Maggie took it and thanked him and when she got the top off, she drank some.

"I know you are confused, Maggie. I brought you here so I could take care of you. I wanted to protect you and I promise I will keep you safe. Nothing will ever hurt you again. As long as you do as I say, I will not harm you. I hand-picked you, Maggie. We have our whole future to look forward to," he told her.

Maggie tried to keep the shock from showing in her face as she heard the words. "This man wanted to protect me from harm, so he drugged me, brought me to a shed in the middle of nowhere, tied me to a bed, and locked me in. And, I am supposed to feel safe," her mind silently screamed. "I have to do what he says since I really do not know what he is capable of."

Her thoughts are broken when she heard him tell her, "I didn't want to tie you, Maggie, but I didn't know if I could trust you. If you try to trick me, I will know. You have to promise me you will do as I say because I want you to be different from the others. They did not listen to me and I had to hurt them. I know you will be good, right Maggie?"

Maggie looked at him and nodded her head yes, which seemed to please him. He reached to touch her arm. His touch sent chills up her spine and she pulled her arm away. He saw the look of fear on her face and said, "Maggie, don't be afraid of me. I love you."

Maggie's head snapped up, her jaw dropped. It did not seem to faze him in the least.

He continued, "I know the two of us will be so happy together. We have our whole future ahead of us. I am so excited."

He ruffled in the bag again and gave her a hairbrush and a mirror. "I have a surprise for you too. I bought you a new wine colored blouse, and I would love to see you wear it. I thought it would look good and bring out the hazel in your eyes. Your beautiful eyes and the way your lips curl up at the corners drew me to you the first time I saw you. I also got some make-up for you to try out. I want you to look your best when we get married. I will be so proud to have you as my wife. It sure will surprise all the guys at work that I could get a knockout like you. Won't they be so jealous?"

Maggie gritted her teeth and did her best to stay calm. She had to find a way out of this madness.

Maggie said, "If I am to be your wife, shouldn't I know your name?"

He said, "My name is Walter. Walter Mills, and soon you will be Mrs. Walter Mills."

Maggie thought and wanted to say aloud, "Who in the heck is Walter Mills? What makes you think I want to be Mrs. Walter Mills? I am Mrs. Maggie Taylor." She bit her tongue and instead said, "I don't even know you. How can we be married?"

Maggie saw the anger redden his face. She drew back as he glared at her.

Walter said, "Maggie, I told you before that I love you. When I saw you, I had to bring you here to protect you. I would appreciate a little gratitude. Everybody else hurt you. That is why I rescued you. Why are you questioning me?"

Maggie was afraid not to respond so she said, "I am sorry, but I've known you a few hours."

"Yes, you are right. I will be patient with you. We need a little more time to get to know each other. We have every day from now on to grow close. I can't wait. We have wedding plans to make. We deserve a perfect wedding."

A terrible realization occurred to Maggie, she was in trouble. Walter Mills captured her from her own home, and now he says she will spend the rest of her life as his victim.

"I've read about this happening to other people, but I never thought it would be me. Is this person so evil he does not care that I had a life before? In this dangerous situation, will I have the courage to take his life to protect mine? I need to come up with a plan to outsmart him before he kills me," Maggie thought.

Walter reached into his bag and gave her some lipstick and perfume. He said, "I had the girl at the counter sample the perfume to make sure I got the right one for "my Maggie." I want you to make sure you brush your hair everyday. My mother taught me to brush your hair at night so it will be shiny. Everyday before I get here, I want you to put make up on and look your best. See, Maggie, if you are nice to me, I will be nice to you. If you listen to me, nothing will happen to you. I promise to take care of you."

*Your Maggie!* she thought. How dare you call me your Maggie? I hate you. I will never belong to you. I have a husband who is waiting for me and loves me. I will return to him or die trying.

Instead of screaming, she took each item from him and started brushing her hair. Each stroke sent spikes of pain down the back of her head, but she continued brushing.

The fear caused her heart to skip beats, and she thought she was going to faint. She remembered back to a happier time with her husband Jim, and her daughter. Her heart broke all over again when she thought of Sarah. She whispered softly, "Sarah, please forgive Mommy. I am so sorry for what happened. I wish I could go back, and I would not have left your side. I miss you baby."

Walter spoke to her and broke her train of thought, "I have something in my car I want to show you. I will be right back."

As he went out, Walter was smiling with a smug feeling. "Mother, I finally got it right. Maggie is the perfect girl, and now she is all mine. I did

14

good, and I did it all by myself. Those other girls were a waste of time. I really did not want to hurt them but they wouldn't listen to me. I really did like the second one. I tried to warn them that I would hurt them if they disobeyed. It's not my fault. Oh well, I have Maggie now and she really is the perfect one."

Walter went to his car and headed back to the shed. He was excited and so proud of his handy work. He made sure he cut each picture straight, and did not close the book until all the glue dried. He hurried to give Maggie his treasure.

Maggie took the book from him and opened it to the first page. She saw photos cut from a magazine of a young couple getting married. She stared in disbelief when she saw that Walter had pasted her picture over the face of the bride and his picture on the groom. How hideous!

As she looked closer Walter said, "On our wedding day you will look better. I know you look awful in this picture, but with some rest, you will be beautiful again. You will have every day to relax and when I get here, we will just enjoy each other's company. I have never been happier than I am now."

Maggie's mind shot back to the day the reporter took the picture. Sarah had been missing for one week and the trauma showed on her face. The memory tore at her heart and her anger grew against this poor excuse for a man who thought nothing about reminding her of that day.

"What kind of a monster am I dealing with here?" Maggie thought.

Walter said, "I have to leave now, but I filled this lantern for you. I hope I don't have to remind you again what I said. You cannot get out, and if you try, I will know. Do not make me mistrust you, Maggie. If you try something stupid then I will punish you. Believe me when I say you will not like the punishment."

His facial expression changed from anger to exhilaration in one second. "I will be back in the morning. See you then, sweetheart," he said. He went out the door and she heard the lock click.

Maggie sat on the bed and sobbed. She missed Jim and her parents. She missed her darling Sarah. The memory of her daughter in her coffin slipped into her mind. A demented child molester took her darling Sarah and murdered her, and after two weeks of torment, the police found her body in the woods. That was three weeks ago. She wanted to die and give up. Losing her only child was more than she could bear. Now, Walter Mills had taken her freedom and locked her in a shed. How much does one have to bear? Was she capable of hanging on one more day? Was life worth fighting for?

Maggie listened after the car left to make sure he did not return. She counted off the minutes and when she thought it would be safe she ran to the door. She pulled and tugged trying to budge it.

She gave up on the door, went to the wall, and tried kicking the slats with her feet. She needed something to pry the boards apart. She spotted the plastic spoon Walter left on the table, grabbed it, and pried on the board with all her strength. She broke the spoon, got down on her hands and knees, and dug at the dirt. Maybe she could dig a hole under the wall and escape. She dug so hard that her fingernails broke and her fingers started bleeding. "This is not working," she screamed.

She desperately dug until the dirt was red from her blood. She got up and kicked at the walls. She slammed her body into them trying to move them. Maggie didn't know that Walter reinforced the walls with two-by-fours running around all sides. She worked and screamed until she fell down exhausted. There she sat. She was all alone. She was locked in. She was scared to death. She could not take any more and accepted her fate.

"I cannot get out. I deserve to die. I am so sorry Sarah. Please forgive me," she whispered.

Maggie went to the bed, grabbed the cover, and crawled to the corner. Her body shook with fear as the tears fell. She finally lay down in the dirt and gave into the fear. You can push a person to a point that the body shuts the mind down to protect it. Maggie went to that place, without pain, without suffering, without fear. She left the damp, cold, filthy hole. Would she return?

CHAPTER THREE

Walter was so happy and giddy driving home. Maggie was going to be just right for him. He wondered to himself, "Did I remember to lock the door? Should I turn around and check? Get a grip Walter, no wonder Mother never trusted you to do anything right. I am not as stupid as you said I was, Mother. I got Maggie all by myself, didn't I? Yes, Mother she is the right one finally. Just wait until you see her."

Another car came around the corner too fast and he swerved to miss it. "Mother, I have to concentrate on what I am doing. I will talk to you later," he said.

Walter talked with his mother a lot. He tried to be careful when he was around people. He made a mistake at work and held a conversation with his deceased mother and all his co-workers still made fun of him. They laughed louder than usual and asked him, "Hey, Walter. Have you talked to your dead Mother lately?"

Walter's mother Naomi died five years before. His father Charles disappeared when Walter was twelve. He did not remember a lot about his father, except that he hated him.

Walter's father, Charles Mills, was one of twelve children. His mother and father lived in upper Pennsylvania. He was the middle child and with all those kids in the same house, he got lost in the shuffle. Growing up in a small coalmine town was a hard life for a family. The money the men made was not nearly enough to afford necessities, and never luxuries.

Charles's father worked sixteen hours a day in the coal mines and at the end of the week, the money ran out too fast. The food did not satisfy all the twelve kids and they went to bed hungry some nights. Charles was afraid of his older brothers. They would dunk him the bathtub just to hear him scream.

Charles got along with Sandy the best out of all five sisters. She was closer and kinder to him. Sandy married Robert Gaines, a Viet Nam Vet. Robert received a Purple Heart for losing an arm in combat. Charles spent a lot of time with Sandy and Robert until Sandy got sick from a rare form of cancer. She battled it for two years but died when Charles was nineteen.

Charles left the coalmine town to escape being poor and hungry like his father. He wanted more money, more fun, and more girls in his life. One of his buddies begged him to move to a town west of Philadelphia, Pa. They applied for jobs at the Chrysler auto plant, and felt like rich men making $11.00 an hour.

Charles met Naomi when he was twenty-two. When she became pregnant, Charles agreed to marry her. They found a small, dumpy apartment. Charles had a problem with his temper. He broke Naomi's arm while she was pregnant with Walter. He spent many nights abusing his wife and the doctors advised her to leave, but where was she going to go. She was simply stuck in a real bad situation. She did her best to stay out of her husband's reach.

Naomi started having labor pains on a cold, frosty night. Charles agreed to drive her to the hospital but told her he would not go in since the kid probably wasn't his anyway.

Naomi brought Walter home from the hospital after a three-day stay. Charles took a few glances at the cute baby, but Walter's smiles went unnoticed. His cries could instantly irritate him, especially at night. He knocked Naomi across the room many times yelling at her to shut the kid up.

Charles found ways to occupy his time, telling himself that his wife got fat and ugly after giving birth to that kid. He found a few bars and a few ladies, who for the price of their drinks would spend a couple hours with him. Naomi knew what was going on, but after many bruises, she quit harping at Charles.

Unfortunately, Naomi's mothering skills were inadequate for raising a normal young boy. She rarely showed Walter any attention. The habit of showing love missed the Mills' household completely. Naomi's doctors suggested she should not have any more children. Naomi knew it was from Charles kicking her in the stomach while she carried Walter. She felt embarrassed to tell the doctors.

Walter would often think about the time he went to his friend Billy Harper's house. Billy lived three streets down from Walter. Billy told him to ask his mother if he could go fishing with him the next day after school. Naomi was glad to have him out of her hair and told him to go. Walter and Billy ran to Billy's house and rushed in to get the fishing poles.

Billy's mother was in the kitchen baking peanut butter cookies. Walter stared at the funny clothes she wore. He never saw an apron before. His mother never baked and he would never forget the smell of those fresh cookies.

Billy's mother, Diane told them to wash up in the bathroom, and then they could have some milk with the cookies. Walter followed Billy's example and even hung his towel neatly back on the rack. He did not want to jinx the promise of those delicious homemade cookies. Diane asked the boys about their day at school and actually listened to their answers. She beamed with pride when Billy told her he got an A on his spelling test that day.

The boys gathered their rods and before they left, Billy's mother hugged him and told him she loved him. She told them to be careful and be back in about an hour.

Walter sat on the creek bank thinking how wimpy Billy was, but at the same time envying the love he saw from his mother. He had no idea that mothers hugged their boys for a simple reason anytime of the day.

When Walter got home, his father was sitting in his chair watching football. Walter tried to sneak past and hurry to his room. His father caught sight of him and yelled for him to get him another beer. "And while you're at it, tell that mother of yours that I am waiting on the sandwich I told her to make me an hour ago," he said.

A commercial was playing so he took time to tell Walter how stupid he was and what a lame brained woman he married. Walter dreaded the lecture he usually heard when his father had too much to drink.

"One of these days I am going to leave and then what will the two of you do? Stupid people need somebody to tell them everything. Just wait and see, I will take off one day," Charles told Walter.

He brought a beer for his father and finally headed for his room. He told himself not to dwell on what a creep his father was, but started playing a new game he wanted to beat on the computer.

Walter turned the game off and tried to do his homework. He hated school almost as bad as he hated being home. The kids made fun of him all the time. The teachers all tried to help Walter with his work, but they thought he was a troubled and strange child. The school did not have the staff to help the troubled kids, but moved them on to the next grade just to get rid of them.

His sixth grade class went on a field trip. Walter found a rabbit and skinned it in front of a group of girls. The girls ran screaming to tell the teacher, but they had too many other things to worry about than to correct Walter, and told the girls to ignore him. If someone would have bothered to try to talk to him, things may have improved for Walter. But, a young boy fell through the cracks of an overworked education system.

One day when Walter was eleven, he was out in the back yard climbing on the tree. He got thirsty and went inside to find something cold to drink. His father was feeling good after drinking all afternoon and yelled for Walter to come in the living room. He told him to stand beside his chair and offered him a beer. Walter was shocked and looked dumbfounded.

"Boy, shut your mouth and take it," his father said. Walter brought the can to his lips and took a big drink, but almost choked to death from the awful taste. He finally got his breath back and waited for his father to speak.

"Boy," he said. "It's time I told you about sex. Let me tell you about women. They only thing they want from you is money. First, they get knocked up, get their claws in you, then they get fat and flabby. So, you have to find fun somewhere else. I know many ladies, and as soon as you are old enough, I will take you to meet them. I guarantee that my ladies will treat a kid of mine just fine. When you want satisfaction, just let me know. That's all I got to say. Now, move out of the way of the TV."

This ten-minute education lesson from his father did not do much to ensure that Walter respected women, as a young man should. That night after Walter got in his bed, he thought about what his father said.

One night Walter heard his mother crying in pain. He went to the door and listened. He heard his father cussing his mother, and heard the crack as he slapped her. The noise quieted after a while and he listened for a few seconds to his mother's sniffles and went back to his room. He vowed that he would treat his girl better.

Walter tried to stay out of his father's way but sometimes no matter what he did, his father came looking for him. If his mother didn't cook his meat right, he would spend a half an hour shouting and beating her. Most of the time, his anger was so out of hand, he would beat on Walter to kindle the fire. Walter made a promise to take care of him someday.

Walter began to understand how degraded his parent's marriage was when he came home from school one day and saw a man in his mother's bed. He was scared to death his father would come home before he left. Walter believed that his father would have killed his mother if he caught her with another man.

When Walter was twelve years old, Naomi's boyfriend lost track of time. Charles came home a little early. He was angrier than Naomi ever saw him. Charles beat her so bad that Naomi was bleeding and screaming in pain. Walter was in the kitchen eating a hot dog at the table. His father came into the kitchen and flipped the table over. Walter tried to escape out the door, and his father pushed him against the kitchen counter. When he fell back, Walter's hand hit the knife block and it fell to the floor beside him.

His hand closed on one of the knives and he grabbed it and lunged at his father. The knife sunk deep into his chest, killing him instantly. Naomi heard the commotion, came into the kitchen, and looked down at her husband's bloody body on the floor. Neither Walter nor Naomi made a sound for a long time.

Eventually, Naomi reacted telling Walter to roll the body in the kitchen rug. She told her son to help her drag the body out to the garage and they loaded the body in the trunk. Naomi drove to the river a few miles away, and they threw the body over the bridge waiting until the body sank into the murky water. Walter stood and watched his father's body disappear. He was only twelve years old and his own mother did not even take the time to deal with the trauma that a normal boy would carry from this tragedy. The act of murder should make any normal person react with some remorse, but Walter Mills just put it out of his mind.

They got in the car and drove back home. Naomi told Walter not to tell a soul what took place. She told him to tell everyone that Charles took off and left them. The story got easier to tell each time someone asked.    After a while, Naomi and Walter believed it too, and never once mentioned what really happened to Charles Mills. The police never came to investigate, and life at the Mill's home got easier. Walter relaxed without looking over his shoulder waiting for the beatings to start. He did not regret what he did to his father at all. Life was simply easier without him.

Naomi got a job at a nearby bar waiting on tables and she seemed a lot happier now. She loved to drink and the men that flowed through the house, stopped bothering Walter.

At the age of twelve, this young boy did not have much of a chance to learn what life should be. He never knew affection from his parents, and true examples of leadership and parenting was non-existent. No one instilled morality and a spiritual conscience in his young soul. Love and respect for another person was a strange site to Walter. He had absolutely no respect for anyone of authority.

Walter started noticing how pretty the girls in school were, and tried to find the nerve to speak to a couple of them. No one would give him the time of day. The girls thought he was a weirdo. The boys made his life miserable every day. Walter did not have one single friend he could talk to. He tried to fit in but in reality, he had no idea what a normal kid should be.

He heard the other boys talk about a new girl named Kyrsten that moved into the area from Oregon. She sat beside Walter in three of his classes. She did not know anything about him. He worked up the courage to ask her if she wanted to go to the movies with him, and she said yes. Walter was elated. She was so beautiful.

He borrowed his mother's car to pick up Kyrsten. He could hardly contain his eagerness when she was sitting beside him at the movie. It was a feeling so new to him, and he wanted it to last forever. Kyrsten talked freely during the movie and Walter finally relaxed and was having the best day of his life. He asked her if she wanted to go back to his house. She said yes, as long as she got home by 10:00.

They were sitting on the living room sofa when Naomi arrived home. Walter knew by the look in her eyes that she was already drunk. Naomi talked to Kyrsten and Walter smiled to himself the evening was perfect. He lost track of the conversation while he was daydreaming, but when he tuned back in to the two of them, he heard Naomi ask Kyrsten what she saw in a loser like Walter. From then on, the conversation got worse. Walter got upset and asked Kyrsten if she was ready to go. Naomi's drunken laughter followed them out the front door.

Walter asked Kyrsten if she wanted to see his favorite place in the whole wide world. She said yes, and Walter headed for the local spot to park. He reached for Kyrsten and she did kiss him, but he started pulling at her blouse and she got upset and a little scared. Walter shouted at her and tugged on her clothing.

She told him to stop and he said, "What did you expect. I took you to a movie, bought your popcorn and now you tell me you did not know this would happen?" He got angry and told her, "If you don't want to undress; I will do it for you."

Kyrsten managed to get the door open, crawled out of the seat, and ran to the next car yelling for help. The couple in the car wanted to call the police, but Kyrsten begged them not to. The driver went to confront Walter and told him to leave or he would call the police. Walter was furious, but left the lot and headed home.

Kyrsten's father wanted to go find Walter but she begged him not to and promised she would not get near him again. She did not want the reputation of a tattletale.

The next day at school, the story got around to all the students. The girls shunned Walter more than they had before. The boys threatened him saying if he came any where near their girlfriends, they would hurt him. They called him a rapist, which was not far from the truth.

Walter became more of a loner in school. He looked at the girls and fantasized about what he would like to do to them. He was determined to find a perfect girl that would love him and not make fun of him. He saw all the other boys with their girlfriends and felt more alone than ever.

In the eleventh grade, he dropped out of school and got a job as a bus-boy at the bar where his mother worked. Most nights he worked late mopping the floors and washing dishes. Many girls came in the bar and Walter joked with a lot of them, but they thought he was just a creep, so they never warmed up to him.

Since he didn't have much luck attracting attention from any girl, he had a brainstorm idea. He devised a plan to build a place where he could keep his *"girls"*. His uncle had a piece of remote property nearby that had some outbuildings. He drove to the VA hospital to see his Uncle Robert. He asked him if he could fix up the old shed on his property to work on his newest project, a '67 Mustang. His uncle felt sorry for him, was glad to see him take an interest in old cars, and told him he could do whatever he wanted. Walter told him he wanted to reinforce the walls. He told him he needed to do some other work to the building so he could change motors.

Walter went to the hardware store and bought the material. He applied for a security position in a nearby plant and agreed to take the night shift. He got the job and they asked him to start the following week. Working nights gave him a chance to work on the shed during the day.

Walter's hide away was coming along just like he wanted. He worked during the day and dreamed all night about his "Perfect girl."

Walter overheard a conversation at work one night with Chris and another guy named Bill. Chris bragged constantly about all the girls he dated and what they would do for him. Walter started sitting next to Chris in the break room and got the nerve to ask one day, "Hey, Chris, will you give me some pointers on how I can get girls like you do?"

Chris laughed and told him, "Sorry Walter, the only way you can get a girl is if you drug her and hold her captive in your house. What girl would want to go out with you?"

The realization of how true his statement would be soon never crossed Chris's mind. He had no idea the horror that was in store for the girls that caught Walter's eye.

Walter turned and thought to himself, "I'll show you! I will find a girl all right. I will love her and she will love me back. I just want somebody to love me. Is that too much to ask?"

## CHAPTER FOUR

Maggie was born in Clarkstown, Pennsylvania, to Fred and Belle Fracheska. Her father's parents were from Yugoslavia and moved to the U.S. when he was three. Fred dreamed of being a lawyer while he was in third grade. When he graduated, he attended law school and finished in the top ten of his class. He soon became a partner in a downtown law office.

Fred met Belle at a social dinner given by his firm. She was a third grade school teacher, at the Locust Hill Elementary School. Belle was one of the favorite teachers and the kids loved her.

They dated for two years, and when Fred asked Belle to marry him, she said yes. They were married in a small church with all the trimmings. They both enjoyed life and each other's company. Fred bought a two-story home in a modern community park in the suburb of Clarkstown. Their dream came true when Belle got pregnant. Fred was overjoyed when he first laid eyes on his brand new baby girl Maggie, and was a devoted father from the first day.

Maggie was a bright eyed, energetic child. Her beauty as she became a teenager astounded her father. She had the personality to match her beauty. She was the light of the world to both her mother and father.

When Maggie was growing up, her parents wanted her to see the world. They traveled across every state in the United States. Every year they took two whole weeks, jumped in their RV, and saw all the sights they could squeeze in. When she was in the tenth grade, the three of them went to Paris. Maggie was fascinated.

Belle loved to teach, and Maggie loved to learn. They discovered new things together. They knew the names of all the trees. They studied every bug and insect they could find. They studied every flower, and knew the names of the bushes and even the rocks.

Fred was always amazed at how much fun his wife and daughter had with each other. They were never at a loss for things to learn, and since they loved to cook, they took cooking classes together. They cooked so many different dishes, Fred always stayed a little overweight. The more they cooked, the more he obliged by sampling everything.

In high school, Maggie was a cheerleader. Her beauty, mixed with her sweet personality, won over the teachers and the other kids. She usually did not pay much attention to the boys but one of the young men captivated her. He was Jim Taylor, one of the football players. She followed him with her eyes at every game. She tried not to be obvious, but couldn't help herself.

One day Maggie caught Jim glancing her way, and he finally asked her to a movie.

He told her later that he thought a girl as beautiful as she was, would never go out with him. Maggie told him that she thought he was the most handsome guy in the whole school. They got a kick out of telling this story through the years, and most people would tell them that they made the perfect couple and envied them the love they had when they finally got married.

Fred was the proudest papa in the whole universe. They gave their blessings to Jim and loved their son in law dearly.

Jim Taylor was born in Lansing, Pa. His parents, William and Martha were thrilled with Maggie. William owned a dry cleaning business and Martha helped him part time. She loved to dabble in antiques and made quilts by hand. After Jim was born, they looked for a bigger home and found an old mansion. Martha spent a lot of time restoring it and when she was done, it was a showcase of beauty.

The four parents spent many weekends in each other's back yard for barbecues. Maggie and Jim were so pleased that their parents got along so well.

Jim spent his days just looking at Maggie. He could not get over the fact that she would agree to spend her life with him. She satisfied his every desire in what a loving wife should be. She kept telling him if he did not treat her right she would find another handsome man to take care of her. When the look of fear would cross Jim's face, Maggie would laugh and call him a silly goof. She reassured him that he was a wonderful loving husband and she would cherish him forever.

After they got married, they moved into Jim's apartment. His advertising business was doing well, and they started looking for a house to buy. When one became available on the same street as her parents, they were thrilled and they bought it and started making it their own.

Maggie took a job at her father's law firm. She wanted to take night classes to study law. Her father was excited and loved having Maggie work with him. Everyone at the office grew to love Maggie too. She was as dependable and as charming as her father was. Life was good.

Maggie's best friend since first grade, Gwen Donnelly, lived down the street. As kids, they were inseparable. Now as adults, they spoke to each other every day. They promised they would be friends for life.

Jim's company grew and he needed a partner. He hired Tom Ness, a friend he went to business school with. When Tom and Gwen met, it was love at first sight. They soon made plans and were married. They bought a house on the same block as Maggie and Jim.

Maggie would say a prayer of thanks every morning to God for giving her such wonderful parents, a loving husband, in-laws that she thought of as second parents, and her best friend Gwen. She felt blessed.

They all attended the local Methodist Church. Faith and prayer were a big part of all their lives.

Jim and Maggie worked on their home in their spare time. Maggie was an avid gardener. Her flowers blooming in the spring took her breath. When the sunlight hit the different colors, it made her smile. God's earth was so full of wonderful colors and beauty.

Jim's passion was woodworking. In his spare time, he re-did the cabinets and all the moldings. Their home had three bedrooms and he would remind her often that they would have more fun re-doing the room across the hall into a nursery.

Maggie knew a child would complete their family, and she wanted to get pregnant soon. In her heart, she knew that Jim would be the world's best father, just as he was the world's best husband.

Gwen surprised Maggie in the spring with the news that she was pregnant. Maggie was a little jealous for a few seconds, but was so happy for Gwen she hugged her in delight. Immediately, they shopped at all the new baby stores in town.

One month later Maggie discovered she too was pregnant. Her mother told her she was not shocked at all. She said to her, "Maggie you and Gwen have done everything else together since you were six, and I am surprised you did not get pregnant the same day."

Both husbands were just beaming with joy. They patted each other on the back and like the girls, started making plans for their upcoming children.

Jim made two cribs that were so elegant, both of the women cried. Even Tom had tears. Maggie remembered every morning to thank God for the privilege to become a Mother.

Maggie and Gwen both were radiant while pregnant. Each grandparent grew more excited in anticipation. Jim and Tom went to the birthing classes faithfully with their beautiful wives. They wanted to be a part of every day's activities. They even loved going shopping with the women for each item to fill the nurseries. As time got closer, they practiced breathing with the girls and became old pros at coaching.

In November, Gwen started having contractions and they all were at her bedside when her daughter, Jill, was born. Tom told her that he was glad that Jill looked just like her mother with her dark hair and sparkling eyes.

In December, it was Maggie's turn. Again, all were right there with her. Maggie's parents and Jim's parents had already spoiled the baby with all the gifts they could fit in the nursery.

When Maggie's daughter, Sarah was born, Jim passed out cold three seconds after he first saw Sarah. The doctor's assured Maggie they had not lost a father yet. When Jim could finally stand on his feet, the tears in his eyes touched Maggie so deeply. Her world was complete. A husband who loved her and a daughter that was the most beautiful baby she had ever seen, though maybe she was a little prejudiced.

In the maternity ward, people marveled at Sarah's beauty. They commented on how she looked just like an angel.

Maggie remembered many times how her own mother would lightly touch her cheek and smile with love. Now she understood what it meant. She wanted to be a good mother, just like her own mother. She appreciated her mother in a special way now.

Maggie always imagined having her own child. The love she felt when she held Sarah was a different kind of love than she had ever felt before. It was as though God filled a hole in her heart with sunshine. She was so elated. She could not wait to take Sarah home. Maggie and Jim would stand over the crib and watch Sarah sleep.

Jim had a hard time going to work. He did not want to miss any time with his two beautiful girls. Maggie, like her mother, wanted to teach Sarah about everything. They waited impatiently for her to walk and to talk. They took every opportunity to watch her learn.

When Sarah was two years old, Maggie would take her to the park. She would meet Gwen and Jill, and they would sit on the bench, as the girls would swing. Their daughters were close like the mothers, and Maggie and Gwen hoped they would be like sisters forever.

Jim was expanding his business and was working a lot more hours. Maggie and Sarah missed him in the evenings. Maggie felt guilty for neglecting Jim at times. She had so much to teach Sarah and did not want to spend a minute without her.

Jim asked Maggie to go to Hawaii with him when Sarah was three years old. He already made all the arrangements and begged Maggie to leave Sarah with her mother so they could catch up on all the time they had missed with each other. Their love life slacked off some after Sarah was born, and Maggie was eager to make it up to Jim and bring back some of the romance. They had such a great time and promised each other they would take a vacation every year.

Maggie had missed Sarah a lot. She worried while they were gone that Sarah might be upset with Mommy and Daddy when they got home. When they went to Grandma's house to pick her up, she was so content, and having a great time that she wanted them to take another trip and stay a whole month. Maggie felt a little jealous because Sarah had not missed her more. She got over her jealousy quick and was so glad that her mother loved Sarah as much as she did.

Sarah had inherited Maggie's beauty. She had soft blonde hair with copper highlights. She was a model child and wherever they went, everyone just loved Sarah. Maggie and Gwen put the girls in pre-school at the local church day care. Sarah adjusted so well Maggie thought about going back to work part-time. Jim encouraged her to go back and said he would share the chores at the house.

Her father was happy to have her back and discussed Maggie taking night school classes to get her degree. Maggie wasn't sure if she could handle school, Sarah, and Jim, but she did start classes and managed like the pro she was. She made sure that they had dinner together every night, and Sarah held them captive each night with her stories about the day care.

On the afternoons Maggie had free, they would call Gwen and Jill to meet them at the park. The girls wanted to swing, and climb on the jungle gym. They loved to play in the sand box so much, it was usually a chore to get them to go home.

One Saturday afternoon when they had gone shopping at the local mall, Sarah spotted the largest play set that Maggie had ever seen. As soon as she started begging to Daddy, it was a lost cause. Jim took one look at the puppy-dog pout on Sarah's face and bought it for her. They spent the next two weeks in the back yard setting it up. Sarah loved to swing and when Maggie would push her, she would tell her, "Higher, Mommy, I want to touch the sky."

Maggie loved to bake, and she taught Sarah how to make her special cupcakes, and brownies, hot homemade bread. Every free moment they had, they were baking. The Taylor house overflowed with goodies and Gwen, being the good friend that she was, told the neighborhood where to find the best home-baked cookies, and brownies, and cake, and pies, and hot homemade bread. Maggie and Sarah had so much fun together in the kitchen; they started setting up the dining room table filled with all their treats. The neighborhood often stopped by to sample what they had.

Eventually, people put in orders for the baked goods, and Maggie set up a basket on the table where they could "contribute" to Sarah's college fund. Most everyone was overly generous with paying and stopped at the Taylor house before they would go to the grocery store. The town folks just loved Maggie's home baked goods. Homemade is always better!

CHAPTER FIVE

David Adams lived a few blocks from the Taylor house. Maggie met him often at the summer activities around the community. He took to Sarah immediately and asked Maggie if he could stop by and sample her hot bread. David requested two loaves each week and Maggie worked extra to have the bread ready for him.

After several weeks, he started bringing her a little gift each time he came. Maggie kept telling him he was spoiling Sarah, but he said he was practicing for when he had his own daughter. He asked Maggie if he could take Sarah and Jill to the park. The girls begged to let "Uncle David" take them, and finally after Maggie and Gwen discussed it, they agreed to let the girls go with David.

Sarah and Jill would come home and tell them how much fun they had with "Uncle David." Looking back now, Maggie was sure that there were warning signs of David being too close to the girls. She noticed that David often wanted the girls to sit on his lap, but Maggie thought it was all normal fun. When she spoke of David to the other women in their neighborhood circle, they all seemed to think David was just a friendly bachelor, and almost like "one of the girls.

Sarah and Jill started kindergarten when they turned six. The teacher was excellent with the kids and the mothers loved her as much as the kids did. Sarah got along with the children in her class so well, and she begged Maggie to let her have a back yard party so she could show off her new gym set. They worked extra hard to make sure the kids had a good time, and when the twenty-five kids left, they all said it was the best party ever.

Sarah and Jill spent almost every day in the back yard. Sometimes they begged to go to the playground at the park. Maggie would make a point of taking her several times a month. Sarah and Jill spent half their time watching the bunnies and the birds. She knew when the weather turned cold Sarah would miss it.

On a Wednesday afternoon, Maggie had made plans to meet Gwen and Jill after they picked the girls up after school. Gwen called Maggie and told her she would be a little late because she forgot about a dentist appointment. Gwen assured Maggie that she and Jill would be there right after the appointment.

The sun was shining so bright, and the leaves were just starting to turn. Sarah, like Maggie, loved this time of year. Together they took walks through the woods behind the park looking for the different shaped and different colored leaves.

That day when they arrived at the park, Sarah wanted to swing for a while. Maggie spotted a maroon bush in the grove behind the sliding board. She needed a dark colored flowering bush to fill a space in her own back yard garden.

She glanced at Sarah, who was oblivious to anything but the swing going higher. Maggie grinned at her and said, "Sarah, honey I'm going to go right back here to look at this pretty flower. If you need me, just yell, okay?" She saw Sarah shake her head yes, so she headed in that direction.

A thorn from the tree stuck in her arm so she went to the other side to see if she could reach an easier branch. She was able to break off a piece that had a perfect flower on it. She started back to the swing, and noticed another bush that had a darker flower, so she stopped to get a branch off it too.

Maggie headed back to the swing and didn't see Sarah right away. "That little stinker probably went looking for me," she thought. She glanced over at the slide and thought she should check the other play areas. She walked the few feet to the sand box, and she didn't see any sign of her. "Surely she didn't go too far in the woods," she thought. "I wasn't gone but five minutes."

Maggie yelled for her, and walked to the edge of the trees. She hoped Sarah hadn't gone very far, she wanted to keep an eye out for Gwen. She called out, "Sarah, you need to come back to the swing." She didn't hear her answer and decided to go into the woods on the other side where the swing set was. She continued to call for her. "Sarah, mommy needs you to come back now." She walked a little further. She would stop and listen to see if she could hear footsteps in the leaves. She heard nothing but the birds singing.

Maggie walked and retraced her steps. She would walk and then call for her. She didn't want to go too far and retraced her steps back to the swing set, hoping that Sarah was there. As she was looking around at the playground, she heard a car pull in the parking lot. She saw Gwen get out of her car, and she hurried over to her.

"I can't find Sarah," she told her.

"What do you mean you can't find her?" Gwen asked.

Maggie said, "I went in the woods over there to get a piece of this bush," holding it up for her to see, "and when I came back to the swing, Sarah wasn't there."

"She must have gone to find you," Gwen said. "Let me get Jill out of the car, and we'll go find her."

When they got to the edge of the woods, Maggie told Gwen to walk in one direction, and she would go in another. They separated and Maggie could hear Gwen calling Sarah's name. They searched for a half hour, and as Maggie heard Gwen coming out of the woods, she began to get scared.

"How long has it been since you saw her?" Gwen asked her.

"I was only gone about five minutes," Maggie told her. "Where could she have gone?"

Gwen headed back to her car. "What are you doing?" Maggie asked.

"I am going to call the police," Gwen said.

"The police, don't you think it's a little too soon? We have to look harder," Maggie replied.

"I don't want to take any chances," Gwen told her. "The more people that we have looking for her, the faster we will find her before it gets too dark."

Maggie looked at Gwen and said, "I am going back to search for her, she is probably getting scared by now. Maybe she saw a bunny and followed it. She did that to me the last walk we took."

"Okay I will yell for you when they get here," Gwen told her.

Maggie went back into the woods and started calling for Sarah. "Just keep calm and she will hear you and come back," she told herself. "Sarah, can you hear me? Please answer me Sarah. You are starting to make Mommy scared." She would walk a few steps and stop to listen. She started counting her steps.

Maggie would walk two hundred steps in one direction and then turn and go the opposite way. She kept repeating the pattern. Walk and count, turn, and walk and count. She tried not to think about what Sarah would think when it got later. She needed to find her. She must keep looking. At one point, she thought maybe Sarah had laid down. She got down on her hands and knees and began to look under the shrubbery.

That is where the first police officer found her. He introduced himself as Officer Paul Garret. He reached down to help her stand. His voice was soft and comforting. Officer Garret was forty-five years old and worked at staying fit and trim. He asked Maggie to come back to the park bench with him so he could get some information.

"But I have to find Sarah," she told him. "She has wandered into the woods, I guess, and she will be waiting for me to come and get her."

He gently touched her arm and said, "Mrs. Taylor, I understand, but we need to get a picture of Sarah, if you have one with you."

Maggie nodded her head and followed him back to the bench. She told him her purse was in her car, and she had a picture in her wallet. The number of people gathered to help with the search shocked her.

The search teams split in four groups, and the other officers were instructing them to stay close together, as they approached the edge of the woods.

Maggie got her purse and headed back to Officer Garret. She handed the picture of Sarah to him. Maggie watched Officer Garret's face as he looked at the picture in his hand.

The feeling she got as he looked at Sarah sent a chill up her spine. "I don't like the panic I am beginning to feel," she thought.

Maggie said, "Sarah is just lost. She will come running out of the woods shortly, and will want to tell us all about the little bunny that she followed. The baby bunnies making noise as the mommy bunny feeds them fascinated Sarah. Officer Garret, I have to go now, and find Sarah. I think she might have fallen asleep waiting for the bunny to come out of the hole."

Officer Garret's hope was to find her daughter. "Mrs. Taylor, I know you want to go back and look, but we have our teams searching, and I need you to answer some questions for me."

"No," Maggie said, "I have to go and get my daughter. You don't understand. She will be frightened when she wakes up and I have to be with her."

Officer Garret said, "Please, Mrs. Taylor, I need you to stay with me. Please have a seat on the bench. I won't take long I promise. Right now that is the best way you can help. Can we call your husband for you? I am sure he would want to be here with you. If you give me his number, I will have an officer pick him up."

Maggie looked at him with pure fright on her face. "I don't want to worry Jim with this since Sarah is just lost. I will find her in a few minutes and then I can take her home. My husband does not need to know that I lost our daughter," she said in a sharp tone.

"Mrs. Taylor, I am not blaming you in any way, and your husband won't either. I think that he should be here for you. We need the people who are closest to us at a time like this," he said.

"Please call me Maggie," she said to him. "What does in times like this mean? Are you saying you think something happened to my daughter?"

Officer Garret said, "No Maggie. That is not what I meant. Until we find your daughter, you need someone to help you stay calm."

"I assure you Officer Garret," she said, "I am very capable of taking care of myself." With that, she walked away and headed back to the woods.

Gwen heard the conversation, and went over to Officer Garret.

"I will give you Jim's work number. I am positive he wants to be here." She gave him the number and asked if he would excuse her a minute. She had to call her mother to come and get her daughter, Jill. Gwen did not want Jill to be here if they heard any bad news.

"Sure," he said to her. "Could I ask you a question?"

"Yes," Gwen said. "Ask me anything."

Officer Garret said, "I wanted to ask how well you know Mrs. Taylor."

She waited for a second to answer. "You don't think for one minute that Maggie is lying about what happened to Sarah, do you?"

41

"No, I don't. But how well do you know Mrs. Taylor?" Officer Garret asked.

Gwen said, "Maggie and I have been best friends since we were in first grade. I would trust her with my life, and might I add, I would trust her with the life of my own daughter."

Officer Garret said, "I have to ask the difficult questions, I hope I don't offend you."

"I'm sorry. I appreciate you getting here so quickly," Gwen said.

Officer Garret said, "In these cases, acting quickly sometimes makes a difference. Sarah has been missing for less than two hours. That is a good thing. We should be able to find her soon. If she went into the woods, she could not have gone very far."

Gwen thanked him and opened her phone to call her mother. It was hard for her to tell her that Sarah was missing. Her mother assured her everything would be fine and she should be there to pick up Jill in a short time. Gwen went back to Officer Garret and asked him where Maggie had gone.

Officer Garret told her Maggie had insisted on going back in the woods, and he sent a female officer to go to be with her.

"As soon as my mother comes to get Jill, I will go and stay with Maggie," Gwen said.

Officer Garret said, "I am glad she has a friend with her. If you will excuse me, we need to get out an Amber Alert as soon as possible."

Gwen was shocked as she asked him, "Do you really think that is necessary?"

He said, "It is always better to get a lost child on the airways as soon as we can. I would rather be cautious than be sorry we did not act faster."

Officer Garret contacted the department and ordered an alert for a missing six- year-old girl. He gave a description of Sarah Taylor from the picture he held in his hand. His heart went out to Maggie. He could not imagine what she would be dealing with in a few hours if they had not found her daughter.

The female officer, Cari Johnson, came out of the wooded area. As she approached Officer Garret, he could see her troubled expression.

Officer Johnson said, "I am very sorry sir, but I cannot convince Mrs. Taylor to come back with me."

Officer Garret said, "We will wait for her husband to get here and maybe he can convince her. In the meantime, could you please wait for the reporter from the local news station to arrive so we can get this picture on the air as soon as possible? Hopefully someone in this immediate locality can provide us with vital information to help locate this child."

Officer Garret paused when he saw a fast approaching car pull into the parking lot. He saw a man get out of the car and hurriedly run in his direction.

The man introduced himself to Officer Garret. "I am Jim Taylor, are you in charge?"

"Yes, I am Officer Garret."

Jim said, "I demand to know what has happened. I received a call that my daughter is lost."

"Mr. Taylor, please let me assure you that the best way to help your wife and your daughter is to remain calm. Under these circumstances, I know it is difficult. We should not panic until we have good reason to believe that your daughter, Sarah, is anything but a missing child who has wandered off from her mother. We have several search parties scouting the woods, and patrols searching the roads in the vicinity. Your wife needs you to be calm. As you can imagine, she is very upset."

Jim said, "Yes, of course, and please call me Jim."

Officer Garret said, "I was given a picture of Sarah by your wife, and as soon as we can we will get it on the air."

Officer Garret continued, "I also have contacted our department to put out an Amber Alert for your daughter Sarah. As I told your wife, we want to make sure we do not waste time in locating you daughter."

Jim shook his head that he understood and asked the Officer if he knew where his wife was.

"She is in the woods looking for Sarah. We tried to have her stay here at this command post, but she insisted on searching for herself," Officer Garret said. "We do have four different search teams in the immediate wooded area, and they will continue until the sun goes down. We are doing everything we can to find Sarah soon. If you would please report back to me in a few minutes, I will certainly keep you up to date on what my department is doing."

Jim said, "Of course. Right now, I need to find Maggie and make sure she is all right. I will try to bring her back here as soon as I can. I appreciate all that everyone is doing. I did not mean to question your methods."

Gwen walked to Jim and hugged him. "I am so sorry about this. My mother picked up Jill for me, and I was just now going to find Maggie. I am glad you are here to be with her. She is beginning to fall apart. She was so worried about calling you. Maggie thought you would blame her for letting Sarah out of her sight for a few moments."

Jim looked at Gwen sadly. "Why would she think that?" he asked. "There is no way that I would blame her. I need to go find her now, if you will excuse me."

Gwen said, "Will you tell Maggie I will be right there. I got a call from one of the women at our church. They are bringing sandwiches and coffee for everyone and as soon as they come, I will find Maggie. Please

44

don't worry Jim. We will find Sarah shortly." Gwen reached to hug him again and as she pulled away, she could feel his shoulders tremble. She smiled at him and headed back to the parking lot.

Jim walked to the edge of the woods and asked one of the searchers if they had seen his wife. They pointed to the left of where they were standing. Jim hurried to find Maggie, and as he followed the trail, he saw her with a stick lifting the branches and calling to Sarah as she searched. He went to her and when she saw him, she hesitated as if she was afraid of what he was thinking.

He reached her and held her in his arms. "Maggie, I am here now. I love you. Don't worry, we will find Sarah." As he held her, he felt her whole body shake.

Her knees buckled and she started to fall to the ground.

Jim lowered her gently and sat beside her. "Maggie, look at me, honey. I am here. I will make sure Sarah is all right. You have to believe me. I would never let anything happen to either of you. You and Sarah are my life, and without you two, I am nothing. Please tell me what happened."

Maggie wiped the tears and said, "It is my fault. I went to look for a bush I had spotted for our back yard. Sarah was on the swing, and when I came back in five minutes, she wasn't there. I called for her and I searched everywhere I could think of. When Gwen got here, she called the police. I did not want them to call you until I found Sarah. I thought she had run after a bunny and I would find her sleeping on the ground waiting for the bunny to come out of a hole."

Maggie said, "Last week, we did that and she fell asleep, because she knew the mommy bunny was feeding the babies and she wanted to see them. We waited for a half hour and finally when the bunny stuck her head out of the hole, she agreed to go home. You know how she loves animals, Jim. I just want to find her. Where is she? How could I lose my own child?"

Jim held her as she cried. He said, "Maggie you have to calm down. Please, you are getting yourself way too upset."

Maggie pulled away as she said, "I have to get up. I know she is waiting for me to come to her. She will be scared to death if she is alone any longer. Jim, grab that stick over there and help me look. She must be lying under this brush. Listen, I hear footsteps. Sarah, is that you? Sarah, Mommy and Daddy are right over here. Follow the sound of my voice, sweetheart. Sarah, can you hear me?"

Jim went and gently wrapped his arms around her. It broke his heart to see her so upset. He could tell she was getting near a breaking point.

As they stood there, Officer Cari Johnson came around the bend. "I wanted to tell you that there is coffee and sandwiches back at the picnic tables. Mrs. Taylor, would you go with me and eat something?" she asked her.

Maggie asked, "Why would I leave? Has someone found my daughter? Is that what you are telling me? Can we see her? Where is she? Is she okay? I knew we would find her."

Officer Cari said, "No, Mrs. Taylor, I am sorry, no one has found Sarah. Won't you please rest and let the officers search? They are very capable and trained to know what to do in these situations. I want you to go back to the picnic area. Officer Garret has some questions for you and your husband," she said.

Maggie looked at Jim and said, "You go, I have to stay here in case Sarah calls for me. I cannot leave her in the woods alone."

Jim reached for her hand and said, "Maggie, listen to me. You need to go with me. The police are trained to find her."

They heard several voices calling in the woods. "Sarah, Sarah, can you hear us? If you can, please answer. Sarah, Sarah, we are here to help you."

Maggie looked at Jim with raw emotion. Her heart was beating so fast, she began to weave on her feet. Jim caught her as she toppled sideways. "Please, Maggie, you have to sit down. Please, let me take you back," he pleaded with her.

Maggie agreed and as they left the woods, they could still hear the voices calling, "Sarah, Sarah, can you hear us?"

Jim walked Maggie back to the picnic tables and went to look for Officer Garret. He was on the radio when Jim got close to him, and he could hear his conversation on the police radio.

"Yes sir," Officer Garret was saying, "We have widened our search, we had no luck within a five mile radius. We will expand to ten. I will keep you posted."

Jim stood beside him until he was finished and asked, "Does this mean you think something has happened to Sarah?"

Officer Garret replied, "No, but we do not know how far your daughter may have gone." He reached for Jim's arm and led him back to the picnic tables. "I need to ask your wife some more questions. Your church has supplied the food, and wanted me to let you know that if there is anything else you need, just let them know. The congregation has planned a prayer service for 7:00 tonight. Prayer can work. Trust in your faith, Mr. Taylor."

Jim said, "Thank you Officer Garret. My wife is trying to hold up, but I can see it is beginning to wear her down. She is a very strong person, and I promised her that I would not let anything happen to her or Sarah."

Officer Garret looked at him and said, "Mr. Taylor, I must ask you if you think your wife would ever harm your daughter. Before you get angry, let me assure you, and I told your wife the same thing, I have to ask these questions. I have to determine that we are dealing with a stranger, and not a member of the family. In cases of abducted children, the first suspects are the parents. I need to talk with Mrs. Taylor for a few minutes."

"Certainly, we finally got her to sit down for a few minutes," Jim said.

Officer Garret went to Maggie and asked, "Mrs. Taylor, I need to go over a few things with you. When you arrived here at the park today, was there anyone else here?" She thought for a second and said, "No, Sarah and I were the only two here."

Officer Garret asked, "Did you hear anyone close by? Did you see anyone or a strange car in the parking lot?"

"No there were no other cars," Maggie said.

Officer Garret asked, "Maggie, are you sure you did not see or hear anything? Sometimes we hear things and are not aware of it until later."

She thought again and said, "No, I pushed Sarah on the swings for a while and then I went to the woods to get a piece of a bush. I wanted to see if I could find one like it for my own garden. I was only gone five minutes. I told Sarah before I left to yell for me."

Maggie hesitated then continued, "When I came back to the swings, she was not there. I did not mean to leave her. I thought she would be fine for that few minutes. If anything has happened to her, how can I live with the fact that it was my fault?" As she finished her voice broke.

"I know this is difficult for you," Officer Garret said. "If you can remember any noise or anything out of the ordinary, please let me know."

Maggie shook her head and rose to go back in the woods.

Jim said softly, "Maggie, would you like for me to take you home? You need to get some rest. You will not be any good for Sarah if you are exhausted."

Maggie had terror in her eyes. "Please don't make me leave. Sarah will come back and wonder why I left her again."

Jim said, "Maggie, you did not do anything wrong. Sarah does not think you left her."

Maggie said, "Yes, she does." Her eyes filled with tears. "She thinks I walked away and now she is trying to find me and she is lost and can not find her way back. Jim, I have to stay. Please I have to stay."

Jim said, "Okay Maggie, but I want you to stay here and I will go look for her too." He motioned for Gwen and he asked her to sit with Maggie while he went to join the search party.

Gwen said, "Of course I will stay with her." She brought back a cup of coffee and handed it to Maggie. "Here, you need to drink this," she told her.

Jim thanked her and hugged Maggie. "I will be back soon. Don't worry, okay?" Maggie stared straight ahead.

Jim thought, God, please let us find her. We are lost without her.

As Jim headed into the woods, he heard voices and he followed the sound. As he entered a clearing, there were several people gathered around something on the ground. As Jim came closer, he saw a bright yellow hair ribbon. He stared at it; he knew Sarah wore two yellow hair ribbons with her yellow striped top. His heart froze and he reached down to pick it up.

One of the officers stopped him and said, "Do not touch it. We have to treat it as evidence and check for prints on it."

Jim could feel his chest tighten and could not contain himself. He turned to try to hide his sobbing.

The officer said, "Mr. Taylor, please do not take this as a bad sign. This shows us in which direction your daughter went. We will follow this trail and hopefully your daughter is safe but just lost."

Jim said to him, "Please do not show this to my wife. She is fragile right now, and I want to protect her until we find Sarah."

"Of course," the officer said, "but I need to inform Officer Garret."

Jim asked the others if he could join their search. They explained what to do, and tried not to let him see their fear.

The searchers spread out in a line with a foot in between them and walked slowly in a straight line. Jim was in the middle. He copied the actions of the others, and as they walked, they turned their heads from one side to the other. As they went along, they used their feet, brushing along the ground to see if they could uncover anything else that belonged to Sarah.

Officer Garret hurried to examine the hair ribbon. He stooped down to check for any further evidence. When he was finished, he took out a plastic bag and carefully placed the yellow hair ribbon in it. He handed the bag to another officer and asked him to take it straight to the lab for testing.

# CHAPTER SIX

The local news contacted Officer Garret by phone and told him they would certainly run the story of Sarah's disappearance on the evening edition. They requested an interview with Mr. and Mrs. Taylor as soon as possible. Officer Garret expressed his gratitude and said he would have one of his officers take them to the station.

In the cases of missing children, it helps to put the parents on the news. He hoped it would bring new information. The yellow hair ribbon was the only clue they had. He hoped that the exposure would help in the search for Sarah Taylor. In many cases of missing children that are lost, someone that has seen them can help the police locate them quickly.

Officer Garrett went to look for Jim and Maggie. They were not at the picnic area, and he asked if anyone had seen them. One of the bystanders told him they saw Mrs. Taylor head back in the woods. Officer Garret headed in that direction. He heard Mrs. Taylor as he headed into the wooded area.

A few feet from where they found the hair ribbon she was calling, "Sarah, can you hear me? Honey, it's Mommy. If you can hear me, yell loud and I will find you. Sarah, please answer me. Sarah, Sarah, can you hear me? It's Mommy. Sarah, Sarah."

Jim was looking under the brush. He had a stick in his hand. He was searching frantically for any sign of his daughter. He looked up when Officer Garret got close. Officer Garret knew that Mr. Taylor was aware of the yellow ribbon, and he was not sure if he had told his wife, so he avoided the subject.

"Mr. Taylor," Officer Garret said, "I just spoke to the local TV station and they want you and your wife to do an interview for the evening edition as soon as possible. I have arranged for one of my officers to drive you both there. We do not have a lot of time so if you could both come with me, I will notify them that you are on your way."

Jim went to Maggie and spoke in a soft voice, "Maggie honey, Officer Garret arranged for us to do an interview for the evening news. He needs us to go with him so we can go to the station."

Maggie looked up at him and said, "Jim, I need to stay here. Sarah is somewhere in these woods. I want to be right here so I can make sure she is okay. I have to keep looking. She will be frightened if I leave."

Officer Garret went to Maggie's side and said, "Mrs. Taylor, I will keep looking. If we find Sarah, I will radio my officer right away and you can come right back. If someone knows something that can help us find your daughter, we need to make the evening news cast."

Maggie was irritated, "What makes you think that someone else will know where Sarah is? I have to look for her. She is just lost!"

Officer Garret paused for a second and said, "Mrs. Taylor, I don't want to upset you without a reason. If Sarah has wandered out of our range, maybe someone has information. Someone may see Sarah's face and recognize her. If someone has taken her, it will make a difference if they see Sarah as your child, and not just an object."

Maggie and Jim followed him back to the picnic area. The squad car was waiting for them. They met the officer and as they got in the car to leave, a group of the search party was standing nearby and wished them luck as they drove away.

The station was a twenty-minute drive. As soon as they were on their way, Jim could feel Maggie's impatience. She wanted to stay at the park in case they found Sarah.

Jim reached for Maggie's hand and softly said, "Maggie, Sarah will be fine, I promise. Look at me Maggie. You and Sarah are my world. I could not live without either of you. I love you with all my heart. Please don't shut me out. I need you."

Maggie turned to him and brushed his face with her hand. "I am so sorry, Jim. I know you love me. I need you too. You are my pillar of strength," she said.

Jim leaned over and put his lips on hers. "Maggie, I will protect you and Sarah. We are in this together. Please trust me."

Maggie's head dropped and Jim sees she is on the edge. "What would we do if something has happened to Sarah? I cannot live without her," she said. She gives him a faint smile and leans against him for the rest of the drive.

The officer pulled up at the station and opened the door for them. The manager showed them to the studio where the interview will be taped. As they take a seat, one of the newscasters came and introduced himself, "Mr. and Mrs. Taylor, I am Jerry Kline. I will be doing the interview. I know this is an emotional ordeal for you. I have a picture of your daughter, Sarah. We will be running it on the air. Now, if I can walk you through what we would like to say, we can get started. I understand you last saw your daughter at the Clarkstown Park. We need you to tell the time of your daughter's disappearance, and what she was wearing. Anyone with information can contact us here at the station. So if you are ready we will get started."

Someone came and put the microphones on each of them.

Maggie had no idea what she looked like. She had crawled on the ground and looked under every bush. Right now, she did not care.

They asked them to tell the story of what happened in their own words. Jim started. "I am Mr. Jim Taylor, and this is my wife Maggie. This afternoon around 2:30 p.m. our daughter Sarah went missing when my wife was with her at the Clarkstown Park. Sarah is six years old. She was wearing blue jeans and a yellow striped shirt." He remembered finding the yellow hair ribbon and could not continue.

Maggie spoke, "I am Sarah's mother. We were at the park today, and I left Sarah alone for five minutes. When I came back, she was not on the swing and I could not find her. Sarah will be afraid when it gets dark. She is our only daughter. Please help us find her. She has never been alone. Please, I beg you, if you know where she is, bring her back to us." Maggie lost her composure and started crying. Jim reached for her hand.

Jerry took over and repeated the information about Sarah. "We have a picture of Sarah Taylor and will run it for the rest of this evening. If you know anything that can help locate this six-year old child, please call this station. If you have seen something that can help in the search, please call us."

They ended the interview and Jerry assured them that they would run the story that night on the news. "I hope your daughter is found safe. I cannot imagine what you are going through. My wife and I have a three-year old son named Mikey. If he was missing, I do not know what we would do. Please believe me that everyone here at the station will be praying for you and your daughter."

Jim stood and shook Jerry's hand and thanked him for taking the time to help. "We will be waiting to hear from you. I hope someone has information to help us find Sarah. It will be getting dark soon and we need to find her. She will be so scared when it gets dark."

Jim took Maggie by the arm and they went to find the officer to take them back to the park.

"Maggie, you need something to eat. We can get the car and go to the restaurant down the street. Would that be okay?" Jim asked.

She said, "I do not think I could eat a bite, but I will go with you if you want. We have to tell Officer Garret where we will be."

They went back to the park to find Officer Garret. He was talking to his men and they waited until he finished. He turned to them and asked, "How did it go at the station? I know it was hard on both of you. Maybe we will get some information that will help."

Jim answered, "Yes, it was very hard. We do appreciate what you do. Your job is not an easy one."

Officer Garret smiled and said, "No, this is the hardest part of our job. The helplessness we feel is hard not to show. We do try to make it easier on the family. I want you both to know that every person here would like to find your daughter as soon as possible. These men will not give up as long as there is a chance of finding her."

Jim told him that he was taking Maggie to get something to eat. They left their cell number with Officer Garret and he assured them that if he had any news at all, he would call them immediately.

"Have you found anything at all?" Maggie asked.

Officer Garret glanced at Jim and when he shook his head no, he said to her, "Mrs. Taylor, so far we have found nothing. But the searchers are still out and we will do all we can to find your daughter." He also did not want to tell them about three missing teenage girls over the past three months.

Jim went to get Maggie's car and waited for her to get in. They went to the restaurant and found a seat. Jim ordered the dinner special, but Maggie was not hungry and she ordered coffee. Jim got her to share some of his salad and he could tell Maggie was anxious to get back to the park, so they headed back.

Maggie started walking towards the woods and saw Gwen heading her way. Gwen hugged her and asked her how she was doing.

Maggie told her, "I do not think I can take one more minute without knowing where Sarah is. Why would anyone take her Gwen? She is my child. No one has the right to take another person's baby. I will not rest until I see her."

Gwen wiped a tear away and said, "Maggie, you are my best friend in the whole world. You and Jim do not deserve this. I will be here with you no matter how long it takes."

Maggie stared bluntly at Gwen and asked, "Do you blame me, Gwen? Sarah is missing because of me. Why didn't I stay right by her side? Why did I leave my child for one second? I am to blame and I do not want to live without her."

# CHAPTER SEVEN

Walter was beside himself with excitement. He hurried through his rounds. He needed to get to the shed as soon as he could get through his shift. He daydreamed about Maggie all night. She was his. Finally, he picked the right one.

Walter thought to himself, I have so many plans to make. She will not betray me like the others. I know she wants to be with me. No one ever loved me before, but now I have Maggie. I cannot wait to see her. His smile widened, as he grew impatient to get back to her. There was not one thought in his mind about what he was doing was wrong. To him it was right just because it was what he wanted.

Walter rushed out to his car when his shift ended. Dan, his co-worker noticed his good mood and asked him, "Walter what has got into you lately? Did you finally find a girl who will give you the time of day?" The whole plant made fun of Walter. He was just so weird. They knew he did not have much luck with women.

Walter smiled and answered, "Actually, yes I found me a special lady." He smiled to himself all the way to the shed. He got the key and unlocked the door. He was in one of the best moods he could ever remember.

Maggie was still in the corner with the blanket. The far away look in her eyes did not register with Walter. He jabbered away and started telling her about his day.

"Maggie, I rushed to get here just to see you. I had the best day ever. Actually, I think it was the best day of my life. I brought you some more chicken soup. I hope you are hungry. Maybe I will let you outside today. The weather man said it was going to be a bright sun shiny day."

He looked at Maggie and noticed she had not moved at all. He went over to her and leaned down. "Maggie, sweetheart, can you hear me? Here let me help you up." He reached down and lifted her up to sit on the bed. He smoothed down her hair with his hand, spit on his palm, and tried to rub her hair in place.

He got the soup from the basket. "Now I will find your spoon and you can eat. Where did you put your spoon? It was right here beside the bowl." He looked around and found the broken spoon on the floor.

"Maggie, what were you doing with the spoon? It looks like you were digging in the dirt with it," he said. He saw the marks she put on the floor the night before. "I told you that you can never escape, didn't I? If you try anything else I will have to hurt you, and you will not like it," he said.

Walter is very angry now, and it has ruined his mood. "You act like you don't appreciate the trouble I went to in bringing you here. It's your own fault, Maggie, if I hurt you. I told you if you try anything stupid I would know."

He paced around the tiny room and said in a hateful voice, "You have spoiled my day. I thought you were different Maggie. I am so disappointed in you. I am going to leave. You can spend the whole day thinking about what you can do to make it up to me. I told you to listen, didn't I? You really do not want to find out what I am capable of, Maggie."

He went to the door and she heard the lock, and it penetrated the fog in her head. She listened for the sound of the car leaving and let her breath out. The fear she felt before was nothing compared to the terror she now feels.

She thought to herself, what did he say about hurting me? I have to get out of here. I want to go home.

Maggie started to cry and lies on the bed. She felt something under her and she reached for it. She pulled out the photo album and opened it. The picture of her makes her stare again in disbelief. However, the terror had only begun.

She flipped the pages and stared at the other pictures with pasted faces. The first girl looked around sixteen. The second girl was a little older. The third picture looked a lot like her when she was younger.

Maggie thought back. He said there were others. Oh God, did he hurt these girls? Where are they now? She felt a hatred building in her heart. First Sarah was taken, and now these beautiful innocent girls. It was not fair. "I must stop him," she said to herself. "Maggie, you have to pull yourself together. You must figure out how to get away from him. He will keep on if I don't do something."

# CHAPTER EIGHT

Alan and Ashlee Harris were so proud of their daughter, sixteen-year old Shelly. The local paper ran the story when Shelly and her team won the championship soccer match at the local high school. The team picked Shelly as the most valuable player of the season. She looked so cute in the picture. Her mother bought extra copies to put in her scrapbook she started when Shelly was born. Shelly's sweet personality made her well liked by all her classmates. She felt so proud of the nomination, but was a little embarrassed about all the publicity. She had a good time just being able to play on the team. She never thought of getting her picture in the paper.

Shelly's mother, Ashlee, gave a party and invited the whole team to a back yard barbecue. The Harris' loved having a house full of energetic teenagers. The other kids often came to hang out at the Harris's house. They always felt welcome. Shelly was the all-around typical American sweetheart.

Shelly's father was very protective of her. He made sure he knew where she was all the time. Wherever she went, Shelly had a cell phone, and kept in close contact with her parents out of respect.

One Saturday night, Shelly asked if she could go to the movies with a few friends. She liked a boy named Shawn, and she was to meet him and a few other friends at the theater. The movie was over at 10:30, and she told her parents she would be home by 11:15 p.m.

Her father woke up at 12:30 and went to get a glass of water. He thought he would check and make sure Shelly arrived home safely. When he checked her room, her bed was empty. He went to question his wife to make sure Shelly had not made other plans that he did not know about. Mrs. Harris agreed that she should have been home.

They went into Shelly's room to find Shawn's phone number and when Shawn's father answered, he too was concerned and woke Shawn up. Shawn told Mr. Harris that he had said good-bye to Shelly after the movie and the last time he saw her, she was walking to her car. He was certain that she had told him she was heading straight home.

Mr. Harris thanked Shawn and out of fear, they called the police. The officers arrived in a short time, and took all the information on Shelly and the vehicle. They assured the parents they would go immediately to the theater and would keep them informed.

When the officers arrived at the theater, it was almost bare. The only people were the few workers cleaning up and closing for the night. None of them could recognize Shelly's picture. They had seen hundreds of teenagers come to watch movies that day, and could not remember her specifically.

The officers searched the parking lot and found the car locked. Shelly had left with someone else, or someone prevented her from getting into her car. The police officers reported to Mr. and Mrs. Harris and told them that Shelly probably went with another friend, and would be in touch with them soon. That was three months ago and they still did not know where their daughter was, or if she was still alive.

Mrs. Harris's routine changed instantly. Before Shelly's disappearance, she was active in many things. She went to the gym three times a week, attended a neighborhood sewing class, and worked at the library part time. She was a troop leader for the girl scouts.

Now Mrs. Harris never left the house. She sat by the phone waiting for it to ring. Should she walk the streets looking for her daughter, or wait by the phone twenty-four hours a day? Three months ago, her life was relaxed. Now fear controlled her life. Where was her daughter and what had happened to her? Her life was in limbo. Her marriage was breaking apart.

Mr. Harris was not much better. His daily routine took him to the police station. He could not believe that a sixteen-year old girl vanished and no one, including the police, could tell him what happened to Shelly. He often got in his car and drove through the town just hoping he would see Shelly. His emotions were all scrambled. Most days, he felt nothing. If he gave in to the roller coaster, he may never get off.

Three months ago, he looked forward to coming home. No one could understand how it had changed. He would come in the door, and expect to hear Shelly's laughter. He used to head to the kitchen. Ashlee and Shelly loved to cook together. They were more like sisters; they picked on each other all the time. He would join them and the three of them would spend hours having a fun time and enjoying each other's company.

Life was good, then. Life was carefree, then. Life was normal. Now, if he did go to work, he could not concentrate. He waited, every second of every day. News of his daughter, and that she was well, was the only thing he thought about.

When he opened his door to his own home now, it was like a tomb. There was no laughter, no kids hanging out. The fun around the dinner table was gone. No more anything! Now, it was silent. His wife was not well. She did not smile anymore, she just cried. One day ran into another. He did not know how to help Ashlee. His wife had become a stranger to him. She woke up in the night screaming like a wounded animal. The mere image of what their daughter may have suffered was driving her crazy.

A mother cannot heal when one of her children disappears. They had no closure. There were no leads. It was as though Shelly evaporated into thin air. For sixteen years, she had been their reason for living, and now someone had taken her from them. There was no explanation as to why. There was no excuse for a human being hurting a young girl just because they felt a desire, a desire that person claims they cannot resist. Shelly had a right to live, everyone does.

A stranger forced Alan and Ashlee Harris, two loving parents, to feel agony. Once they were a normal family, striving everyday to be kind and loving, now it was a struggle to face the next day.

# CHAPTER NINE

Walter was reading the local paper to pass the time at the power plant. His job as a security guard allowed him plenty of time to read. He was feeling lonely, and saw a picture of a pretty girl. He heard his mother tell him, "Walter, don't bother looking at her picture, she would never have anything whatsoever to do with you." "Mother, leave me alone," he said.

A thought popped in his mind. "Why don't I go find her? The old abandoned shed on my uncle's farm would make a great hiding place. I could keep this girl there and when she agreed to be my wife, I could finally have a perfect family."

Walter devised a plan. The paper gave her address. He could figure a way to drug her and take her to the shed. He researched the internet to find the best way to drug someone. You could purchase the drug chloroform on line. He read the best way to administer it, and the dosage to use.

Walter placed his order and waited anxiously for it to come in the mail. He went to the shed and put in a bed. He bought some rope at the hardware store. He reinforced the walls and locks to make sure no one could escape. The shed was isolated. No one lived nearby. The closest houses were two miles away on each side.

After two weeks, his plan was coming together. He followed Shelly for a week. He knew she usually went to the theater on Saturday night. He would hide behind her car. The parking lot was not well lit, and no one would see him if his plan worked out right.

By the time Saturday rolled around, Walter was so excited. He made sure he had a cloth ready and at 10:30, he saw the kids coming out to get in their cars to go home. He poured the chloroform on the cloth, and when Shelly came out, and headed to her car, he was waiting. She never saw him. He crept up behind her, and placed the cloth over her face. Within minutes, he headed to the shed with Shelly in his trunk.

"Boy," he said, "that was easier than I thought. Now I have her all to myself. She is such a pretty girl."

Walter parked his car a few feet from the door at the shed. He unlocked the door and lit the lantern. He went back to the car and unlocked the trunk. Shelly was oblivious to what was happening.

He carried Shelly into the shed. He laid her on the bed and tied her hands and feet to the bedposts. He placed the lantern on the table, sat in the chair, and watched her as she slept.

Walter really was not sure how long the drug lasted. Since this was his first time, he hoped he did not use too much. He went to the side of the bed and ran his hands over her hair. The thrill of it was what he waited for all his life. She was his perfect girl.

He fell asleep around 4:00 am and woke up around 6:30 when he heard her moaning.

Walter stood by the bed and when she roused from sleep, she looked around trying to figure out where she was. She turned and saw him standing there and she started screaming.

She tried to move her arms and legs. Terror crept into her body. She pulled on the ropes and wildly thrashed on the bed. The drug had slowed her mind.

"Where am I?" she screamed. "Who are you? Are you going to kill me? Help, please, somebody help me."

He tried talking to her. "Don't be afraid." he said. "I won't hurt you. I brought you here so we can be alone. I think you are so pretty. My name is Walter. Shelly, I just want to get to know you. Please, stop screaming."

Shelly became hysterical. She had no idea who he was. She had no idea how she got here, and fear was taking over her mind. "I want to go home," she screamed. "Please let me go."

Walter reached out and touched her arm. "You are so soft," he said.

Shelly screamed louder. She was thrashing around on the bed pulling at the ropes.

Walter wanted her to stop screaming. He put his hand over her mouth. "You have to be quiet," he told her. "Don't scream or I will hurt you."

This made her scream and fight more. He took the pillow and put over her face. Shelly fought harder and beats at his chest. She manages to free one hand and her fingernails rake down across Walter's face.

He pushed the pillow down, her screams stopped. He wanted to make sure she did not scream anymore so he held the pillow down for a while.

Shelly stopped moving and finally was quiet.

Walter removed the pillow and told her, "See, isn't that better. I had to stop you somehow." He watched her face to see if when she looked at him again, she was calmer. She was not moving at all. He leaned down to listen for her breathing. He heard nothing.

There was a blank look in her eyes. Walter shook her repeatedly. He waited a few minutes and accepted that she was not coming back.

"Oh this is just great," his mother said. "I told you that you were stupid. Now you done went and killed her."

Walter sat on the bed looking at the girl's body. "Now what am I going to do?" he asked. The old well on the property would come in very handy now. "Well, you may as well get to it. You know what you have to do now."

Walter rubbed his hand over her hair. She was so soft and beautiful. The necklace she was wearing was a little angel on a silver chain. He took a minute to admire her. He leaned over and kissed her gently on the lips. He said, "Good bye Shelly. I am sorry you made me do this."

He has to hurry before the sun comes up. He went out to the well and removed the heavy slab on the top. He looked in and could not see the bottom. If I throw her in here, no one will ever know what I have done, he thought.

He headed back to the shed, stood over her, and felt her face. "I wish you wouldn't have made me do this to you. I have never been close to someone that is so pretty. Why did you make me hurt you? Why couldn't you just stay here so I could spend my time with you? It's not my fault. I had to make you stop. I am so sorry, Shelly. I have to get rid of you."

Walter picked the body up and carried her to the well. He laid her on top and pushed her over the side. He heard her hit the water.

Walter straightened up the shed and went to his car. As he drove home he thought, I will just have to try again. Maybe I will have better luck next time.

He was whistling by the time he arrived at the house he used to share with his mother. He went in the kitchen and started fixing breakfast. As he waits on his toast, he thought to himself, if at first you don't succeed, try, and try, again.

# CHAPTER TEN

Maggie tried to recover after looking at the pictures of the three girls in the photo album. The face of each of the girls was so precious. Each one looked so young and so innocent. It brought what happened to Sarah back to her. She was only six.

She thought, I know who took Sarah. Did Walter kill these three girls? Did this town have two killers on the loose? Why wasn't the public informed? Has God put me here for a reason? Maybe it will be up to me to stop both of them. The determination was building in her. She hoped she would be ready.

She felt so drained. Her head hung down and she gave in to the despair again. Her heart could not take any more pain. She was not sure what Walter had in store for her. If he had killed the other girls, what chance did she have to survive?

She needed to hang on to what was waiting for her if she ever went back home. Jim was there. Her parents, and Jim's parents, were there. Gwen, Tom, and Jill were there. As she thought of Jill, the realization that she would never see Sarah again caused her to break. The sobs racked her body.

Will I ever get over losing my beloved daughter? Do I want to go on living? Do I have the will to survive? Or do I want to give up? Again, she curled up on the bed. Somewhere inside of her, she remembered when they found Sarah's body, and thoughts of taking her own life seemed like the answer. The night when they took Sarah away, she had the bottle of pills in her hand. She wanted to end the pain. How easy it would have been.

She laid there for a long time. She was numb. Could she ever feel anything now? How long until a heart broken by grief mended?

68

All the other girls had mothers and fathers and as she thought of them, she knew what they were going through. I am not the only one to lose a child. How does a mother go on?

She thought back over her life, how she never once gave a thought to others who lost children before.

Was I so blinded by my own selfish wants and needs? Is this world that selfish? I thought I had done my duty. I went to church. I gave to charities at Christmas. I donated food to the poor. I didn't hurt anyone. I did not steal or cheat. All I ever wanted was to be a good wife and mother.

She hung her head in shame as she thought, Yeah, pat yourself on the back. My life has been so sheltered. I promise if you help me God, I will never take for granted the privileges I have again. Please help me. Please let me know what to do.

She tried to stay focused but her mind went back to the two weeks of terror waiting to find Sarah. All the details seem so real. The terrible memories flooded her mind. She started to sob again. "God, don't leave me here," was her prayer.

Maggie relived the two weeks searching for Sarah.

# CHAPTER ELEVEN

Maggie and Jim went back to the park. Officer Garret met them and talked with them for a few minutes. Jim asked if there was any news.

Officer Garret told him "No news yet. We are going to keep the search parties out a while longer. When it gets dark, I will have to pull them out of the woods. We have sent another group over to the wooded area across the street. Maybe Sarah wandered over there. We are expanding the search area. I have heard from the agency and the Amber Alert is on the airwaves. If anyone at all has seen her, we will know."

Jim asked him, "Do you expect to hear from the news cast? Do you think anyone has seen Sarah?"

He replied, "I hope it helps us. Maybe if someone sees her picture, and remembered seeing her in the area, they will call. Mrs. Taylor, I know you have had time to go over this afternoon's events. Have any other details come to mind yet?"

Maggie shook her head. "No," she said. "I have played it out over and over in my mind. I do not understand where she could have wandered in just five minutes. I am going to go and look. I have to find her. She has to be in the woods."

Maggie walks toward the woods. Jim stays with Officer Garret and asks him what he thinks the chances are of finding Sarah before it gets too dark.

Officer Garret says, "I cannot believe we have not found her yet. If she is lost here in this wooded area, we should have found her by now. The search parties are very diligent in checking in every place they think she could be."

Officer Garret said, "We will keep looking. I have called in extra patrols to canvas the roadways and neighbors within ten miles of the park. When they return, I will set up another briefing. I am not sure what the other agencies present will want to do next."

Jim thanked him and went to find Maggie. He saw Gwen on his way and went to her.

"How is Maggie?" she asked him. "I took her to the diner down the road, and she ate a little of my salad. So far, she is being strong. I hope we hear soon. I do not know what to expect if night comes and we do not find Sarah. That is when Maggie will fall apart."

Gwen leaned in to hug Jim and said, "I spoke to Tom a while ago. He said to tell you that everything at the office is going fine. He will take care of the business unless you need him here."

Jim said, "No, I appreciate him taking the responsibility of the office. Maggie and I both could never want better friends than you and Tom. Maggie loves you, you know. She thinks of you as the sister she never had. I am glad you are here."

As Jim was walking towards Maggie, he heard her ask Officer Garret. "Officer Garret, have your men found anything at all? Please don't hide anything from me!"

Jim approached Maggie and wrapped his arms around her. Officer Garret turns to look at Jim, and is relieved when he heard Jim tell her, "Honey, it's not Officer Garret's fault. I told him not to tell you they found one of Sarah's hair ribbons."

Maggie screamed at Officer Garret, "Give it to me! I need to keep it!"

Officer Garret calmly replied, "I'm sorry Mrs. Taylor, we have to keep it as evidence."

"Evidence of what?" she shouted.

Jim reaches out and holds her. "Maggie, please let Officer Garret do his job." Maggie stands and demands. "Tell me right now what this means. Do you think someone took Sarah? I left her for five minutes. How could someone have taken her without me seeing him? I was only over there. Did they hurt her? Tell me, I need to know."

Jim holds on to her and asks Officer Garret, "What do you think this means? Has someone kidnapped our daughter?"

Officer Garret hesitates to tell them what it really means to him. He did not want to take the hope of finding her away from them. He knows that he had recently received a bulletin from the next county about a seven year old taken from the mall. The report did not go into detail. He would have to wait until he got back to the office to read it. He hoped that this was not the second little girl kidnapped. How was he going to tell these two parents that a child molester might be in the area? It was a town's worst nightmare. He also wanted to get back to work on the three teens that were also missing.

What was happening in their hometown? How many lives would this destroy before they solved it and took the predators off the street? Were they looking for one man?

Officer Garret asks the Taylor's to follow him back to the picnic area. He would call his men and decide what would be the next step. If he was looking for a body, they conducted the search a little different. A child that is alive will answer when you yell for them. There were too many places to bury a body.

Officer Garret left the Taylor's at the picnic table and went to his squad car. He sent a radio transmission for his officers to come back to the command post. He needed to do this away from the Taylors. He goes to find Officer Cari Johnson. She will have to occupy the Taylor's so he can question his men. If they had uncovered any other pieces of clothing, the prospect of finding her alive was not likely.

Officer Cari Johnson asked the Taylor's if they would please go with her to the station. They needed to file an official report of Sarah's disappearance. It was standard procedure, but she also was following Officer Garret's instructions to keep them busy until he could speak frankly with his men.

Jim agreed but Maggie did not want to leave. She told Jim to go so she could stay and search more. He convinced her she had to go since she was the last one to see Sarah. Jim had a bad feeling, and in order not to upset Maggie until they had to, he wanted to put some distance between her and this place. Maggie agreed finally and they went to get in the car with Officer Johnson.

As they were driving away, Maggie turned in her seat and as she looked at the park site she thought, "I will never feel the same about this place. How can I ever come back here with Sarah? We will have to find another park close by."

Officer Cari Johnson pulled into the station and opened the door for the Taylors. She led them into the station and told them to wait in a seating area until she found someone to take the official report. She came back and led them to a desk nearby.

One of the officers introduced himself as Officer Sam Collins. He told them he was going to tape the interview just to make sure they had the information right. He asked their names and then asked for the description of Sarah's disappearance.

Maggie broke into tears as she told them she could not believe that she only took her eyes off Sarah for five minutes and it led to this. As the officer recorded the information, Maggie tried to stay calm. She kept telling herself that she could not lose her composure until she knew where Sarah was. She had to hold on to the belief that they would find her wandering somewhere lost but safe.

After they were finished, Officer Cari Johnson took them back to the park. Officer Garret met with the men and gave them the information about the hair ribbon. He hated to tell them that he was considering the possibility that someone had abducted this girl. He relayed the information about the previous abduction in the next county. He wanted his men to be prepared and search for a body. It never came easy, this part of his job.

Officer Garret had to stay focused and lead the other men. He did not have the luxury of walking away and hiding in the woods and screaming at the top of his lungs, which is what he wanted to do. He had been a police officer for twenty-two years, and he never felt this inadequate before.

# CHAPTER TWELVE

Three weeks before in the next county, Mrs. Burns took her daughter Candy to the North Mall in the square of town. Every Saturday they spent the day there.

They lived in the bad section of Shawsville, Pa. The young teen boys in the downtown area belonged to city gangs that caused too many problems for the police. The ambulance transported three boys to the hospital in the last six months with life threatening injuries relating to the gang fights. The council and the law enforcement warned all the parents to keep their children off the street.

The officials set up an 11:30 p.m. curfew. The Shawsville people met with the council and the board members of the mall. They proposed building new play areas for the kids. The project took two years, and when it was finished, many parents took their kids to the mall for the whole day. They felt safer in this environment.

Mrs. Burns and Candy arrived Saturday morning around 9:30. Candy looked forward to the Kids Room. She loved to spend hours in the ball pit. Mrs. Burns took Candy to the desk and registered her. She told the attendant she was going to do her grocery shopping and would return to pick Candy up around 10:30.

It took a little longer than she had expected to finish grocery shopping. It was 10:45, when she finally went to get Candy.

Candy asked her mother, "Can I stay one more hour?" Mrs. Burns shook her head and told her they had to stop at the pharmacy and the groceries might thaw out, so they had to hurry. She promised that next Saturday she would give her extra time.

This satisfied Candy so they headed for the pharmacy. On the way, Candy asked if she could get an Oreo Blizzard at Dairy Queen. Her mother looked at her and smiled.

She said, "I really do not understand how you kids eat those things. I get a toothache immediately. You young kids have stomachs of iron. Okay, since you have been good, I'll let you have one."

Candy was thrilled and yelled, "Yipee" all the way to the counter. Mrs. Burns ordered the ice cream and handed it to her. Candy spotted a few girls from school and asked if she could sit at the table across from them to finish her Blizzard while her mother went to the pharmacy.

Mrs. Burns looked at her and said, "For being only seven years old, you are getting mighty independent." She helped Candy find a table and waved to her as she headed for the pharmacy to refill her husband's prescription.

There were four people ahead of her and finally it was her turn. She handed the prescription to the girl who asked if she was going to wait for it or come back later. Mrs. Burns asked how long it would take and the girl told her fifteen minutes.
She told her she would wait for it so she would not have to make a special trip back later.

Mrs. Burns went and looked down the mall lobby to check on Candy. She was eating away at her ice cream. Mrs. Burns chuckled to herself and waved to her. Candy waved back and continued taking big bites of her Blizzard.

Mrs. Burns went back in the pharmacy. She wanted to check on a new eye shadow color she saw advertised, and went to find the right aisle. She looked at several lines of cosmetics, but did not see the new color. She continued browsing until she heard her name called over the intercom.

76

She returned to the desk, paid for the medicine, tucked it in her bag, and went to find Candy so they could head home.

She glanced at the tables and did not see Candy at first. She readjusted her bags, which were a little heavy, and walked around all the tables, but could not find her. She thought she may have gone to the bathroom and went to ask the attendant where the closest bathroom was.

He told her it was down the hall on the right. Mrs. Burns found it, opened the door, and called for Candy. She got no response so she looked under all the stalls for her pink sneakers she wore that morning. She did not see them and went back to the counter to ask if anyone remembered seeing her daughter. The attendants and the other customers said they did not remember her. Mrs. Burns was a tad bit irritated. Candy usually listened to her. It occurred to her that Candy might have gone back to the ball pit, so she headed back.

Mrs. Burns approached the desk. The attendant that was there when she checked Candy in that morning was on break. Mrs. Burns told her she was looking for her daughter and asked if she could go to the ball pit and check for her. The attendant told her sure, and when she did not see her, Mrs. Burns went back to the desk. The attendant told her the other girl would be back in five minutes so she said she would wait.

When the first girl returned, she told Mrs. Burns that she remembered checking Candy in at 9:30, but had not seen her after she had picked her up. Mrs. Burns told her she could not find her daughter, and the attendant asked if she would like to call security and have them make an announcement to see if Candy approached any other desks for help. Mrs. Burns told her she would be grateful and the girl made the call.

When the security officer arrived, he took her to the main desk in the center of the mall. He asked for a description of Candy. She gave him a picture, and told him she was seven years old. He asked what she was wearing. She told him, a rose-colored T-shirt, jeans, and pink sneakers. He made the announcement and asked Mrs. Burns to take a seat. He informed her they waited a half hour before they should start to worry.

Mrs. Burns took a seat and picked up a magazine to read. She got so involved in the story about "What to Feed Your Pets" she was surprised when the thirty minutes were up.

The security officer called her up to the desk and told her he had informed his supervisors and they were going to shut down the mall, just in case. He said a manager would come to get her and take her upstairs to the main security office to make a report.

She heard the intercom announcement about Candy missing and as her heart started to flutter as she followed the manager to the main office. She told Mrs. Burns the police were on their way, which was standard procedure.

The officer arrived shortly and escorted Mrs. Burns to a private office. He gathered the necessary information from her and told her that the security offices were scanning the tapes for the approximate time that she last saw Candy. He assured her that most of the time the children wandered while browsing at the windows full of toys.

It took twenty minutes to get the tapes ready for her. She sat at the screen and as she viewed the last few frames, she spotted a girl that looked like Candy. The operator rewound the frames and zoomed in on the picture.

As Mrs. Burns looked closer, her heart stopped. She stared at the computer screen and her world changed instantly. The image was of her seven-year old daughter leaving the mall with a strange man. Mrs. Burns did not recognize the man, and would never forget the image of Candy's hand in his.

The alert went out to all the counties surrounding Shawsville. The news of the abduction of a seven-year old girl spread quickly. The law enforcement gave a description from the security tape. An all-points bulletin was for a male, thirty to thirty five years old, brown hair, wearing a gray hooded sweatshirt. Roadblocks were set up around the mall. Too much time had elapsed since Mrs. Burns last saw Candy. The best chance comes within minutes of the abduction.

Mrs. Burns called her husband and he met her at the mall. Guilt was tearing her apart.

All she could say was, "I should have kept her with me. Why did I let her out of my sight? It was only for a few minutes."

The detective assigned to the case was Martin Wallace, a veteran of the police force. After twenty-five years, he never stopped wondering how humanity can be so cruel.

He met with Mr. and Mrs. Burns, and drove them to the station. He went over the details with Mrs. Burns and made sure that all his officers had the picture of Candy. They called in the news team and put the abduction and pictures on the newscast.

The phone calls from the crackpots started almost instantly. So far, the leads had not panned out. Searching for an abducted child taken by an adult male who could have posed as her father is hard to trace. It could have been anyone off the street, and he could have gotten a hundred miles from Shawsville.

Detective Wallace knew the statistics. It only takes thirty seconds to persuade a child to go with you. Thirty seconds that changes a family's life forever.

Unfortunately, the manhunt ended quickly. A janitor spotted Candy's body behind a dumpster within a matter of six hours. A young life so brutally ended. The stranger from the video convinced her to go with him and then assaulted and strangled Candy. Her mother and father were devastated.

Three weeks later, Detective Wallace received a phone call from Officer Garret checking the facts about the abduction and murder of Candy Burns. Officer Garret informed him that his case was a six-year old girl taken from the Clarkstown Park. If it was the same man, the two towns harbored a serial child molester.

# CHAPTER THIRTEEN

Maggie tried to brace herself for the turmoil when Walter returned. She does not know how long she has, but there is no doubt he would return. He was angry with her when he left because she tried to dig under the wall, and he threatened her when he found the spoon. In his mind, he felt betrayed by her attempt to escape.

She was almost positive he had harmed the other three girls. If Walter killed them, where were their bodies? She remembered him telling her that he would hurt her, as he did the others.

Maggie Taylor had no idea what she would have to do to save her own life. Hopefully, she is strong enough to endure until she figures it out. She barely withstood the loss of Sarah, and she wondered if her willpower to fight was strong enough.

Maggie drew on her inner strength she inherited from her parents. In all her life, she tried to be a good person, and up until now, she was extremely lucky with the things she held dear and all the pride she felt about the example of what a person should be. In her heart, she muttered a prayer. Her thoughts went to Jim and she said, "Jim, I hope you haven't given up on me. I need to feel your presence with me. If you can, send me your love. I need you now more than I ever have before."

The trauma of the past few weeks was playing havoc with her emotions. She looked bad; her complexion was white as a sheet. The bags under her eyes were black, and her hands shook constantly. In the past few days, she had not eaten hardly anything. Her stomach was so upset and her head was pounding.

The medicine Walter brought her was on the table and she swallowed some of the Pepto. The rest of the things Walter brought her;

the make-up, the perfume, the hairbrush and the mirror, sat neatly on the table.

She picked up the brush and the mirror. She tried to smooth down her hair and with her fingers, tried to wipe some of the dirt off her face. When she looked at her image, she knew she had aged ten years.

What is the outcome of this trial I have to bear? she thought. When Walter does come back, do I have the ability to con him into believing that I am happy to be here? I know that is what I must do if I am going to beat him at this horrible game. Am I going to get out of this alive? I must not think about what it will take. I have to get back home.

She took a few minutes to let the heaviness on her shoulders weigh her down, and shook herself to relieve some of the tension. "Okay," she said, "I am ready to start the next episode in this nightmare." She sat on the bed and waited until she heard the car pulling up beside the shed. She counted to ten, forced her breath to slow, and closed her eyes and tried to put all her fear aside.

Maggie heard the car door close. She heard the key turning the lock. She fearfully waited as Walter opened the door and came inside. He looked at her and she saw the anger and hurt on his face. She must make him believe she was sorry for what she did. "I am sorry for upsetting you. Please forgive me," she said while her head hung down. "I will not try anything else, I promise."

Walter hesitated and within seconds, she could see his demeanor change. He came to the side of the bed and said to her, "Maggie, I told you that I would not put up with you not listening to me. Your life depends on you doing exactly as I say. I am trying to show you that you are the only woman for me. I want to take care of you. I need you to appreciate all I have done. No one else cares for you as I do. Now, we will start over. But, remember, you only get one more chance. Do not spoil it by trying to get away. You will never be able to get out. I made sure there is no way out of here. You have to get it through your head that you are now mine. We will have a great life together. Do you promise?"

"Yes," she said, "I promise."

This makes him happy and he actually giggles with glee. "I am glad I picked you, Maggie. I know we are soul mates, and in all my life, I have never had one person that I could count on. You are that person for me, Maggie. I just know it."

Maggie cringed inside. She asked herself, what have I done? I have committed myself now, and I must keep up with it until I get away from this sick monster.

Walter told her he brought her a tuna sandwich from home. He walked to the cooler. He gives her the sandwich and a can of soda. "I hope you like tuna," he said. "I hated the way my mother used to make tuna. She always put celery in it and I told her over and over, that I hated onions. I make it with salad dressing. Do you like it?" he asked her.

Maggie took a bite, and even though her stomach wanted no part of food, she nodded her head yes.

Walter picked up his sandwich, and sat in the chair beside the bed. He chatters about how beautiful the weather is.

"If you feel like it, I may open the door and let you look outside today. Would you like that?" Walter asked.

"I would love to feel the sunshine on my face," she said.

"Well, eat your sandwich, and after that we will see," he told her.

When she finished the tuna sandwich, Walter handed her a flyer from a shopping center. He opened it and showed her a picture of a wedding band.

"I want us to have matching rings, and I am going to get these two if you like it. We have to have matching rings. It wouldn't be right if they don't match."

She looked at the picture and said, "I have my own rings." She pulled back as he stood.

His face turned beet red. "You have to forget about your husband. You belong to me now."

He grabbed her hand and ripped the rings off her finger. He went to the door and threw her rings as hard as he could.

"We will never speak of your husband again. If we are going to be happy, you must devote yourself completely to me. Do you understand?" he asked her.

Maggie willed herself to remain calm. Inside she is shaking. "I understand," she told him.

Walter paced around the room for a few minutes. He rubbed his hands together as he walked.

It was as though he has the absolute right to claim her and she had no say. He looked back at her and a smile appeared on his face.

"I know you love me. I knew when I chose you that fate brought us together. The day I was at your house and you looked at me, I knew then that I would bring you here. It was meant to be."

Maggie frantically searched her memory. He must have been among the people that were searching for Sarah. I do not remember seeing him there, she thought to herself. Did I look at him? Those days are like a blur. I do not even remember anyone being there. I went through torture then, and I am not finished yet.

Walter sat down in the chair. "Now," he said, "we must decide on the rings. I will get these for us. Now if you want, I will let you go outside the door for a few minutes before I have to leave for work. Only if you promise you will not try to run away. Mary made that mistake, and you don't want to end up like her."

He went to the corner and got a long rope. "I am going to tie this rope around your neck. I will not hurt you unless you make me. I will let you stay outside for five minutes. So stand up and I will fix the rope," he told her.

Maggie stood up and turned her back to him. He took the rope and tied a noose around her neck. It was all she could do to stand still. She wanted to scratch his eyes out, but she knew he would kill her if she tried. She stood perfectly still until he finished with the knot and he led her to the door and opened it.

Maggie stepped outside and the sun on her face was a wonderful feeling. She only took a few steps. She did not doubt that he would tighten the rope and her life would be over.

The dampness in the shed was void of sunshine or warmth. Being outside gave her hope as the sun beats on her head. "I will survive. I will survive. I will survive," she repeats repeatedly in her mind.

Maggie suddenly thought back to what he said, "Mary tried that, and it was a mistake." What did he mean? Was Mary one of the girls in the album? And where is she now, her mind raced. She would check the book as soon as he left. Until then I will just stand still.

Walter held the rope and watched Maggie as she stood in the sun. She is more beautiful than all the others. I love her, he thought. He watched the time and when five minutes was up, he told her to go back in the shed. He untied the rope.

Walter found the lantern and told her she has enough oil for the night. As he prepares to leave, he said, "I left you a sandwich for later. I have to go but I will be back in the morning. Try to get some sleep. Tomorrow is another big day and we have so many plans to make. I will go now and I will see you tomorrow."

He looked around to make sure he did not forget anything. He started for the door, turned to her, and said, "I know you are the right one Maggie. I am so glad I brought you here." He went out the door and she heard the lock fall into place.

As soon as she heard the car pulling away, she went to find the photo book. As she flipped through the pages she silently prayed, "Please don't let me find Mary." The picture of Shelly is first, and as she turned the page, she saw the story of Mary Hollister and her heart broke.

What did he do to her? Am I next?

# CHAPTER FOURTEEN

Mary Hollister set her clock in her room for 6:00 a.m. She wanted to get to school early to set up her science project. Her mother told her she could drive to school that morning instead of riding the bus.

Mary was an excellent student, and she had devoted a lot of hours and time into her experiment. The teacher submitted Mary's project, and it won first prize.

The local paper ran a story about the science fair, and when her mother read the article, she was proud of her daughter. She showed it to all her friends.

Mary was a little surprised about how many people read the article and how different some of her classmates treated her. They used to call her a geek, but mostly because she was so smart. Now, they sat with her at lunch and asked her to go out that weekend with them.

She asked her mother if she could go and her mother said to her, "Mary, go and have a good time. You spend too much time on your computer. Take time off and enjoy being with the other girls."

She told them she would meet them at the bowling alley Saturday morning. She had a great time bowling, she had not done it for years. One of the boys she had talked to before asked her to go to a movie Saturday evening. She hesitated but finally said she would go.

Her parents were going out Saturday evening with another couple but they told Mary she could have her mother's car. They left around 7:00.

Mary was meeting her friend, Tyler at 8:00. She took extra time to get ready. She hoped Tyler would like the new sweater she had bought. Mary did not realize how pretty she really was. All the boys noticed her, but she was so busy with the books they never got her full attention.

Tyler was glad she was going with him, and he thought she was a real nice girl.

Mary met Tyler, and they had a wonderful time at the movie. She hated to see the evening end. They said goodbye to each other and made a date for the next Saturday night. Tyler said he wanted to take her to the football game their team was playing at a school in the next district. She told him she was looking forward to it and she got in her car and headed home.

Mary pulled into the driveway and got out of the car. She was so happy thinking about the movie and she did not hear someone coming up behind her.

Mary's parents arrived home around 11:00. They were going up the walk when Mary's mother noticed Mary's purse lying on the ground beside the car. She bent down and picked it up. She showed it to her husband and said, "Why did Mary not take it in with her?" Her mother called for Mary. Mary did not answer, so she went to her room. Mary's room was empty.

She called to her husband and they searched all the other rooms. There was no sign of her. They tried to remember whom she was meeting that evening, and they called a few of the other kids in her class. One of the girls said she was there at the movie and she saw Tyler say goodbye to Mary around 10:00. They did not know Tyler's number and they decided to call the police.

The local station was on alert after the disappearance of Shelly Harris so they acted quickly.

Two police officers arrived at the house around 11:30. They checked the car for any sign of prints, and came up with nothing. Mary's parents were beside themselves with fear. Who would take their daughter?

The officers checked the information and told them that someone from the station would contact them the next morning and they could come to the station and fill out a report.

The officers met with their superiors and put an alert over the airwaves about another missing teen girl.

Mary's mother was not aware of the other girl's disappearance. When she talked to her friends and found out that the girl was still missing, her heart could not take it.

Mary's mother had heart trouble for the past few years, and the doctors were concerned with her last stress test. Her heart was weak and the knowledge that someone took her only daughter and meant to harm her was more than her heart could take. She had a massive stroke in the middle of the night and died.

One blessing in all this tragedy, a mother would not have to find out her daughter was no longer living.

Mary's father buried his wife and if that wasn't hard enough, he waited every day for news of his daughter's return. He lost both of his jewels that gave him a reason to live. Why did it have to happen? Was there an answer to that question?

The whole town started to panic. The news of the two disappearances spread quickly. Everyone looked at each other with a little more suspicion. Was there a serial killer in their midst? What did a killer look like?

The schools sent bulletins to the parents. They advised the kids to travel in pairs. The town they lived in all their lives began to look less appealing. What were the police doing to catch this guy? The newscasts ran the stories of Shelly and Mary night and day. The pressure was on law enforcement to catch this person and bring the two girls home.

Unfortunately, they did not realize the magnitude of the problem. They were unaware they were dealing with a child molester and the kidnapper of two girls. The department authorized overtime. They patrolled the streets in hopes of seeing something that would give them a lead to solve these horrible crimes. Everyone locked their doors and barred the windows. Mothers were afraid to let their daughters go on dates. Panic ran rampant.

## CHAPTER FIFTEEN

Walter was grouchy at work thinking about what happened with Shelly. The other guys made fun of him and asked him if his big date ended with the girl finding out he really was a dork. They poked fun all night unaware that Shelly lay at the bottom of the well. Walter ignored them and promised himself that one day they would envy him when he finally got the girl that would be his *perfect* mate forever. He went right to the paper to look for another prospect.

Walter spotted Mary's picture that night spent several hours fantasizing about her. He liked this one better anyhow.

He got the address and the next day went to look for her house. He spent Friday night sitting outside across from her house to watch for her.

Her father came home from work and later Mary and her mother pulled into the driveway after shopping. Walter was thrilled when he saw Mary in person. He could not wait until he could take her to his hideaway.

He spent Saturday getting the shed ready. He ate an early dinner and was across the road from her house by 6:30. He watched her parents leave. He was watching when Mary left at 8:00.

He went to the diner down the road and drank coffee wasting time, and was back outside her house at 9:30. He waited and was pleased when he saw Mary coming down the road at 10:30. He prepared the chloroform and sneaked up behind her when she got out of the car.

He did not notice when she dropped her purse. He was on his way to the shed long before her parents arrived after 11:00.

Walter parked, opened the door, and lit the lantern. He went back and opened the trunk. He carried Mary in and laid her on the bed. He got the rope and tied her hands and feet. He used less chloroform this time. He thought maybe he gave Shelly too much and that is why she woke up and he could not get her to stop screaming.

"Maybe this one would be a little bit less hysterical," he thought. He got her situated on the bed and waited for her to wake up. Within a few hours, he heard her moan.

When she opened her eyes, she was not sure where she was. She turned her head and saw Walter sitting on the chair. Terror burned in her soul. She fearfully asked, "What am I doing here? Who are you? What are you going to do to me?"

Walter stood and went to the side of the bed. "I am not going to hurt you, so don't scream. If you will be quiet I will explain," he told her.

She looked like a scared rabbit. She considered her options, and did not scream. He waited for her to look at him and he said, "I brought you here so I can get to know you better. We can be friends if you promise to be good. I can hurt you, but I really don't want to."

Mary stayed silent and waited for him to speak. "My name is Walter. I saw your picture in the paper and I thought you were so pretty and I chose to bring you here. The last girl screamed and she was sorry. You don't want to be sorry, do you?" he asked her. She could not get her voice to work enough to answer him, so she said nothing.

Walter took it to mean she agreed and he sat back down in the chair. As she looked at him, she could see the crazy glaze in his eyes. She had never seen him before.

Mary was scared to death. She wanted to live. She needed to get back to school. I have stuff I want to do. I have to finish my project. I made a date to go out with Tyler next week. My mother and father will miss me, she thought.

Walter stood and came to the side of the bed. He reached down and caressed the side of her face. "You are so soft and smell so good. I just want you to love me. I saw you with the other boy. He does not love you. I will keep you here forever and we can be happy. Would you like that?" he asked her.

Mary's mind could not understand. "I do not want you to touch me, you are crazy. Let me go. I want to go home. Please don't hurt me. I never did anything to you. Why did you bring me here?" she said to him.

Anger instantly consumed Walter. He stopped and looked at her. "I chose you. You are mine now. You will never go home. I brought you here because I need you to understand. I planned this all very carefully. We are all alone here. No one can bother us. We can spend every day with each other. Why do you question me?"

Mary is numb. What is he saying to me, she thought. I am going to be his prisoner forever? I do not want to be here. She stayed silent for fear of anything she might say making him angrier.

Walter's mood changes to a happy one. He went to the table and brought back a soda. "I got you this because I know all you kids love Pepsi. Would you like a drink?" he asked her.

Mary's throat is burning from the drug he used on her. She nods her head yes. He lifted her head off the pillow and gave her a drink. He sat the soda down and went back to the chair.

"Now, let's talk," he said. "What do you kids do for fun now days? I used to love to listen to my music. My mother always screamed for me to turn it down though. Do you like a certain group?"

Mary shook her head and said, "I do not listen to much music. I am too busy with my schoolwork. I want to go back to school. They will be looking for me. My mother is sick. Please let me go," she begged.

He stood again and started pacing around the room. "I will just leave you alone if you keep asking the same stupid questions. I told you that you have to stay here. I do not understand why that is so hard to get.

93

Didn't you hear what I said? You are mine now. Get used to it," he yelled at her.

He went out the door and slammed it behind him. He walked towards the well. He stood beside it and looked down and said, "Well, Shelly. I hope this one does not end up like you. I really like her. She is not as loud as you were. However, it seems like she don't get it either. Oh well, I will wait and see. If she forces me to hurt her, I guess you will be seeing her soon."

He turned and walked back to the shed and unlocked the door and went inside. He walked over and told her, "Mary you have two choices. One is to shut up and behave. The second one, keep this stuff up and you will wish you would have chosen the first."

Mary's eyes get big. She is so scared. She cannot breathe. She gulps for air and starts choking.

Walter rushed to the bed and tried to hold her head up a little. He does not want to lose her so he told her to hold on a minute. He untied her hands and feet and scooted her to the edge of the bed. He threw the rope around her neck and stood her on her feet. "I will take you outside so you can get some air," he said.

Mary is still choking and he untied her. He wrapped the rope around her neck and dragged her out the door. She tried to take in as much air as she could. He steadied her and waited for her to stop choking.

Mary calmed down a little and her breathing got a little better. As soon as she realized she was outside, she started running. The rope around her neck gets tight and Walter jerked on it to try to get her stopped.

Mary struggled to get away from him. The rope tightened and crushed her airway. She couldn't take in air. He watched as she dropped to the ground. He tried to loosen the rope. It took him a while to get the rope to loosen up a little. By the time he manages to get her airway open, it is too late. When he jerked the rope, it crushed the bone and before he could help her, she suffocated. It was almost accidental. He did not want to kill her. He had not wanted to kill Shelly either.

Now, he rubbed on his head as he looked down at her lying on the ground. Walter said, "I have to take her to the well. I told her. She did it to herself. Now she is dead," He rested for a while and finally took the rope off and put her over his shoulder. "I really did like you, Mary. I warned you, and you wouldn't listen."

He carried her to the well and laid her on the ground. He sat down beside her and rubbed her hair. She was so beautiful. He was frustrated and angry with her for making him do this.

As the sun comes up, Walter repeated the scene one more time. He took the lid off and scooted it to the side. He picked Mary up and laid her on the ledge. One shove and she fell to the bottom. He heard the water splash. He waited for a couple minutes to rest. He covered the well and made his way back to the shed.

He made sure that everything was back to normal as he leaves and locks the door. Walter got in his car and headed home. Within minutes, he is already making plans for his next victim. Shelly and Mary to him were just two mistakes.

Walter sings a silly song and makes up the words to include, "Next time will be better. I will find my perfect girl." He reached the house, washed his hands, sat in the chair where his father used to sit, and turned on the TV.

CHAPTER SIXTEEN

Maggie's thoughts after Walter left drifted back to hunt for Sarah. For her, time stood still. When she couldn't find Sarah, her head tried to tell her heart that something was amiss. She told herself, "Just keep looking for her, she is still in the woods. Why will no one believe me? You cannot give up hope."

Jim, on the other hand was trying to face the possibility that someone must have taken Sarah. He knew if she were just lost in the woods, they would have found her by now.

Jim braced himself for the dreaded discovery of her body. The search parties were still combing the woods. He needed to find Officer Garret and talk with him frankly about what was going on. He told Maggie to stay on the bench. He wanted to have a talk with the police.

Maggie blankly stared at his face, and he knew it was not registering what he was telling her. He knelt down in front of her and took her head in his hands. "Maggie, I need you to focus. Are you listening to me? I am going to find Officer Garret and I need you to stay right here until I get back. Okay?" he asked her.

Maggie shook her head yes, but had no idea what he was saying. Her mind was running in high gear and she knew she could not stop to think or she would fall apart.

Jim saw Officer Garret at the command post that was set up at the entrance to the park. He approached him and said, "Officer Garret, I need to know if you think Sarah is missing or has someone taken her? I want you to be honest with me. I have to know the truth so I can prepare my wife if something has happened to our daughter."

Officer Garret cleared his throat and sadly told him, "Mr. Taylor, if you want me to be blunt, I will. But you must understand that what I tell you may change if we find evidence that Sarah is still a missing child."

Jim took a step back. He told him to be blunt, but he was afraid to hear what may be coming next.

Officer Garret reached out and steadied Jim. "I certainly do not want to give you false hope. Unfortunately, what I say to you will not change the outcome of what may have happened with your daughter. Another child was abducted in a county nearby recently."

Officer Garret reluctantly continued, "A seven year old girl's body has been found behind a dumpster at a shopping mall. This may have no bearing on your daughter's case. Nevertheless, we do need to consider the possibility that a child molester is in this area. Now, after I have said all that, we may still find your daughter, Sarah. I have my men searching all the areas within a ten-mile radius. The newscast tonight may lead to more information. We will keep searching as long as it is light."

Jim's face showed his shocked reaction. The color had drained and left his face white. His eyes misted and he tried to regain his composure. He wiped the tears and said, "I know you have done this before. How do you know when to give up the search? Sarah may still be lost. We know she was with Maggie except for five minutes. I really do not understand how someone could have taken her in that little amount of time. Was someone waiting for Maggie to leave her alone? If that were the case, wouldn't my wife have seen someone? Maybe Sarah wanted to find her and wandered too far and did not know how to get back to her."

Officer Garret said, "Yes, someone must have been lurking a few feet away, and when he saw Sarah swinging by herself, he took the opportunity to rush in and grab her. He may have driven by the park and noticed her alone. Sometimes, we cannot explain the why's or how's."

Jim's shoulders sagged and he wanted to turn and run. "How am I to help Maggie if I cannot deal with this myself? I hope I have the courage to face this for her," he said. "If I could, I would take all this back. I wish a person could turn back the time and start this day over again."

Officer Garret again reached out to him and said, "Mr. Taylor, I have been in law enforcement for years. I have dealt with tragedy of my own. I can tell you that facing this kind of a situation does not come easy. I have no idea what is going through your mind. I think I can empathize with you, but I do not have any idea how a person can prepare themselves of harm of one of their children. I wish I could fix the world. Men that take children are the most evil creatures that roam this earth. I hope that before this day ends, we will have some good news about your daughter. I told you before to keep up your faith. Even no matter what the outcome, God is still in control and he is with us through all the valleys. My prayers are with you and your wife. My prayers are with the other parents that lost their seven-year old daughter. God certainly does not cause this to happen. He lets tragedy enter our lives for a reason. I know you and your wife attend a good church, and I am sure that the prayers for your daughter are heaven bound as we speak."

Jim noticed a tear running down Officer Garret's cheek.

Jim thanked him for his concern. "What is the next step? Are there any clues to track the person that took Sarah? She may be alive if we can find her. Do you have any leads about the man who took the other girl? In this day and time, you would think that a man cannot hide if the whole town is looking for him."

Officer Garret told him. "I cannot go into the details of the other case. There may not be any relevance to your daughter's case. I have to contact the other department and investigate the leads they have. We may still find your daughter. Do not give up all hope yet. Please, tell your wife for me that we are doing everything we can. I know it does not seem like much, but as soon as I do some checking, we will get out bulletins for the description of the other suspect."

Officer Garret put his hand on Jim's shoulder, "In the meantime, the news cast should air in an hour, and we may get some leads. If we do not have any solid evidence by tomorrow afternoon, we will follow up with another TV interview. The best way to have the public to help is to stay on the airwaves. If you will excuse me, I have to do a briefing with my men in fifteen minutes. I will let you know if anything else comes up."

Jim thanked him for taking time to talk to him, and went back to find Maggie.

The last time he saw her, she was on the bench. When he went to look for her, she was not there. He called for her and went to ask if anyone else had seen her. One of the women serving the coffee told him that she saw a woman head for the woods. Jim knew in his heart that it was Maggie. He headed to find her. He heard the voices of the fellow searchers calling for his daughter. He silently thanked God for leading these people here today to selfishly search for his missing Sarah.

As he walked the path he had searched earlier in the day, he thought, why can't I see Sarah looking for the bunny? Please let her be here. Maybe we overlooked her. If I search a little harder, maybe I can find her and take her to her mother. Please, let me find you Sarah. Daddy needs to know where you are.

He went around the bend in the trail and saw Maggie sitting on the ground. With her head bowed, she was silently praying. His heart broke and as the tears ran down his cheeks. Silently he turned and walked in the other direction. He wanted to give Maggie her privacy. Right now, he would upset her more. He had to get himself under control so she would not see his tears. He wanted to be strong for her like he promised. They had to find Sarah. His heart could not take it.

Maggie prayed silently. Her strong belief in God wavered slightly as she prayed, "God please help us find Sarah. I am so sorry I left her alone. I need you now more than I ever have before. Please, if she is in these woods, let someone find her. We need to find her. Please, help us all." She could not go on.

She wanted to search some more but her body was exhausted and she had to sit to rest. "I will sit here for a minute and then I will look for you Sarah. If you can hear me, sweetheart, let Mommy know where you are."

Maggie sat still for a few more minutes. She turned around when she heard someone coming up behind her. She looked up and Jim was standing there. It looked as though he had been crying.

"Did you get some news?" she asked him.

He knelt down beside her and took her hands. "No, I talked with Officer Garret, but they don't know anymore. He is hoping that the TV interview will get us a lead on where Sarah may have gone. Will you come with me and get a sandwich or a hot cup of coffee?" he asked.

Maggie stood up and wrapped her arms around him. That small gesture from her made him sob. They stood together and held each other while they cried. No one could imagine what awful torment Maggie and Jim were going through. They built their life on love and goodness. They finally got their beautiful daughter Sarah. The circle was complete, two loving parents, and Sarah. A family based on goodness and faith.

Now they stood in the middle of the woods holding each other. If Sarah were gone, the circle would never be complete again. They stood still until Jim stepped back and took her hand. "Let's go and get you something to drink. I could use some strong, hot, coffee." Maggie let him lead her back to the tables.

Gwen came to her and hugged her. She cried some more with her. Gwen reached up with a napkin and wiped some of the dirt and tears off Maggie's face.

Compassion showed heavily on Gwen's face and Maggie hugged her again. "I love you Gwen," she said.

Tears fell from Gwen's eyes, "And I love you too, Maggie. I would give everything I have to make this better. Have you heard any news of Sarah?"

"No, we haven't heard anything new." Maggie told her, "Officer Garret promises to tell us as soon as they find her. Gwen I cannot go on without her. Do you think someone hurt her? I see a picture of her in my mind of how sweet and innocent she is. Why would anyone want to harm a beautiful young girl like Sarah?"

Gwen took notice that Maggie said, "As soon as they find her." She hoped for Maggie and Jim's sake that it was soon. They did not deserve this awful trial they had to bear.

She handed Maggie a cup of coffee, led her to the bench, and sat beside her. Jim came and sat with them. Gwen told them that Tom was closing the office and should arrive in the next half hour.

They sat in silence for a few more minutes. One of the women came over to Maggie and gave her a shawl. She told her that she used the shawl quite often. She had knitted it when her own son was sick. He had brain cancer at the age of fourteen and she wore the shawl each night at the hospital. She told them that her son had died six months ago, and she lent her shawl of love to a lot of others since then. She told Maggie to keep it as long as she needed to and when she was done with it, she would get it back from her and pass it on to the next person she met that needed the comfort.

Maggie touched the soft yarn and thanked the woman. "What is your name?" she asked her.

"My name is Bonnie Blevins. I have seen you, your husband, and your daughter in church. I wish I had spoken to you before. I meant to introduce myself several times. I do want to tell you that everyone is thinking of you. You and your family are constantly in my prayers. My earnest prayer is that God will help us find your little girl."

Maggie hugged her and wrapped the shawl around her shoulders. "I will wear it until my daughter comes back home. Thank you, Bonnie."

They looked across the parking lot and saw Tom get out of his car. He headed for them. Tom reached them and hugged Gwen. He went to Jim and grabbed him in a tight hug.

Tom told him. "I wish I would have been here sooner, but I wanted to take care of a few things before I left. I knew you would worry about them, so I stayed and took care of them. What can I do now that I am here?" he asked Jim.

"I appreciate you staying at the office for me. I am glad you are here now, and that is all we need. Our friend's supports means more than you know."

Tom went to Maggie and hugged her for a long time. He usually was afraid to show emotion, but she saw the tears in his eyes and kissed his cheek.

"You and Gwen are the two best friends we would ever need. Thank you so much," Maggie said.

Jim filled Tom in on all the details so far. They went to get a sandwich and coffee, and told the girls they would bring one back to them. Jim and Tom brought Maggie and Gwen a sandwich and a drink.

It touched their hearts to see all the women willing to give the time to people they did not even know. How different in ones that wants to help others, and ones that want to hurt others.

Jim's mind was still reeling from what Officer Garret told him about the seven- year old girl found behind the mall. He would have heard it and ignored it before, but now he had to face what may have happened to his own daughter. His thoughts went out to that mother and father.

Officer Garret came across the parking lot to talk to Jim. "Mr. Taylor," he said, "I wanted to let you know that it will be dark soon, and I have to call off the search until tomorrow morning."

Officer Garret was hoping Mrs. Taylor would not object as he continued, "If I need to talk to you later, will you be at home? I do have your cell number too. I am going to give the men another fifteen minutes and then I will call them in for the night."

Jim told him, "Yes, I am sure we will be home. I do not know what else to do. I do not want to go home and leave Sarah alone wherever she is. I do not have any idea what I can do. I feel so helpless."

"Mr. Taylor, do not blame yourself or your wife. I spoke to one of the men from the agency we are working with. He said that it only takes thirty seconds to take a child. Sometimes they bribe them. Often they tell them that their parents are hurt and they need to go and be with them. Children are too trusting. Unless you make them afraid of everyone, what can we do to stop them from taking our children? I will contact you if I hear anything at all."

Jim went back to Maggie and filled her in on what Officer Garret had told him. Since they were going to call off the search for the night, he wondered if she was ready to go home. She looked at him. He could see the terror in her eyes.

"How am I supposed to go home?  Sarah is still here somewhere.  I do not want to go home.  What if she comes back and it is dark?  I have to stay here.  She will be so afraid.  I can't leave her here after dark.  One of the wild animals may hurt her.  I have to stay, please Jim I have to stay.  Don't make me go home," Maggie cried.

"But Maggie, Sarah is not here.  The search parties would have found her by now.  I do not want to upset you, but I have to tell you that if Sarah were in these woods, they would have found her.  She is not here," Jim said firmly.

Jim could see Maggie pull away from him.  She did not accept what he told her.  He knew that if he was going to get her to go home, he would almost have to force her to go.  He went to take her arm and she pulled away from him and started running as fast as she could towards the woods.  It took Jim by surprise.

Jim knew she was just beginning to show the stress that the next few days may have for all of them.  He stood with his head down.

Gwen and Tom went over to him and asked him if they should go after her.

"No," Jim said, "she will come back when she wants to."

Maggie kept running until she got in the middle of the woods.  She literally fell down on the ground and cried, "It is not fair.  Why did you take Sarah?  She was the only child I have.  Please, bring her back to me.  Please, bring her back."

The sobs racked her body.  The sounds that came from her were like a wounded animal.  She beat on the ground.  She beat on herself.  The thought of Sarah being hurt was a thought she would not give in to.  "I have to find her.  I have to save her.  What am I going to do?  Sarah, where are you?" she screamed over and over.

The few people that were still in the woods heard her cries. They stopped where they were and cried with her. A child taken by an evil man had disrupted and harmed so many people's lives. It was just the beginning.

# CHAPTER SEVENTEEN

Jim went to find Maggie. He could hear her sobs, as he got nearer. His heart broke as he bent down beside her. He put his arms around her and lifted her up. She was in a trance. Nothing could penetrate the sorrow that settled in her. He led her back to the car and put her in the passenger seat. He went back to Gwen and Tom and told them he was taking Maggie home and calling her doctor. Gwen and Tom said they had to go and get Jill, and they would call later.

Jim drove home and took Maggie inside to the sofa. He laid her down, covered her with a blanket, and went to the phone and called the doctor. He explained what happened and the doctor said he could come right over. The doctor gave Maggie a shot to help her sleep. Jim thanked him and promised he would call him again if he needed him.

Jim had to call Maggie's parents and his own mother and father. They both cried with Jim on the phone. Both sets of parents wanted to come over and check on Maggie. Her mother sat on the couch and cradled her head in her lap. She could not imagine the fear and pain that her daughter was going through. She sat with Maggie for a long time. Jim made coffee and they gathered in the kitchen.

Maggie's father told Jim he was going to call and see if he could find information on the other cases in the area. Since he was a lawyer, he could cut through some of the red tape. They left around 12:00. Jim hugged them all and told them if he heard anything at all, he would call them immediately.

Jim carried Maggie upstairs and helped her undress and put on pajamas. He climbed in beside her and held her as she slept. Finally, he drifted off but the nightmares haunted him. He woke up in a sweat around 4:00 a.m. He reached for Maggie and she was not there. He jumped out of bed and went to find her.

Jim looked in the bathroom and did not see her. He went to Sarah's room, looked in, and saw her on Sarah's bed. She lay curled up in a ball holding Sarah's favorite stuffed bear. He lay down on the floor and slept another two hours. When he heard Maggie stir, he got up and sat on the bed beside her.

Jim asked Maggie if she was all right.

"No, I will never be all right again," she said.

He helped her into the bathroom, turned on the shower, helped her get dressed, took her downstairs, and sat her at the table. He made the coffee and asked if she wanted breakfast.

She shook her head no. He gave her a cup of coffee, sat, and held her hand.

The phone rang and he went to answer it. It was Tom checking on a few things he needed Jim's advice for work. Tom asked about Maggie, and Jim told him she was not responding to anything. He told him that Gwen would be over later in the morning to see her. He hung up and went back to the table.

When he sat down in front of Maggie, it was as though all her soul and spirit had vanished. She had such a blank look on her face it frightened him. Maggie used to be a person that loved life and had a light in her eye constantly. What would happen to the real Maggie? He did not know what to do to help her.

Jim hoped they would get good news today. He believed that if Maggie lost Sarah, then he would lose Maggie.

Jim was startled when the doorbell rang. Two women from the church brought food and wanted to know if they needed them to do anything. Jim took them to the kitchen so Maggie could speak to them too. She stared straight ahead.

Maggie did make eye contact with them for a second, smiled, and hugged them both. The women left and Jim made Maggie some toast and almost forced her to eat it. She did not have an appetite and did not eat much at all.

Jim put the dishes away and straightened the kitchen. They went back to the living room and Jim tried to talk to her.

"Maggie, honey, what can I do for you? I cannot stand to see you hurting this way, please, talk to me," he said.

Maggie looked at him and she said, "I know you want to help me, but can you assure me that we will find Sarah? I do not mean to turn you away, and I know you are as worried as I am. Please, I just need to know she is fine. I need to know, Jim. Please help me find her. I need to find Sarah."

Jim wanted to tell her that he knew beyond a shadow of doubt they would find Sarah today, but instead he hung his head and stayed silent.

Maggie said she wanted to go back to the park as soon as possible. If Sarah was coming back, they had to be waiting for her.

Jim did not want her to go anywhere near the park, but he was afraid he could not stop her if she made up her mind to go. He agreed and he said he would make a few phone calls and then he would take her.

Jim called Officer Garret and left a message for him to call as soon as possible. He was hoping that they had discovered news through the night that would end the nightmare.

Jim told Maggie they would wait for Officer Garret to call before he took her to the park. She told him she had to go to the bathroom, and she went upstairs.

He called Maggie's father, and asked him if he found out any new information on the other abduction. He told Jim that another officer was going to call him shortly and he would call him back as soon as he heard from him.

Jim did not hear anything from Maggie and he went upstairs. He found her in Sarah's bedroom. She had a picture of Sarah they had taken a few months ago. She was holding the picture and tears ran down her face. He sat with her and they both cried. Jim talked to her about the day they took the picture. The three of them spent the day at an amusement park. Sarah loved the rides and he could still hear her laughter as she went from one to the next. He played a shooting game and won the biggest stuffed lion they had for her. It was a happy day.

Maggie talked about the cotton candy and the ice cream the three of them had. She remembered that she and Jim had a stomachache from it all, but Sarah wanted more. The park fascinated Sarah and she loved seeing all the people. The clowns and the jugglers were her favorites. She told them she wanted a clown for her next birthday.

Suddenly, reality set in. They both realized that the next birthday was in question. If they did not find her there would be no birthday party. Maggie sobbed from the thought of never seeing her daughter again.

The phone rang and Jim went to answer it. It was Officer Garret. He told him they planned to bring helicopters later in the day and circle the area to see if they could find Sarah. The organized search parties were to start at 10:00 that morning. He did not want to give any details on the phone and said he would talk to him later at the park.

Jim and Maggie left for the park around 9:30. When they arrived, the search parties were preparing to enter the woods in fifteen minutes.

Another police vehicle arrived and a canine team got out. Jim asked what was going on. Officer Garret explained they were sending the dogs to pick up Sarah's scent.

Jim found a jacket in the car that was Sarah's and gave it to them. Within another half hour, the woods were full of sounds and yells for Sarah.

Maggie walked to the place she last saw Sarah and sat down. It was as though if she waited, Sarah would come out of her hiding place and Maggie would be right there to see her. Jim left her alone and went to find Officer Garret.

Jim walked over to him and asked, "Did you get any information on the other suspect and who it may be?"

Officer Garret told him, "Yes, I did get the description from the officer handling the case, but it is too general. It did not distinguish any certain suspect. His back was to the camera and they could not see his face. It may not have any bearing on Sarah at all. We have the canine team out and we will search a wider area today. I hope someone sees the broadcast you and your wife did, and gives us a lead. We will play the day by any further developments. How is your wife doing?"

Jim said, "She did not have a good night. Right now, she is waiting in the woods for Sarah to find her. I could not convince her to stay at home. Maggie is strong willed and she has to be here or she will go crazy with thoughts of missing her. I hope we hear good news today. If not, I do not know if she will withstand it all."

Officer Garret said, "I guess if it were my child, I would feel the same way. I will keep you posted if anything else turns up."

They looked up when they heard the helicopter overhead.

Jim could not fathom that they were actually looking for his daughter. Two days ago, their world was safe. Two days ago, he knew what to do. Now his wife was sitting in the middle of the woods, waiting for their daughter to come back. Today a helicopter was circling, and teams were scouting the woods looking for Sarah. No one can be sure of what a day may bring. He thanked Officer Garret and went to find Maggie. He hoped she would hold on until they could find Sarah and all three of them could go home again.

Maggie was looking in all the bushes. She was frantically digging in the dirt. It was as if she could dig and search to find Sarah. He went to her and firmly stood her up.

"Maggie, you are doing yourself no good. You have to come back to the bench. Please, I need you to come with me."

She looked at him like a crazy person. Her eyes were as wide as saucers. Dirt covered her face and her hair knotted with briars. He took her by the arm and led her out of the woods. He sat her on the bench and called Gwen on his cell phone. He asked Gwen to come and be with her.

Jim said, "Gwen will be here in a few minutes. I want you to stay here. You cannot go in the woods anymore. You are driving yourself crazy. Maggie, look at me. Please, sit here with me."

Gwen arrived within fifteen minutes. Jim asked her to make sure Maggie stayed with her. He went to find Officer Garret. He requested a meeting with all that were involved in the case.

Jim called Maggie's father and asked if he could come and meet with the rest of the officials. He needed someone who knew the legal side of the law.

Officer Garret asked Jim if he would mind going to the station for the meeting in one hour. Jim agreed and asked Gwen to take Maggie home. He needed to make sure she was safe and away from this park.

Jim called Mr. Fracheska, Maggie's father to meet him at the police station. Gwen promised she would take care of Maggie, and would call her mother to help her. At least he felt like he was doing something.

Jim met the men at the station. Officer Garret introduced all the other officers involved. He had the files of the other abduction. Mr. Fracheska looked over the file and asked if they knew about the earlier abduction before Sarah was missing. Officer Garret assured him that the news of the former case did not get to their office until after the day Sarah went missing. Mr. Fracheska asked if they thought it was the same person in both cases. Officer Garret told him there was absolutely no evidence to be positive it was the same man. If they uncovered any evidence, they would certainly make it known to the families.

Officer Garret said, "Until we find Sarah, or her body, we have no evidence to support or disprove it was the same suspect. We are shooting in the dark in both cases, and we cannot warn the public that it may happen again, unless we have a better description of the molester. It puts us all on edge until we take the next step, whatever that may be. I hope it is good, I hope we find your granddaughter. And most of all, I hope the person that is responsible in either case is apprehended quickly."

Officer Garret spoke with authority and determination, "I will promise you that I have all the men at my disposal, and all the hours I need to take this case apart until we solve it."

Mr. Fracheska spoke and said, "Officer Garret, I am sorry to seem as though I don't trust you or this department. I just do not want anyone to hide an important detail that may help us find Sarah. If we can find out who took the other little girl, it may lead us to Sarah. If it is the same man, can't we put out a bulletin with his description so that your officers will be looking for him in case he may still have Sarah alive?"

Officer Garret tried to explain that sometimes if they do not have the right description, an innocent man might be harassed.

The men took a second to gather their thoughts. They all felt inadequate and restless sitting in a room while Sarah was out there. If it was the same man, was he looking for his next victim? The only thing they had to go on was a picture of the back of the man on a mall security tape. It was a general description. It could be anyone on the street. It may even be someone that Jim and Maggie knew.

Jim said, "I wish I knew who he was. He would certainly not be breathing very long if I got near him. I want to kill him if he has hurt my daughter." Each of the men saw the fury in Jim's face and could understand the frustration.

Officer Garret thanked them for coming. He told Jim he was going to the command post and check on the latest news from the helicopters and canine teams. He told Jim he would see him there later.

Jim went to Gwen's house to check on Maggie. She had settled down a little. She asked him if there was any news and he shook his head no. He asked Gwen if she could keep an eye on Maggie for a while. He wanted to take care of some things. She agreed readily. He kissed Maggie good-bye and left for the park.

Jim drove to the park. He walked over to a group of men that came out of the woods. He asked if they had found any sign of Sarah. They did not have anything new to report.

Jim waited for Officer Garret and asked him, "How long will the search parties be out? If nothing turns up now in this area, are you going to change the locations of the search?" he asked.

Officer Garret told him, "There are many fields and pastures nearby and the helicopters may spot something. If not, I do not want to search the same area over again. The search parties combed the whole woods here behind the park. We will expand to the next wooded area and stay out part of the morning. The men need a break. They have been at this for many hours. I cannot know what we will do next until we have completed the search by air."

Jim went to the park bench and sat for a while. His heart was breaking. There should have been an easy answer. Sarah was here yesterday. Now, there was no sign of her. They needed to have something, anything, about Sarah. Was she here just out of their reach? Had someone taken her and left the area? If so, was she still alive? He slumped over, held his head in his hands, and cried for him and Maggie. "God, please help us get through this trial," he prayed.

## CHAPTER EIGHTEEN

The helicopters circled the park area and saw nothing. They expanded the search wider and swept the area again. They could see no sign of a six-year old girl or her body. They stayed in the air for four hours.

The emergency team received a distress call to cover air transport for an accident on Route 67, so they left the area and responded. Officer Garret thanked them and asked them to contact him later for instructions for further air searches. Reports had come in for a storm that was developing for the second half of the day.

The search teams stopped for lunch and gathered at the command post. They found no sign of a six-year old girl. There was absolutely nothing to indicate that Sarah was anywhere close.

Officer Garret called his supervisors and they told him severe weather was brewing and the search may have to stop until the next day. Sarah had been missing for forty-eight hours. As they were eating their lunch, it started to pour rain. He told the men he was putting the search on hold until the following morning. Officer Garret thanked them and told them to wait for further instructions.

Jim could do no good here, so he went to Gwen's house to pick up Maggie. She ran to the door when she saw him pull in the driveway. He met her at the door and embraced her. He said, "I am sorry Maggie. There is no sign of Sarah. Because of the storm, Officer Garret postponed the search until tomorrow. I can think of nothing else I can do. I wish I could tell you more." Maggie broke down and walked to the other side of the room.

Jim could feel her slipping away from him. The pain was too much for her. Maggie knew she should go back to Jim, but she just couldn't.

Her whole being ached and she did not know what she was going to do now. Her beautiful Sarah was gone. Nobody knew where she was or what happened to her.

"How can this be? It is entirely my fault. I should not have left her alone. I did not mean to leave you, Sarah. I did not know that stupid bush could cost your life," she cried. Maggie would have to live with what she did for the rest of her life. She would never forgive herself.

Jim went in the kitchen to find Gwen. She had coffee ready and he sat at the table with her. He said, "Gwen, what can I do? Maggie is pulling away from me. I do not understand. She is my wife and I love her. How can I help her?"

Gwen looked at him with sorrow in her eyes. "Jim, I wish I knew the answer. I do know that sometimes the pain is so consuming, your heart will not function. I have never been in the midst of anything this tragic. I can hardly handle the thought of never seeing Sarah again. I cannot imagine what you and Maggie are feeling. You have to give her space. She is a strong person, and I do believe that she will come back. Maybe you should call the pastor and he could talk to both of you. I'm sure he has more advice than I can give. You need his help now, and so does Maggie. If you do not find Sarah, what will Maggie do, Jim? I do not have answers. Remember that Tom and I love you both. I told Maggie, whatever you need, please let us help"

"Thank you Gwen," Jim said, "We love you both too. I know that somehow Maggie and I will find the strength to get through this. If we do not find her, we will not come out of this the same people we were."

Jim wiped a tear and said, "We do need you. Tell Tom that I am so glad he is my partner and I cannot ever repay what he has done for me with handling the business. I am going to depend on him a lot until this is over."

Jim stood and went back to Maggie. "Maggie, do you want to go home now?"

She turned and said, "I never want to go in my own house again."

Jim was shocked when he thought of Maggie hating to go home to the house she used to love.

Maggie said, "There are reminders of Sarah everywhere. When I walk in our door, I expect her to come running to me. When I go upstairs, I pass her room. When I lie down to sleep, I see her face."

Maggie's eyes went from Jim to Gwen, then back again." Do I want to go home? No, but where can I go? How far do I run to get away from this agony? I am not sure I can do this, Jim. What am I supposed to do? Please tell me," she said.

Jim walked to her and took her in his arms. The rigid position of her body surprised him. "Yes, if you lose Sarah, then I lose you," he thought.

They went into the kitchen and Gwen brought Maggie some coffee. She smiled faintly and thanked her. "The two of you are the closest people in the world to me," Maggie told them. "Please understand, I do not mean to hurt either one of you. Where ever I may go to be able to cope with this, remember I will come back. Can you do that for me?" She looked at them both and through their tears they held her hands and promised they would help her and love her no matter where she went or what she did. It was almost as though Maggie looked into the future and needed them to believe in her no matter what happened.

Jim asked Maggie if she wanted to go home or stay with Gwen. He wanted to stop by the office and check on Tom. Maggie said she needed to go home. He dropped her off and told her he would be back in a couple of hours and then they would check in with Officer Garret. Since it was raining, there was no one at the park. He told her he would call her and make sure she was okay.

Jim left and went to the office. Tom had it all under control and Jim asked him if he could handle the next few days by himself if he had to take off for any reason. Tom asked if there were any new developments and Jim said no.

Jim called Maggie and told her he would be home in an hour. She was waiting by the phone, and no one else had called.

Jim left the office and went by the grocery store. He knew Maggie would not want to leave the house, and if something did happen, he was sure that people would be stopping by. He drove home and Maggie helped him put the groceries away. She was so restless; she would walk from one room to the other. If this was an indication of how the next few weeks would be, they just had to play a waiting game.

Officer Garret called Jim around 5:00. He told him that he was driving to the county sheriff's office the next morning to speak with them about the abduction of Candy Burns. He needed to hear firsthand if any thing new turned up with the description of the man at the mall. As long as it was raining, they would not be searching for Sarah until it stopped. He did tell Jim if there were any clues, the rain most likely would have washed them away. Unfortunately, the rain was still falling.

Maggie fixed them a sandwich for dinner. When they were finished, they sat in the living room staring at the walls.

Maggie's parents stopped in to see her. Jim and Mr. Fracheska talked about the abduction of the girl found at the mall in Shawsville. They wondered if the same man was responsible for Sarah's disappearance.

Then the phone started ringing. All their friends wanted to tell them how sorry they were, and that they were all praying for Sarah's safe return. Jim thanked each one as they called.

Maggie's parents left and when it got dark, they got ready for bed. Maggie went into Sarah's room and lay down on her bed. When Jim was changed and ready, he went and lay down beside her. That is where they spent their second night without their daughter, lying in her bed waiting to hear news.

The next morning, they got dressed and went through the motions like zombies. In the late morning, they drove to the park and waited. Maggie got out of the car, walked straight into the woods, and sat on the ground. Jim begged her to go home after a few hours. Maggie sat like a statue. She looked into space with a blank expression. Every hour seemed like forever.

Jim brought her something to drink and at lunch brought her a sandwich. He forced her to eat at least some of it. After it got dark, Jim would go to her and pull her to her feet. He held her as they walked out of the woods. When they arrived home, Jim sat her at the table and talked softly to her until she ate. He would walk her to the sofa and after he finished clearing the table, he sat beside her and tried to get her to talk to him. Maggie was non-responsive to anything.

For two weeks, this was their routine. Jim tried to help Tom at the office as much as he could. He did not want to leave Maggie's side.

Their entire existence was literally in limbo. Every day they waited with no news, made it more real that Sarah was actually gone. They needed to know what happened. As parents, they needed closure. One way or the other, it was better than not knowing.

For two weeks after Sarah disappeared in the park, Jim drove Maggie to the park. She sat on the path she often walked with her daughter. Jim fed her, sat with her, and watched as he lost more of his wife each day.

Then the closure came. Officer Garret came to their door. When Jim opened the door, he knew. Maggie was standing behind him and held her breath. They asked him to come in and have a seat. Officer Garret asked Jim to call his parents, and Maggie's parents to come to the house. He wanted them to have support for what he had to tell them.

Jim offered some coffee and went to prepare it while they waited for the parents. Within a half hour, all four parents arrived. Officer Garret asked them to sit and began to tell them the news they had dreaded to hear for two weeks.

Officer Paul Garret's deep emotion and compassion poured forth as he said, "Your daughter's body was discovered in a ravine three miles from the park. We found her wrapped in a blanket. Two young men found her while hunting for squirrels."

The room was deathly quiet. No one moved for a few minutes. Suddenly Maggie stood and ran upstairs. Her mother and Jim's mother went after her. She was in Sarah's room and holding her picture and sobbing. All three women held each other. Nothing would ever be the same.

Officer Garret asked Jim if Maggie was okay.

Jim said, "I asked her that same question a week ago. She told me that she would never be all right again. What chance do we have of catching the person that took Sarah? Do you have any leads at all? It is so unfair that someone takes your child just to hurt her. What do we do now?"

Officer Garret told them, "I am sorry to say that we do not have leads on the cruel person that took Sarah."

Mr. Fracheska said to Officer Garret, "I read the file on the little girl that was strangled in Shawsville. The man that took her, only kept her five or six hours. Do you think that Sarah was alive all this time? Did he kill her that first night?"

Officer Garret replied, "We will have to wait on the autopsy. I do not know what condition she was in, but the coroner was able to identify her from her picture."

Officer Garret turned to Jim, "Mr. Taylor, whenever you are ready, I will take you to the morgue to identify the body. Maybe your father and father in law will go with you. You should not do this alone. I don't think your wife should see her yet. It is best to remember your daughter before this happened. As soon as you make a positive ID, we will let you know when you can make funeral arrangements for her."

Officer Garret put his hand on Jim's shoulder, "I am so sorry I brought you this awful news. I was hoping this time would be different. You never get used to the unbelievable cruelty. I have thought a lot about what makes a person take another couple's child and feel no remorse. I guess if I had that answer, it would bring you some peace. But, I do not know. Everyone at the station wanted me to offer our condolences. Their thoughts are with you and your family."

Officer Garret headed for the door, "I am so sorry," he said.

Jim shook his hand and said, "Officer Garret, I want you to know that the help you gave us in searching for our daughter was above and beyond your duty as an officer. I know that you really do care about people."

Jim told him that he would make sure Maggie was okay and then he would call him and meet him at the morgue. Officer Garret left and Jim went to the bottom of the stairs. He slowed his breathing down and stood still for a few minutes. He wanted to be calm for Maggie. He headed up the stairs to see his wife.

When he reached the door to Sarah's room, Maggie looked up at him from the bed. Jim would not forget that look for the rest of his life. Pure and honest pain showed on her face. He went towards her and she broke. The realization that a stranger took their daughter's life for absolutely no reason was more than a mother can handle. She fell to the floor. He knelt down with her and held her while she cried. Both mothers walked slowly down the stairs.

Jim said, "Maggie, I am sorry. I did not think that we would ever lose a child by someone else's hand. I will find the person that took her. If it is the last thing I do, I will make him pay."

Maggie could not speak. She was slipping and he could see her getting farther away from him.

"How can I help you, Maggie? Please, don't shut me out. I am here with you always," he said. She stood and he held her. He felt her whole body tremble.

The first part of the nightmare was over. Now the second part came. They had to plan their six-year old daughter's funeral.

Jim decided he would discuss that with her later. They went downstairs and Maggie's mother offered to call Gwen. She knew that she could help Maggie. They had been friends their whole life. She went to find the phone and returned a few minutes later. She told them that Gwen and Tom were on their way.

Jim waited for them to arrive and asked Tom if he would stay with the women while they went to the morgue. Tom said, "Of course I will stay. Call us if you need to." The men got ready to leave and Jim put in a call to Officer Garret to meet them there.

Officer Garret was waiting for them in the parking lot. He told them to follow him. The morgue was in the basement and as they rode the elevator down, Jim tried to pull himself together. I do not want to do this, he thought.

The men got off the elevator and Officer Garret opened the door to the morgue. What an awful place. It was so cold and morbid. The coroner met them and introduced himself to them.

"My name is Gary Meadows. I will show you the body and please if you need to leave at any time, let me know. I will be performing the autopsy later tonight. We have done nothing with the body yet. Are you Mr. Taylor?" he asked Jim.

"Yes, I am Sarah's father. Does she look terrible? Will I recognize her?" Jim asked.

Mr. Meadows replied, "Yes, I think you will know her. Her body is still intact. The elements were kind to her. The weather and the body wrapped in a blanket protected her. I do not want to go into how long she has been dead, until I finish the autopsy. I will certainly be in touch with you as soon as I know." He led the way down the corridor.

The double doors at the end made Jim think of a giant monster that was about to swallow him whole. The doors opened and the men followed him to a table. Mr. Meadows pulled back the sheet and Jim slowly looked at the face. It was Sarah. He reached out and brushed her hair with his hand. The others stood quietly and watched as the father identified his daughter's body. Jim shook his head yes. His father put his arm around him and held him up. Jim leaned on him as the tears ran.

Maggie's father stepped up to the table, leaned down, and kissed her on the forehead. His only grandchild was gone. "We all loved you so much, Sarah," he said to her. "We will miss you every day for as long as we live."

Jim took a few more minutes to look at Sarah and then his father led him back out those big double doors.

Maggie's father asked the coroner how long he thought it would be until they released the body. He told him it should be in two days. They could plan the funeral for Saturday. He thanked him and told him to take extra care with his beautiful granddaughter. Mr. Meadows clasped his hand in his own and promised he would treat her with the utmost respect.

The men left the building. Officer Garret shook each man's hand, told them how sorry he was, and to call for whatever they needed.

The men went back to Jim's house. Gwen was upstairs with Maggie. Jim told the rest how they had slept in Sarah's bed for the past two weeks. Now they had to go on with life without her. Jim's mother told him that she had called the pastor and he should arrive shortly.

They started making a list of the people they would have to notify.

Jim took a minute to go on the back deck. He looked up at the sky and thought, Sarah, your life has ended. You were only six-years old. I wish I could have taken your place. I did not want you to suffer at all. Your daddy sends kisses for you in heaven. I love you.

The doorbell rang and it was the pastor. He spoke to everyone and went to join Jim on the deck.

"Jim, I do not have the words to tell you how sorry I am about Sarah. Remember that God said he would never give us more than we can bear. I will be here whenever you need me. How is Maggie doing?" he asked him.

Jim started crying and said, "Pastor Blevins, I think I am losing her. She shuts me out. I do not know what to do to help her. I can hardly help myself. Why did someone take our daughter? Do you think she suffered?"

Pastor Blevins clasped Jim's hands in his and said, "Jim I cannot answer why. I can tell you that I do not think that God lets a child suffer. I want you to remember God is in control. He will not leave you. Hold on to him and he will give you comfort. I must speak to Maggie. I will see you after I have talked with her."

He went upstairs to Sarah's room. He stepped into the room and asked, "Maggie is there room on the bed for me? How are you doing? I am so sorry about Sarah. She was a beautiful child, and Maggie she will make a beautiful angel. She is walking on streets of pure gold, and sitting on Jesus' knee. He is taking good care of her Maggie, until you get there with her. I talked to Jim a few minutes and his question was why. I told him I do not begin to understand why."

He took her hand and continued, "I know the person that took Sarah, is not good. As long as we live on this earth, there will be trials to bear. God will send you comfort. He understands your pain. He knows you will cry for your child. He will not leave you Maggie, no matter how much pain we have, he shares it with us."

Maggie looked at him and said, "Pastor Blevins, I believe every word you said. But I am not sure I am strong enough to handle this." Tears ran down Maggie's cheeks, "How does a mother handle this? Somebody murders my child. I won't ask why, because I know we cannot know what makes a person kill someone else, especially a child. I have no idea how to get through tomorrow, how am I going to handle the rest of my life? I have the guilt of leaving her alone in the park. If I would have stayed with her she would still be here with us."

Pastor Blevins said, "Maggie, let me help you get through this day. We will work on tomorrow when it comes. You cannot and will not ever forget Sarah. You will not forget what happened to her. You must forgive yourself. There is no guilt for you to carry. You did not cause this to happen to your daughter. A mean spirited man hurt her. It was not your fault in any way."

Maggie told him she would try to remember his words. They went downstairs and had prayer. He told them he would contact them tomorrow for the arrangements.

The house grew quiet. Everyone had his own pain to bear. As one by one they left, Jim and Maggie prepared for bed. Jim asked Maggie to sleep in their bed. "We have to get rest Maggie, tomorrow we need our strength. Do you want one of the pills the doctor left to help you sleep?" he asked her.

Maggie thought about it and said that she probably would not sleep without it, so he went to get her one. They got in bed and stayed on their own side. Jim reached to hug her but she was so stiff and he turned over and tried to sleep. He would have to be patient with her. He knew she needed to deal with it in her own way. He would have to stand right beside her and be there when she needed him.

"I love you Maggie," he whispered to her.

The next day the coroner called and asked Jim to come back to the morgue. Jim called his father and Maggie's father to go with him. He had to get this part over. The three men were silent on the trip to the morgue.

Mr. Meadows took them into his office and said he finished with the autopsy. "I have some things to tell you, Mr. Taylor. In this time of sorrow, sometimes we find little blessings we did not expect. Your daughter did not suffer at all. I discovered she had a heart problem. She died peacefully. The fear she felt is what killed her. The person that took her did not get a chance to hurt her. Her little heart just quit beating.

You would have discovered it soon, and she would have needed surgery to fix it. I do not mean to make light of your daughter's death. Please take comfort in the fact that she did not know that the man that took her meant her any harm. I would say she died the night he took her. She did not suffer at all. I hope this helps you to deal with her death a little better. If the man did mean to torture her, she escaped that terrible ordeal. I will release the body immediately. I will list the cause of death as heart failure."

Jim broke down and had a hard time controlling himself. It was good to hear what Mr. Meadows discovered. At least Sarah did not endure the humiliation of any man molesting her.

Jim's father thanked him and they discussed arrangements for the funeral home to pick up her body. Jim tearfully thanked him for telling them what he found.

Mr. Meadows told the men that his prayers and thoughts were with them all.

They planned the funeral on Saturday. Jim told Maggie that he would take care of the arrangements if she were not able to go.

Maggie said to him, "I want to give our daughter the purest and most peaceful burial we can. I will go with you."

They picked out a white coffin. It was hard to get through all the details but it was finally over.

They returned home and spent the next several hours on the phone letting everyone know the time and arrangements.

Gwen stopped by and helped Maggie pick out Sarah's outfit. Maggie asked her if she wanted Jill to have something of Sarah's and she chose a necklace with a silver angel. Jill was having an extra hard time losing her best friend. Maggie apologized to Gwen for not asking about Jill before.

Gwen said, "Maggie, I do not think you need one more thing to worry about. We will have to handle Jill with love and patience. Sarah and Jill would have been best friends for life, just like you and me. I know God had different plans and in time, we will all learn how to deal with it. If you need me to stay with you, Maggie, I will. I will stay day and night if you need me to. I cannot stand to watch you suffer. What can I do?"

Maggie said, "Gwen you have been like a sister to me all these years. I wish I knew what I needed. I know you would do whatever it is. I have to deal with this on my own. I see some big hurdles in my way. I must take one day at a time. Just knowing you are there helps me."

They finished and went downstairs. Jim and Tom were going over some business details. The girls joined them and they spent a while going back over past days of happiness they had with all six of them. It helped them all to talk about happy days.

Jim told them what the coroner told him. It helped Maggie to know that Sarah did not suffer at all. They told Gwen and Tom good night and said they would see them at the funeral. All four hugged at the door. Laughter and joy used to fill the Taylor house, but now it was a somber place.

The service for Sarah was sad. For a child to die like this was hard on the whole community. It would be a long time before the community forgot.

After everything was over, they gathered at Jim and Maggie's house. Maggie tried to hold up, but at one point she wanted to scream and tell everyone to go home and leave her alone. You don't know how hard it is. You have no idea what I will face tomorrow. My daughter is dead. Go away and leave me alone! I have to get out of here. She excused herself, went upstairs, and locked herself in Sarah's room.

Jim came and knocked on the door and asked her if she was okay. She murmured for him to go away and leave her alone.

Jim went back downstairs and told everyone that Maggie was not feeling well and was lying down for a little while. She did not come out of the room, and eventually every one left. Jim went and asked her to unlock the door. She told him again to go away. She knew it was mean, but she could not help it. She did not want to live, how could everyone else act as if it was just another normal day? The thought of tomorrow held no interest for Maggie. She wanted her daughter back home alive, not buried in the ground.

Maggie saw the bottle of sleeping pills on the table. For one second she thought of swallowing the whole bottle. It would be so easy to lie down and go to sleep and never wake up to what her life had become. She forced herself to push the notion out of her head. It would not be fair on Jim. She whispered softly, "Jim, I will come back. Wait for me."

# CHAPTER NINETEEN

Maggie finally came out of Sarah's room the next morning. She did not bother to look in the mirror. She went downstairs and started the coffee. Jim was in the study and heard her in the kitchen.

He went in and said to her, "Maggie, how are you doing this morning? Do you want me to fix you some breakfast? I had toast and eggs, and I will fix you something." She told him, "No, I really do not feel like eating, maybe later."

Jim sat at the table and waited for her to get her coffee. She sat across from him, and as he looked at the face of the woman he loved, he hoped they could hold on.

"We have to talk about a few things, if you don't mind. I need to know what you want me to do today. Should I go in to work, or should I stay here with you? I will stay if you want me to. We need to decide what to do with Sarah's things. If you want to wait for a while, I understand. If you want me to, I will start packing her stuff and move it somewhere where you do not have to look at it every day. I will do whatever you want me to do. I just want you to talk to me."

Maggie took a while to answer. She finally said, "I would rather you go to work. I am capable of staying by myself. Eventually, we have to get our life in some kind of order. I do not want to get rid of Sarah's things yet. I will let you know."

Jim asked her, "You do not want me to stay here today? I am sure Tom can handle things at the office. I know if we both are busy, we will not think as much. Can I call someone to come and stay with you?"

Maggie stood up and went to the kitchen window. "I have to learn how to stay alone. I do not need a babysitter."

Jim said, "Maggie, I did not mean it like that. I realize that you are capable. I do not want you to become depressed. I need you to share this with me. Sarah was my daughter too."

Maggie looked at him with tears. She told him, "Jim, please just give me some space. I know you will miss Sarah as much as I do. Sarah was my world, and I planned my days with her. Now, since she is gone, my world has changed. I cannot cope with this right now. You go to the office and I will be fine."

Jim went over to hug her. She did not hug him back. He turned and left the kitchen and she heard him on the phone. He came back a few minutes later and told her he was leaving and he would call her in a little while from the office.

As soon as she heard the door shut, she sat down in the floor and cried. "Why did I act like that with him? He does not deserve that treatment, Maggie. If you drive him away, you really will be all alone."

She sat down with her coffee and stared into space. To attempt to focus was beyond her. She sat and stared for a long time. She jumped when she heard the phone ring. It was her mother. She asked how she was doing and wanted to know if she wanted some company.

"No, Mom, I would rather be alone. But thank you for calling," she said. When she hung up, she started crying again. She knew her mother wanted to help her too, but no one else could take her pain. It was all too real and consuming.

She did go up and take a shower in the afternoon. It made her feel a little better.

When Jim called later, she asked him what he would like for dinner. He told her that so many people had brought them food and he would warm something up when he got home.

When she got dressed, she walked past Sarah's room on her way downstairs. She went in the door, and that is where she stayed. She sat in the middle of the floor and cried and then cried some more. Sarah had helped her decorate her room. She remembered the day they found the bedspread. Pink and white were Sarah's favorite colors. The room was so cheery. Just like Sarah.

They were planning to update the furnishings soon, since Sarah thought she was getting too old for "My Little Pony" themes. She had not made up her mind what theme she wanted. Maggie promised her that as soon as the weather turned cold, and they were not as busy, they would go shopping for whatever she wanted. Now, she sat in the room. Sarah would never be here again.

Jim found her in a daze on the floor. He helped her up and led her downstairs. He made them both something to eat, and Maggie attempted to swallow a few bites. He knew he should have stayed with her. He could not concentrate at the office any way. He was not much good to Tom. At least he had a place to go each day. What did Maggie have? How was he going to help her mend?

After they ate, they went into the living room and Maggie fell asleep in the middle of a movie. Jim carried her up to bed, and climbed in beside her and held her while she slept. He knew she was exhausted. The last few days were hard ones. He had to think of some way to give her peace. The pain could consume her soul and he would lose her. Maggie and Sarah were his world; at least they had each other, didn't they?

The next morning, Maggie looked a little more rested. Jim told her he was taking the day off and wanted to go for a drive to check out the fall leaves. He thought Maggie needed to get out for a while. They got ready and drove for a few hours. The scenery this time of year was spectacular.

Maggie smiled a few times. In the afternoon, they stopped at a little diner and got a sandwich.

On the way home, Maggie thanked him for the trip. "I do love you, just be patient with me, okay?"

Jim smiled at her and said, "I love you too, Maggie. I cannot stand to watch your pain. Let me take some of it for you. Please, Maggie, we have to get through this together."

Maggie reached for his hand and said, "Jim, I know you would take all my pain for me. But, I am going to have to learn a new way of life day by day. I promise I will try not to hurt you in the process. The countryside is beautiful isn't it? Sarah loved this time of year too."

They both were silent. Even mentioning her name hurt them both. They arrived home and spent a quiet evening. The next day was the same way. Maggie kept telling herself, one day at a time.

She went into Sarah's room one afternoon and got one of her books off the shelf. The daycare that Sarah and Jill attended always needed books. She decided to call them and ask if they would mind a donation. She would rather see someone enjoy them as much as Sarah did. They told her they would appreciate more books, and she could bring them in anytime. The receptionist cried as she told Maggie how the teachers and the children missed Sarah. The books would keep her memory with them.

Maggie went to the basement and found two boxes. She sorted the books and kept some of their favorites and when she was done, she carried the two boxes down to the front door. She was going out to her car when she saw a car pull in the driveway. It was David Adams.

He stopped to see how she was doing. She remembered how much time he spent with the girls and thanked him for caring. He saw the books and asked her where she was going with them. She said she wanted to donate them to the church day care.

"I am going right past there on my way to the bank. Can I drop them off for you?" he asked her.

Maggie said, "I do not want to bother you, you have other things to do.

David said, "Maggie, it is no bother, I would love to help you. We will take them to my car, and I will drop them off on my way to town."

She went to pick up a box and he told her, "You take the key and unlock my trunk. I will carry them out. They are too heavy for you."

Maggie said, "Okay." She went to his car and opened the trunk. She wanted to make room for the two boxes and picked a blanket up that was in the floor. She was going to fold it and when she shook it, something fell on the ground.

She bent down to pick it up. It was a yellow hair ribbon just like the one Sarah wore. She noticed it was dirty and she held it in her hand. David came out with the boxes, put them in the trunk, and shut the lid.

Finding the ribbon got Maggie so flustered, she barely heard him tell her good bye and waved to him as he left.

She stood still for a couple of minutes. Then it hit her. Sarah was wearing this yellow ribbon in her hair the day she disappeared. She thought, what does this mean? Did David take Sarah?

She was so shaken she headed for the back yard and was sitting in front of the swing set trying to understand why David would want to hurt Sarah.

She remembered hearing a noise behind her and the next thing she knew she woke to find herself tied to a bed in a strange place. She knew who had killed Sarah.

# CHAPTER TWENTY

David Adams was born in New Jersey. The doctors diagnosed his father, Carl Adams with a compulsive disorder when he was twenty-one. His mother, Isabelle Parson, was born and raised in West Virginia. Carl worked for a brewery as a sales representative and often took trips for a week at a time. He met Isabelle on one of his trips to West Virginia while he was there for a convention. He liked her and every time a trip to that area of the country came up, he would put in for it just to see her.

Isabelle was shy and had not dated many men. Carl asked her to marry him and they planned a wedding for the spring.

Carl's compulsive disorder affected everyone around him at the office. He had to have his desk arranged in a certain way. His co-workers started changing things around while he was away, but as soon as he got back, he ranted about what they had done for hours. He would not touch any object that someone else touched, unless he wiped it off first.

Carl spent half his time worrying about germs. At the office parties, when he felt comfortable enough to start eating, everyone else was finished.

At home, Isabelle discovered very quickly that she had to spend a whole day pressing Carl's shirts and pants. He ironed his own underwear; he did not want Isabelle to touch them

Her life was not like the blissful marriage she imagined. Her very existence had to revolve around Carl's excessive habits.

It took a full hour every night for Carl to check things over before they went to bed. When Isabelle became pregnant, Carl was not pleased. He would rather not have a dirty baby around, but it was against his beliefs to end the pregnancy.

David was born in June. It was so humid, and Carl wiped his hands every time he came within two feet of David. Isabelle was the soul caretaker of David. Carl held him once, and did not like the baby smell.

David soon learned that his father was not a typical dad. Carl forced Isabelle to bathe David at least three times a day and he developed skin problems. The doctors warned Isabelle about the hot baths, but in order to live with Carl, it was an unavoidable evil.

Carl's obsessions often caused arguments with those he met. He would not shake hands, and he would not use public restrooms if he could help it.

One night Carl attended a company dinner at a high-class local restaurant. He was so good at his sales position that the company presented him with a plaque. After the dinner, the crowd started out the doors. One of the other customers in the restaurant stepped on Carl's spit-shined shoes. He became angry.

The man pushed Carl, and before everyone could stop it, Carl hit the man as hard as he could on the head. The blow fractured the man's skull and cut his main artery in the side of his head. The man died within seconds. Carl went to jail and at his trial; his sentence was twenty years for murder.

The lawyers for the other man's family were good and they made sure that poor Carl would not use his fists as weapons ever again. When Carl went to prison, her fragile mind was shattered. Isabelle was left with the job of raising little David on her own. The woman did not even know how to get through a full day without Carl telling her what to do.

Poor David, at the age of ten, became the parent. It is against the law for a child not to attend school, so David had to make sure every morning that Isabelle knew exactly what she was to do until he got home. David felt like his mother was a child.

She waited on David to tell her even when to take a shower. David spent his youth caring for his mother. He graduated from high school, and since he inherited his father's gift for being a salesperson, he got a good job at a computer manufacturer. He had to call home three or four times a day just to check on his mother

His life revolved around her care. When David was twenty-three, his mother got sick with pneumonia. She was in the hospital for one whole week. The infections took over her frail body and she died. David moved to nearby Pennsylvania. He transferred to another plant his company owned.

He had no self-confidence with girls and never went on a date. He spent most evenings on his computer. He loved to browse the chat rooms and it evolved into things that were not normal. He got his thrills by spending hours looking at pictures of children. He became obsessed with little girls.

Before he learned to curb his appetites, many of his own relatives ordered him to stay away from their daughters. The way he wanted to touch them was too obvious. He moved many times to hide his way of life.

He became obsessed with someone's child, and the mothers often threatened to call the police and report him. His first victim was a girl named Maria who was five years old.

Sometimes he spent the night with his victims. The shame of what he did took over and he usually drowned the girls in his tub and threw their bodies away wherever he could hide them.

If a situation arose where he felt his cover was blown, he moved. Sometimes he tried to stop, but when he would see a little girl alone, his old habit would creep in, and he would steal the child and use her and then get rid of her body.

He had lost count of the number of girls he took.  His job allowed him to relocate often.  His supervisors were thrilled that David was content to move wherever the company needed him.  The fact that he was a bachelor let him come and go without asking anyone.

David tried to take a little boy one time.  When he was in the chat rooms, some of the other men would talk about wanting little boys.  He could not bring himself to touch, Martin, the little six-year old boy he stole from a bus stop.  His preference was girls.  He strangled Martin and threw him off a bridge.

When David turned thirty, his company offered him a permanent position in a division in Clarkstown, Pa.  He thought it over for a while and decided to take the job.  He found a real cute house in a nice neighborhood.  He really tried to stop looking at the beautiful little girls.

When the urge hit him, he got in his car, drove for fifty miles, and rented a hotel room.  When he first started traveling, he did not have much luck finding the children easily.

He thought it must be because he was not familiar with the area and was on edge.  After the first or second trip, he got right back in the swing of it.

When he moved to Clarkstown, Pa, he dyed his hair to dark brown.  He wore layers of clothes when he went hunting for his victims, but he worked out to stay trim.  He changed his appearance in every way he could think of so if the public heard a description of the abductor, it would not fit with his true appearance.  In his line of crime, a man had to take precautions to stay ahead of the law.

Six months after David moved to Clarkstown, he took a five-year old girl from a mall.  He made sure the news died down before he tried again.  He was getting restless.  He knew his obsession was ruling his life.

He could not resist the children on the internet. It was so easy to cover your trail, especially for someone like him who knew computers and how they worked. The more he looked, the more he wanted.

One thing he discovered in Clarkstown, was the women loved having a bachelor join them. He made a point of meeting his new neighbors. He often crashed their parties, which they did not seem to mind. He volunteered for community activities. The more people that were there, the more children were there. He held the little girls and at night dreamt of them.

He learned not to be too demonstrative with their daughters. If he befriended the moms, he could get closer to the girls.

He met Maggie and Sarah, and Gwen and Jill at a soft ball game for the local fire fighters. He saw Sarah the first time and could not believe that she was the perfect idea of what he searched for all these years.

He could have been content with spending forever with her. There was something special about Sarah.

He was beside himself when he found out that Maggie made homemade hot bread. It gave him a chance to see Sarah twice a week. One time he thought Maggie was looking at him funny while Sarah was on his lap. He told himself he had to be careful. Not seeing Sarah was not an option for him.

His frustration of not being able to have her got the best of him. He put on a wig, added some clothing, and went to Shawsville in the next county. He saw a girl sitting by herself eating ice cream. He walked over to her and said he was with the police and her mother had an accident at the shop on the other side of the mall. She had tripped and sprained her ankle and he would take her to the hospital to be with her.

She took his hand and they walked out of the mall together. He left her behind a dumpster after a few hours. It satisfied his hunger for a little while.

He brought Sarah and Jill a few little gifts when he would go for the bread. Once Maggie said she did not mind, he found himself looking for special gifts for Sarah everywhere he went. She was his dream girl. He tried to be content seeing her every week.

Then one day he was driving home past the park and he noticed a little girl swinging. No one was around. He pulled in the lot and could not believe his eyes when he saw it was Sarah. It was an omen. To David it meant that she was there for him.

He went to her and asked her if she would go and help him find his next-door neighbor's cat. The woman was so upset she couldn't find Nappy, her cat. David told her it would only take a minute.

Sarah told him her mommy was in the woods and would be right back.

"Oh, we will only be gone five minutes," he said. "Your mommy won't even miss you. Besides, she won't care if you are with me. You go with Uncle David all the time." Sarah climbed off the swing and went with him. He took her to his house.

Sarah headed back out the door and he asked her where she was going. She said, "We have to find Nappy."

David asked her, "Do you want some cocoa first? I make it real good."

Sarah said, "Okay, but we have to hurry. Mommy will be mad at me."

He took his time making the cocoa. He wanted to savor his time with her. He told her to sit up at the bar and take off her coat. The smell of her hair breezed his nose. He tickled her and she laughed. They were having fun.

After a half hour, she wanted to go back to the park. She got down and got her coat. He couldn't lose her now. He told her he would take her in a little while.

He said, "I know your mommy already went home. We will call her after a while and tell her we are having a great time together and maybe she will let you stay and have burgers and fries with me."

Sarah said, "No, I want to go home now, please."

He saw she was getting worried about being in trouble. She headed for the door and he went and picked her up and took her to the spare bedroom and shoved her in and locked the door.

He heard her crying and hoped she would settle down in a few minutes.

"I can't take you home Sarah. You have to stay with me now and be my little girl. I love you," he told her through the door.

David waited outside the door and when he didn't hear any noise, he thought Sarah must have settled down. He waited a few more minutes and unlocked the door. She was lying on the floor.

David went to her and picked her up. He thought at first that she was sleeping. He shook her but she would not respond. What is wrong with her, he thought. He tried breathing in her mouth to bring her back. Sarah's lips were blue and she was cold. David went hysterical. He finally got his perfect child and now she was dead.

David screamed and held Sarah as he rocked back and forth. After a while, he got a blanket and wrapped Sarah's body in it. He put her in his bed and for a few nights, he slept with her.

Finally David had to make a decision to get rid of the body. Sarah had been dead for two weeks, and he was afraid to be caught with her body in his home. He decided to go back to the vicinity of the park and leave her body, hoping that someone would find it and take care of the burial.

David waited until it was almost dark, took the body and walked deep into the woods. He chose a spot under several huge trees and took a shovel and worked in the dirt trying to make a softer place to lay Sarah in.

He covered her and drove back home. The one time I did not want to hurt a child, and now she is gone. He wanted to keep Sarah forever.

# CHAPTER TWENTY-ONE

After Walter took Mary things went haywire again, and he got perturbed. He just wanted someone who would enjoy being with him. He thought a lot about Mary and Shelly.

"I guess they were too young. Maybe I will try to find an older girl. I have to get lucky soon," he thought.

He spent his time off driving around the town looking for another girl He saw several pretty ones he would have liked to grab, but he resisted. He had decided to look for ones that would not freak out so easy.

He got an idea one evening sitting in his living room. "Maybe I will try the bar where Mother used to work. At least those girls are less hyper, and they are nothing but sluts any way. Why else would they hang at a bar," he thought.

Walter got excited and made sure he had the chloroform and some rope. He double-checked what he needed and started out to set his plan in motion. "This time tomorrow, I will have a new girl and be set for the rest of my life."

He arrived at the bar, went in, found a bar stool, and ordered a beer. He checked out the girls. "This time I have to make sure she is right. I will run out of room in the well if I keep going the way I have so far," he thought.

Walter drank and watched for a few hours. One young girl came in with a friend. They both were very pretty girls. As he watched them, they did a lot of giggling. He figured they would both be screamers so he decided against them. He evaluated every girl that came in the door. He was getting a little impatient.

"How many girls do you have to look at?" he asked himself. Time is running out when he finally sees one he liked. She appeared to be around twenty years old. She had long straight black hair and her eyes were the brightest blue he had ever seen.

Yep, she will do just fine, he thought. He finished his beer and went outside to wait. The parking lot was secluded and hidden from the road. He went to his trunk and found the drug and the cloth.

He was giddy with anticipation. He hoped this one cooperated better than the first two. This one is the perfect one finally, he thought. He chose a spot in the middle of the lot. He crouched down behind a cement pole and waited.

He was daydreaming about the girl he had chosen and almost missed her when she came out. She walked past him without seeing him and headed for her car. He quietly crawled through the rows of parked cars following her. She stopped at a bright red sports car and as she inserted the key in the lock, he rose up behind her.

He quickly put the cloth over her face and within seconds, he had her. She was more beautiful than he thought at first. Her features up close excited him. As he touched her hair when he lifted her to put her in the trunk, he could not wait until he got her to the shed.

Wow, he thought, I really should have thought of this before. I wasted my time with the younger girls and now I am sure this one will want to stay. He hummed as he drove her to the shed.

He checked his watch when he got out of the car. He drugged her at 10:15, so she should wake up before it got daylight. He unlocked the door and lit the lantern.

He turned down the cover on the bed and got the ropes from the corner. Everything is ready for my new girl, he thought. He went to trunk, opened it, lifted the girl up, and carried her to the bed. He tied her hands and feet to the bedposts, and sat in the chair to wait.

This time he remembered to bring a magazine to read. He had restocked the cooler he carried in his car with soda. He opened his soda, got the magazine, tipped his chair back, and began the waiting game.

He read a few stories in the crime magazine. He loved reading about how other men carried out their crimes. It fascinated him that most people were too dumb to figure out what happened right in front of their own eyes.

Walter chuckled and thought, "If people paid attention, they would know when someone was out to hurt them. "Yeah, like me," he thought. "I took three girls so far, and no one has a clue." His attention went back to his story.

He got restless after an hour and paced around the room a while to keep himself awake. He went to the bed and stared at his new girl. She was nice and slim and reminded him of a girl he liked when he was in the tenth grade. Her name was Tina. He tried to talk to her, but soon gave up.

"But now I have a better deal. This one can't get away," he thought to himself.

He sat back down in the chair and fell asleep. He woke up around 3:30 in the morning and checked on his prisoner. She was still out of it.

He went out to his car, fiddled with the radio, and found a rock station to listen to while he wasted time. He fooled around until 4:15, and then went back inside. He wanted to be right beside her when she woke up.

He sat back down in the chair. After a half hour, he heard her moan. He watched her as she forced her eyes to open. His smile was big and wide as she turned her head and looked at him for the first time. He saw the fear, but kept smiling. He hoped she would not be like the others and start screaming.

Walter smiled again and said, "Hi, I'm Walter. Don't be afraid. I do not want to hurt you. If you scream, I will though." He waited for a few seconds for her to focus and as she tried to raise her arms, they would not budge. She was scared to death.

She started yelling and demanding that he untie her. "Let me go," she yelled. "What are you doing? You are a crazy idiot. I want you to let me go now."

Walter was a little shocked by her anger. To him he did not see any reason why they all had to get mad. "If you will shut up and listen to me," he said. "I will tell you why you are here. But as long as you are yelling, I am not going to say a word."

She pulled at the ropes and tried to free her hands. She tried to kick him. She thrashed around on the bed then. She yelled and cussed him for a few more minutes. Finally, she grew tired and stopped to rest.

Walter took a step back and waited. He knew if she started screaming, he would have to shut her up. The other times he did not handle it well and both of the other girls ended up dead.

She lay still and her mind was reeling. "How do I get out of this?" She was a levelheaded girl and surely, she could think of something. She struggled within herself and knew if this man had kidnapped her, he meant her harm.

She remembered hearing stories about others and always wondered what she would do in the same situation. She thought she would try to talk to the guy and eventually he would let me go.

"I would hope somewhere inside every person is some sort of reason. If I can bide my time, maybe I can survive," she thought. She calmed down and looked over at him. Walter approached the bed again.

He started telling her, "You are here because I wanted you to be with me. There is no way you can escape. No one can hear you, and no one knows where this place is, so you have to stay here. I will not hurt you if you do as I say. You and I can get to know each other. I brought you here because I think you are very pretty. I hope you know how lucky you are to be chosen over all the other girls."

She did not respond and Walter continued, "I will give you a few days to get used to it, and then we can spend all out time together. Okay?"

She wanted to scream at him again. Thoughts were running in her head, "I am lucky? You kidnapped me instead of the other girls, and I should feel lucky? You are a sick creep." She did not say a word. "If he takes girls, he does hurt them," she thought.

Walter looked down at her and said, "Now, if you are finished with your tantrum, we can move on. I want you to know that if you try to get out, you will be sorry. I will take care of anything you need, and since I work nights, we can spend our days together. Just think, we are out here in the country and no one will disturb us. I will bring your food every day. We can eat dinner together, and then we can even play a game if you want. I always wanted someone to play games with me."

He continued, "When I was growing up, my parents never once played games, did your parents play with you?"

She nodded her head yes.

"Boy, I envy kids that had parents that did stuff with them. If we have kids, I want to play ball, and soccer, and take them bowling. I can't wait till I have a boy. I would never be mean to him. He would not hate me like I did my father."

He changed moods again and told her, "I have to leave soon to get some sleep before work. I have soda in the car, do you want one?"

She shook her head no.

She was so confused her mind could not fathom that she was here. "I remember leaving the bar last night, but I do not remember anything else. He must have been in the parking lot waiting for me. I wonder if anyone saw him. Maybe they are looking for me right now. Oh I hope so."

Walter was fiddling with something on the table. As he turned around, she saw a white cloth in his hand. He came near her and she smelled a strange odor.

He took a few steps toward her and said, "I cannot take the chance of trusting you until I get to know you a little better, so I am going to put you back to sleep until I can come back. Don't be afraid, it won't hurt a bit."

He came next to the bed and she fought the cloth as hard as she could, but she felt the drug take effect and everything turned black. Walter smoothed the cover and stood looking at her for a few minutes. He was so proud of himself. He finally made a good choice and he knew that this girl was to be his.

His world became right again. Walter made sure the lantern was out. He went out and locked the door behind him. He whistled as he got in his car. Man, he thought, I can finally have a girl that I can spend all my time with. Ain't life grand?

# CHAPTER TWENTY-TWO

The girl that Walter had kidnapped was Susan Halsley. She shared an apartment with two other girls. She would turn twenty-one in a few weeks, and she loved her life. She worked as a lab technician in the local hospital. She moved out of her parent's house after attending trade school. She had a whole slew of friends and was enjoying working and having a good time on her days off. Her parents, Lou and Nancy Halsley, were ordinary people with four children.

The two boys were older and Susan and her sister were only a couple years apart. Her older brothers were both married to real cute girls. They each had two children. Her older sister, Patricia, married her high school sweetheart. They were the most well matched couple she knew. They had two girls, and were waiting for a while to try for a boy.

Susan wanted to be like them when she got ready to get married. Her parents hated her to move out, but taught her to be responsible and trusted her decision to get her own place.

Today Susan planned to go straight home after work, but one of her friends, Janice, called and asked her to stop at the bar and have a quick drink. Susan told her she would meet her for a little while, but she had to be at work early the next day and did not want to stay late. Susan arrived to find Janice waiting for her with a burger, which was the best burger in town, according to Janice. They laughed a little and had one drink.

Susan glanced at her watch and told Janice she had to go. Tomorrow she had the early shift, so they hugged each other and promised to get together again soon.

Susan's mind was on her cat, Jasper, as she headed for her car. He missed her when she did not go straight home. She brought the cat with her when she moved into the apartment. Jasper was an eleven-year old calico. Jasper and Susan spent every day with each other. He was the last thing she saw every night and the first thing she saw in the morning. He slept in a small bed right beside her on the floor. He knew her so well, if she was sick, he lay beside her until she was better. If she was upset, he was upset. If she was happy, he licked her face.

Her family often kidded her and said if she got along with her husband as well as she did with her cat, her marriage would last for one hundred years.

Vanessa Baldwin was one of Susan's roommates. She turned twenty-two a few months ago. She was a jolly girl. She was a little over weight but when you met Vanessa, you usually laughed so much, your attention was not on her weight. She got along with everyone.

Vanessa worked at the hospital as a nurse. She looked forward to work every day to be able to make a sick person feel better. Her parents were as happy as Vanessa was. She had six brothers and sisters and the Baldwin clan loved to eat and loved to laugh. They were one big happy family. She met Susan six months ago and immediately knew she would fit in well at the apartment.

Kathy Bailey was the third roommate. She was a little quieter than the other two. She worked at the Bon Ton in the women's department and was the smartest of the three. She was also twenty-two and was an elegant young woman. She knew about makeup and hair and often treated the other two girls to a makeover and gave advice on how to dress better

She never failed to let them know when the good bargains went on sale at the store. She was an only child and lost her father a few years before. She was close to her mother and checked in with her every day.

Kathy was in her room getting ready for bed when Jasper made his way to her room. He was meowing so she went to find his food. Susan was usually home by 11:00, and fed the cat right away.

When Kathy looked at the clock and noticed it was 11:30, she went to find her cell phone to call Susan. Kathy got Susan's voice mail and she left a message for Susan to call her.

Vanessa was pulling the late shift at the hospital and Kathy made a quick call and asked her if she knew if Susan had plans to be late that night. Vanessa said she talked to her earlier in the day, and Susan had not mentioned being late. She told Kathy to call her as soon as Susan came home so she would not spend the night worrying.

Kathy promised she would and went back to her room and lay down on her bed to wait. She fell asleep and did not hear the phone when Vanessa called at 2:00. When the sun came up, Susan was not in her room. Kathy put in a call to Vanessa. She was to get off at 7:00. She told her when she got home, they would make some calls and give Susan a lecture about leaving her and Kathy and Jasper in the dark about her late night.

Later that morning they called Susan's mother to ask if she heard from her. Her mother said she talked to her the day before around lunchtime. She asked if anything was wrong and Kathy told her they were concerned that Susan did not come home the night before. The three girls kept close watch on each other. In this day and time, you could not trust people. Vanessa told Kathy about the articles in the papers about the two missing teen girls from the area.

After calling a few more friends, they decided to call the police and ask how they should handle the situation. The officer that talked to the girls told them that they should wait at least twenty four hours, and call them back if they had not heard from Susan in that time. He remembered a memo the whole squad received a couple of days before. If anyone in the department wrote a report of a missing girl, Officer Paul Garret requested a copy sent to his department.

Kathy had to get ready for work, so she went to take a shower. She heard a noise outside the door and when she opened it, Jasper was scratching at the door. He could tell something was wrong, so she picked him up and hugged him for a while. She always heard that pets could tell when someone is upset. Kathy knew that he missed Susan. She hoped they heard from her very soon.

## CHAPTER TWENTY-THREE

Walter slept for a few hours. When he woke up, he was in a good mood. He hurried and got dressed in his security uniform. He got off work early and he thought he would go by the shed and check on his latest conquest. He could not wait until this girl settled down and got used to the idea that now she was his.

I do not understand why they have to get so hysterical about everything. Why can't they just accept that they cannot get away and just do as I say? I am getting tired of fooling with ones that don't work out.

He packed an extra sandwich to take with him and grabbed some chips and cookies on his way out.

"I will take her some goodies and maybe she will see I really do care about her," he said to himself.

When he got to the shed, he unlocked the door and went into the room. The girl was awake. Her face was a mess and he knew she was crying. He sat the basket with the food on the table and went to the side of the bed.

Walter said, "I see you are awake. I brought you some food. I cannot stay very long. Do you need to go the bathroom before I leave?" he asked her.

She looked at him and he could see the raw fear in her eyes.

"You do not have to be afraid of me, unless you do not do as I say. As long as you obey me, you will be fine. Would you like for me to untie you so you can use the bucket?" he asked.

She looked at him again and nodded her head yes.

"I will untie you and show you the bucket. I will wait outside for two minutes. When you are finished, I will give you your food. He went to the bedposts and untied her hands.

153

As he was working on the ropes around her ankles, she flinched when he accidentally touched her foot.

Walter shook his head and thought, "Oh, I hope she does not freak out like the last two." When he was done, he pointed to the bucket in the corner, went to the door, and shut it behind him. He looked at his watch and timed two minutes.

When he went back in the door, she was sitting on the side of the bed. He went to the table and got the sandwich. Walter brought it to her and said, "I do not know your name yet."

She glanced at him and did not say a word.

"It will make it easier if you tell me your name. I told you my name, Walter Mills."

She hesitated and was afraid not to do as he said, so she told him. "My name is Susan."

"That is a pretty name for a pretty girl," he said. "Are you hungry, Susan?" he asked her. He held the sandwich out to her and finally she reached back and took it.

Susan unwrapped her sandwich and took a bite. "What if he put poison in it?" she thought. She tried not to think about it as she took the second bite.

He said, "I also brought you some chips and cookies. I will have to leave in a few minutes. I put oil in the lantern for you. Do you promise to behave until I come back tomorrow morning? If not I will tie you down and drug you again," he said.

Susan shook her head yes and softly murmured, "I promise I will behave. Please, don't tie me again."

"Okay, you remember what I told you. If you try something stupid, you will have to pay," he firmly said to her.

"No, I promise," Susan said.

Walter laid all the food on the bed and told her he was leaving but would be back first thing in the morning. He shot her one last intimidating look and she heard the lock click shut. She listened for his car to leave and started shaking uncontrollably.

"How can I get out of here? I have to find a way out. Please I want to go home," she cried. She went to try the door and found it was too strong for her. It did not budge no matter how hard she pulled on it.

Susan was scared to death. She crawled back on the bed and covered up. She was freezing, but she knew it was her terror. She stared into the empty space around her and gave in to her fear. She curled up on the bed and sobbed for the longest time. Finally, she sat up. It was dark outside and she did not have any idea what time it was.

She ate the rest of the sandwich. After she was finished, her stomach started hurting. The smell of the urine in the bucket mixed with the damp dirt floor was nauseating. She lay back on the bed and eventually drifted off. She woke up screaming a few hours later. She was hoping it was all a dream, but she looked around and knew she was still a prisoner in a dark, damp room. "I wish I was home."

After a while, she became upset as she thought, "Jasper will think I've left him."

She drifted back to sleep and tossed and turned for the next several hours. Sometime after the sun came up Susan heard the car pull up. She waited anxiously and heard the lock on the door. She tried to pretend she was sleeping.

Walter came right to the bed and she opened her eyes. "Good morning," he said. "Did you sleep well? I am glad to see you listened to me and did not try to get out. I told you if you do as I say, you will be fine. I brought you an egg sandwich. I did not know if you liked it on

155

toast or plain bread, so I made you one of each. I also brought a brush for your hair. You need to brush your hair everyday so it will be shiny."

He laid the sandwiches beside her and rambled on about when he was a kid his mother brushed her hair fifty times a day. She could not follow some of his conversation. She did not know if it was the drug, or she just was so scared she could not concentrate. He fiddled with the lantern, got the urine bucket, and told her he would empty it while she ate.

She picked up one of the sandwiches and took a bite. She forced herself not to gag and concentrated on taking small bites.

Walter went outside and she thought about running out the door and taking off as fast as she could go. She was afraid if she tried now, her legs were too weak. She might not be able to outrun him.

She slowly nibbled on the sandwich and waited for him to come back. She could hear him whistling and singing some kind of tune outside.

"How can he act like this is normal?" she wondered. "He has taken me as a prisoner against my will, and will hurt me if I try to get away."

She had finished one sandwich when he came back in.

"If you want I will let you go outside and sit on the bench for a little while. The last girl tried to run and did not make it. So, I tell you that and I will let you decide if you can do as I say. If you do, I will let you out today. When you are finished eating let me know."

She felt her heart skip a beat when he casually talked about one girl not making it. "Does that mean he killed her?" she thought. "Will he kill me whenever he is done with me?"

Walter walked to the corner of the room. When he turned around there was a rope in his hand.

"Do you want to go out now?" he asked her.

She found her voice long enough to say, "Yes, I would like that."

Walter said, "Well stand up and I will put this rope around you. If you try to run, you will be sorry. But if you behave today, then you go out again tomorrow."

Susan stood up but was so shaky she almost tumbled to the floor. She reached for the edge of the bed to steady herself and after a few seconds, she stood still.

Walter came toward her and put the rope around her neck like a noose. He finally got it the way he wanted it and he told her to go out the door to the bench.

Susan squinted as the sunlight hit her eyes. She did not realize how damp and dreary the shed was. The sun felt good on her face and she headed for the bench and sat down.

He sat beside and told her to look out to her left. She heard a noise and as she turned to look, a deer stood on the edge of the woods.

Walter said, "Ain't that the most beautiful sight you ever saw? I have some friends that like to go deer hunting, but not me. I could never kill a deer. They won't hurt you so why can't they leave them alone."

Susan's first thought was, "You can't kill a deer, but you could kill me if I try to get away from you and go back to my own life. I can't believe this!" She sat still as a mouse on the bench. She really was afraid for her life. His eyes were so cold when she looked in them. She knew that he really could kill her.

They sat still and watched the deer for a while. Walter started telling her the different kinds of trees that were in the woods. He told her that one field was wheat, and one was corn, and how he spent a lot of time here soaking up the beauty

For the next half hour, he talked about the woods and land and how fascinated he was by how many animals that were living in the woods and how they survived without any human help at all. She tried to listen to what he was saying. Her heart was racing and her knees were almost knocking together. She had to hold on to both her hands so he would not see them shake.

Susan thought to herself, "In some ways it was worse to be sitting in the bright sun listening to talk about everyday things, than it was to be locked up inside like an animal. He really does not know what he is doing is so wrong. To him it is okay to hold me here. How do you reason with a human being like this? Do I stand any of a chance to ever escape?"

Walter told her to go in. "I will go home and take care of what I need to do and will bring you dinner later. I hope you remember what I said about coming out here again. If you want to do it tomorrow, it is all up to you and how well you behave."

Susan stood up and headed back in the door. He spent a few more minutes putting the rope away and checking to see if everything else was the way he had left it.

"I have to go now and I will come back in a few hours. Is there anything else you want me to bring you?" he asked her.

Susan shook her head no and cowered on the bed.

She wanted him to leave and never come back. "I hope you die in a car wreck on the way home," she thought. "I hope you suffer like you make others suffer." She was afraid he would read her mind so she turned away.

Walter told her "I will see you at dinner then." He locked the door and she could hear him whistle again as he got in his car and drove away.

She fell down on the floor and wailed. She rocked back and forth and asked the same question over and over. "Why am I here? What am I going to do? Someone help me, please." She could not yell anymore so she got back on the bed and stared at the wall. Her mind went back to her apartment and Jasper. She knew he missed her too.

"What will he do if I don't go home? What is everyone thinking? My mother and father are probably so worried." She did not pray much but she found herself talking to God. "Please help me. I just want to go home. Why is this happening to me? God, please help me."

She closed her eyes and desperation and anguish flooded her soul. She curled tighter into the cover and tried to warm her body, which was shaking violently. The harder she tried to stop, the more she shook. She felt hopeless.

Later she heard a call pull up. Her mind instantly rushed back to a mode of fear. She knew it was Walter. She tried to prepare herself to stay calm when she heard the door open.

He walked in the room and spoke to her. "Susan I brought you a warm plate of home cooked food. I have chicken and mashed potatoes. I also have creamed corn and a hot biscuit and butter. I thought you might like some hot chocolate and I put it a thermos so it would stay hot. So, sit up here and I will get your fork for you," he told her.

Susan stayed still on her side turned away from him. She tried not to move so he would think she was asleep.

Walter went to the side of the bed and shook her. She turned over and he saw tears on her cheeks. 'Why are you crying?" he asked her. "I told you I would bring you dinner. See, I promised I would take care of you. You don't have to worry now. You are here with me and I will give you anything you want."

Susan shot up in the bed and said, "Then let me go and I won't tell anyone about you. I promise. I just want to go home. Please let me go. You said you would give me anything I want. And that is what I want." She knew she had made a big mistake when she saw the fury in his eyes.

"I told you that you will never leave me. I will take care of you now. You do not need to ever think about anyone else. You have to forget them they are in the past. Now, I will only tell you this one time. You are not going to get out. There is no way to escape. You are mine now. If you bring it up again, I will make you sorry. Do you understand?" He looked straight at her and waited.

She was so frightened her heart stopped beating. She felt as if she would faint. Self-preservation kicked in and she slowly nodded her head yes. She would do as he says. She had to survive.

Susan sat up straighter and he smiled at her. "That is much better," he said. "Here is your fork. Now eat your dinner. I went to a lot of trouble to fix all this food. If you want to show me some appreciation, eat."

She took the fork and took a bite of the potatoes. She forced the food down and he stood and watched her eat. When she finished he took the plate. He walked to the chair and sat down.

He took out a book and told her he would read her a story. He started reading it. She recognized the story of Hansel and Gretel. He read the whole story to her and when he finished he sat the book down and said, "I always liked this book. It was my favorite story when I was a kid. I remember the teacher reading it to my class. I stole one of the copies from her desk and I have read the story hundreds of times. I never get tired of it. Did you like it?" Susan told him.

"Yes, I liked the book. Thank you for reading it to me."

Walter was beaming. He was so happy she listened to him read. He wanted every evening to be like this. He did not consider what Susan wanted, only what Walter wanted. He wanted to keep her here and spend his evenings with her.

He sat with her for a little while longer and said, "I have to leave for work soon. I need to go back to my house to pick up my stuff first. I will fill the lantern with oil and then I will go. I will leave the book for you. You can read it again before you go to sleep." He laid the book on the bed beside her and went to get the lantern. He went outside and she heard him fiddle with the lantern filling it.

He brought the lantern back and lit it. It was dark and dreary in the shed and she was glad to have the light.

Walter asked her if she needed anything else before he left. She thought about raving about going home again, but she remembered what he told her before about hurting her, so she said no. A few minutes later, he left. Susan heard the car start and pull away.

She felt herself drifting into a helpless mood. She stayed on the bed and wrapped in the blanket as tight as she could. She spent the night trying to keep the shadows in the corners from snatching what little hope she had left. The darkness and eeriness seemed like an eternity.

The next morning she woke up when she heard the car.

Walter came in with her breakfast. After she ate, they went to sit on the bench in the sunshine.

That night he brought her dinner again. When Walter left, Susan spent the wee hours of the night so frightened and lonely.

The next two days were the same. Susan was in a daze. She followed what he told her. When he left, she laid on the bed in a state of limbo.

The next day after she ate breakfast they went out to the bench. The sun was warm. The birds were singing. Susan sat and soaked up the warmth from the sun. She knew she would need it to withstand the lonesome night.

While they were sitting there, Walter heard a noise beside the shed. He told her to sit still and not make any noise.

"It is that same stupid ground hog I have been trying to kill him for the past month. This time I'll get him."

He went to his car and took out his shotgun. He told her he was going to kill it.

Her eyes followed him as he went around the shed. Somewhere in the distance, she heard a bird sing. The sound reminded her of the soft meow Jasper made when he was hungry.

Before she thought about it, she was running. She ran as hard as she could towards the edge of the woods. It was so far across the field. She willed herself to hurry before he saw her.

Susan was half way across the field when she heard him call her name. She ran faster. She had to make it to the woods. She heard a blast and felt a pain in her back. She fell to the ground. As her blood flowed out on the ground, she thought of her mother and Jasper and her two roommates. She whispered "Bye" to them as she took her last breath.

Another life ended at the hand of a man who just wanted to have someone he could spend time with and listen to him just for a little while. Walter walked across the field and looked down at her. He knelt beside her and looked at her face. "You did not listen. I told you that you would never leave me. It is your fault," he muttered.

Walter went back to his car and got a tarp. He walked back across the field and wrapped her body in it. He dragged her to the well and removed the slab off the top. He picked up Susan rolled in the tarp and placed it on the ledge. With one shove, her body hit the water below.

Walter calmly recovered the well and walked back to the shed. He went in and put the rope back in the corner. He made the bed and emptied the bucket. He blew out the lantern and sat it back on the table. He locked up, got in his car, and started home.

CHAPTER TWENTY-FOUR

Officer Paul Garret sat at his desk looking at the pictures of the three missing girls. He was exhausted. The faces haunted his sleep for the past few weeks. As he reviewed the files one by one, he studied the faces.

Shelly was a sixteen-year old girl from a very good home. Mary was seventeen and a beautiful girl who should have had a bright future in front of her. He got the impression from her picture that she was a bubbly girl. Dealing with her parents had been extremely hard on him.

The latest victim, Susan Halsley was also a good-looking young girl. She looked to be a little older than the first two. Her mother was falling apart waiting for news of her daughter's whereabouts.

So far, he had nothing to tell the parents and friends of these girls. They had no leads, and found no trace of any of the girls. All three of them had vanished.

The cars had been located, but they had no luck on finding evidence on any of the vehicles. Whoever took them left no fingerprints, no DNA, nothing.

He reached for the other two files on Candy Burns and Sarah Taylor. Finding the bodies gave the parents closure. It did not help the pain of the loss of their children, but they did not have to wonder what happened to their children as the parents of the missing teens did.

He had absolutely nothing to tie the two cases together. The experts he worked with on both cases assured him that for one suspect to take the missing teens and the two children was unusual. Most serial killers stuck to a pattern.

The three older girls were probably the work of one man. A different suspect more than likely kidnapped the two children. How could he assure the people of the town of their safety if there were two serial killers at bay? One took teen girls, and the other was taking younger girls.

He briefed his men that morning and they agreed they had two separate suspects roaming their streets. The press clamored for updates on what the police were doing to catch these killers.

His superiors were expecting him to handle a press conference later that day. What was he going to say? They had no leads on the teens, they were not even sure if they were dead. Without the bodies of the girls, he could not say what happened to them, or if they were still alive.

Officer Garret intently scanned the files on Candy Burns and Sarah Taylor. The closure of finding their bodies was one small blessing for their families. They did not have to live day to day wondering what happened to their children. He wondered if the same suspect took all five victims.

It was a frightening thought that the suspects were normal. If you met them on the street, you had no idea what evil lurked inside these men.

He wired all the surrounding districts for updates on similar crimes. He had no response yet. He hoped no more victims would turn up. He did not want to spend his nights with the images of more young girls that had fallen prey to such maniacs.

Officer Garret begged for all the help he could get on these tragedies. He was glad he had a team of good men. He instructed them to keep digging until they found some evidence that would help solve these disappearances.

One of his officers knocked on his door to let him know that the news conference would start in one hour. He sat down at his desk and started reading all the files again.

There had to be something he was missing. There were five victims in a few months. He picked up Sarah's picture, and remembered the look of fear on Maggie and Jim's face the day that Sarah went missing. He vowed to work extra hard to make sure he did not have to visit any more homes with the tragic news of their children's life being halted by an evil creature that was part of the human race.

Paul Garret hated this part of his job. In his line of work, you never got used to the depravity of some people. His mind went back to his own past and the pain it caused him.

He could still see his wife's face in his mind. She was the prettiest girl he ever saw. They met twenty-five years ago. Evelyn Jones stole his heart the first time he saw her. He spent every waking moment thinking about her, and after a year and a half, she agreed to marry him. She was a petite woman and he was always afraid he would squeeze her too hard.

He loved the feel of her in his arms and hugged her all the time. They both were from Indiana. Paul's parents moved to Clarkstown, Pa. right after he and Evelyn were married. They loved Pennsylvania and his mother wrote him every week begging him and his new wife to relocate here. They made a trip to visit his parents and both of them fell in love with the area.

Paul went into the police academy shortly after graduation, and when a job became available in Clarkstown, he applied for it. His qualifications were excellent. Paul's superiors hated to see him leave but the new job was a great opportunity. Paul and Evelyn moved a few blocks away from his parents.

Paul settled in the new department easily. He advanced quickly and now was the senior officer in the department. All his men had the utmost respect for him. His compassion for the town's people was evident to all who knew him.

As Paul thought about his wife, a smile crossed his face. He remembered the day he came home to find the dining room table set with the fine china and candles.

He wondered to himself, "What did I do to deserve a candle light dinner?" He followed the smells to the kitchen and found Evelyn standing at the stove stirring the sauce. She turned around when she heard his footsteps.

He walked over to her and kissed the back of her neck. He wrapped his arms around her waist and said, "Well Mrs. Garret, did we win the lottery today? Oh, I know. You published another article."

Evelyn was a freelance writer and they always celebrated when one a magazines published one of her articles She looked at him and said, "Mr. Garret, I do not think even winning a million dollars in the lottery could top the news I have."

He turned her towards him and said, "Okay, I give up." The smile on her face lit up the whole room.

"You had better sit down. A lot of new fathers have a tendency to faint," she said.

The meaning of her words sunk in his head and she watched as the biggest grin covered his face. He picked her up and swung her around and around the kitchen. The child like squeals he made tickled her to death. They laughed and hugged for five minutes.

Suddenly a concerned look came over him and he asked her. "Should I be picking you up? Did I hurt you? Do you need to sit down?"

"No," she told him, "you did not hurt me. You can hug me and pick me up any time you wish. A mother's body is able to withstand the hugs and kisses of a happy father to be."

He held her close to him and when she drew back, she saw tears in his eyes. "What a sweet loving man I have for my husband," she said as she reached up and kissed him.

They had a son and named him John. Paul was so proud of his new child. He helped Evelyn with everything. He gave John his bath in the evenings. He helped with the dishes and the laundry. He even changed the diapers when he was home. They were so content.

When John turned three, he got sick. The doctors told them John had leukemia. They fought a good fight, but lost him at the age of five and a half. The loss of their son was extremely hard to cope with.

They wanted another baby right away but unfortunately, the doctors diagnosed Evelyn with breast cancer. Four years later and Paul lost her to the disease.

He threw his energy into work and took all the hours he could get. Going home to an empty house was depressing and Paul knew it would destroy him if he gave in.

His own tragedies taught him how to deal with the pain of others in his job. Losing a son and a wife was hard, but he knew when his son and wife died, it was from natural causes. No one had taken them or harmed them.

He did not know how parents went on after suffering such a devastating blow. All he could do was promise them he would do all he could to apprehend the suspects as soon as possible.

His secretary's knock on the door and the coffee she brought him cut his thoughts short. She put her hand on his shoulder with reassurance before she left. The whole office knew how Paul suffered when he studied the pictures of missing children.

The loss of his own child had softened some, but they all knew Paul took it personal when he had to deal with the death of a child. They loved and respected the compassion Paul used when dealing with people. He thanked her and went back to the files. He had no idea where to start looking for the men who were killing the innocent children and teens in his hometown.

He read the description of the man who had taken Candy Burns. The only thing they knew for sure was that he was wearing a gray sweatshirt and a baseball cap. When he read the forensic report, the hair found on Candy's body was from a man with dyed hair. If a suspect was in question, they could compare his hair to the hair found on Candy's pants. In frustration he pushed back his chair and started to pace around the office.

He decided to check with his men for an update on any other cases. One of the officers was in the middle of a phone conversation. He hung up his phone and informed him of a report of a disturbance at the mall on the north side of town. Officer Garret reached for his jacket and yelled for the men to follow him.

They arrived at the mall in fifteen minutes. The security officers accompanied them to the main office.

A young man sat in one of the chairs and looked up as the officers walked in. The mall security had handcuffed the suspect and escorted him into an office with Officer Garret. The security officer filled them in on the case.

The young man's name was Charles Shifflet. He was seventeen-years old. He told them he was talking to a group of girls. One of the girls started screaming, alerting security. Officer Garret started asking the young man questions. Poor Charles was scared to death. He was just fooling with the girls. He knew them from school and wanted them to go with him to play video games.

He had no idea what he did wrong. He told them repeatedly he did nothing to the girl and did not understand why he could not go home.

It did not take long for Officer Garret to determine that the scared boy was innocent. He did explain to him that other young women had disappeared. After a stern lecture, they released the boy and he promised that he definitely would watch how he handled girls from now on. Officer Garret thanked the security teams and commended their quick response.

Officer Garret went back to the station and prepared for the press conference. He would inform the public of the threat. Until they apprehended the suspects, the public needed to be extra careful. A knock on his door let him know that the press was ready for him.

He stepped up to the microphone and introduced himself. He gave the names of the three missing girls, and that they had no clues of their whereabouts.

He asked if anyone knew anything or had seen something suspicious to call the station. Any lead could help no matter how small it seemed.

Officer Garret proceeded to the cases of the two young girls, Candy Burns and Sarah Taylor. The description of the suspect was very vague. A meeting with all the agencies involved agreed that parents should keep their children by their side. It was better to be over cautious than sorry.

He explained that an abduction of a child could take a few seconds. The abductors led the child away with many excuses. They told the child that a parent had been hurt or an animal was lost. He may offer them ice cream or other treats just to get them to go with them. He told them to talk to their children and explain that they should never go with anyone at all unless they knew them.

Officer Garret waited a few seconds. He said, "I hate to make your children afraid. In these circumstances, it is best to have them be a little afraid of strangers. Also, talk with your teen children and young adults.

Have them travel in pairs. It is harder to take two at a time. A young woman by herself is an easy target for an experienced kidnapper. Please, heed my warnings. These suspects are dangerous and feel no remorse or hesitation. They are the cruelest criminals of all. They are average men with terrible habits. They will not stop unless the community pulls together. I thank all of you for coming and please call the police station if you see or hear anything that may help us."

He ended the press conference and headed back to his office. The stress was taking a toll on his body. He had a headache that just would not go away. Since they found Sarah, he spent long evenings pouring over any information he could get to find a lead to whoever was playing havoc with the young people in this community.

His thoughts drifted back to the funeral of Sarah Taylor. Being there had brought back the memory of his son and his wife. "Oh how I wish I could see them again," he thought.

In times like these, he missed his wife the most. When a case bothered him, he would go home and she would listen quietly and hold him when it got too much to handle.

His co-workers kept telling him to start dating again. They told him he was too young to hide away. So far, he had not met anyone yet that held his interest. He told everyone that his late wife was a hard act to follow since she was the best woman ever made. Anyone that had known Evelyn had to agree.

A knock at the door broke his thoughts and the officer told him that the dispatcher had taken a distress call involving a child. Someone reported a suspect fitting the description talking to a young girl at another mall.

He grabbed his jacket and they headed out the door. They arrived at the mall and interviewed a young mother that left her daughter while she went to order their food at the food court. When she turned around, a middle-aged man was talking to her daughter.

As she hurriedly went to the table where her daughter was sitting, the man ran away. She told them that he wore a black hooded sweatshirt and she saw his face and gave a description of a man around thirty and very good looking. He seemed a little chunky which surprised her. She said it looked like he had too many clothes on. He had a hat pulled over his hair and she could not tell what color it was.

Officer Garret's instinct was that it was the same man that took Candy Burns.

He wanted to get a description out to the media as soon as possible. If they informed the public immediately, it may lead to information. He calmed the mother and told her she had done the right thing. He commended her for making sure she did not let her daughter alone even for a few minutes. These types of abductors are so smooth they can persuade a child to go with them in a short time.

She thanked them for helping and went to take her daughter home. She said to Officer Garret, "I will hug her more now. A child is a precious gift and to almost lose one makes you hang on even tighter." He smiled at her and told her she was lucky, and to tell all her friends to keep their own children in their sight at all times.

He went to the security office and requested a meeting with all the personnel. He warned them of the potential of the suspects striking again and to post a warning and description at all the stations and store fronts to make sure everyone was aware of the danger.

As he headed back to the station, he thought about what the woman had said about the man wearing too many clothes. He figured that the suspect was disguising himself to seem heavier.

He knew it was hard to give an exact description when you see the person only for a few seconds. He would put this fact out on the air so his officers would be looking for someone that was trying to look abnormally heavier. He hoped that the police could apprehend this molester before he could find another victim.

# CHAPTER TWENTY-FIVE

David Adams was restless. He was having a hard time after losing Sarah. He thought if he went to her house, it might make him feel better. When he went in, he could feel the spirit of Sarah and wished he had not come. When Maggie answered the door, he could see where Sarah got her beauty. She had favored her mother a great deal.

He dropped the books off at the day care and just seeing the young girls there made him even more restless. His old habits were hard to break. He went back home and got on the internet.

Seeing the children's faces and bodies on the porn sites made him want to go on the hunt again. He was so uptight. He spent extra time on his disguise and went in the first mall he passed.

David saw the beautiful young girl sitting by herself at a table and almost had her convinced to go help him look for his dog when her mother came back to the table. He ran as fast as he could until he got to his car. He ripped his off his hat and wig. He discarded the extra clothes he wore in the dumpster.

The narrow escape made him angry.

"You are getting sloppy," he told himself. The only way to appease his anger was to drive to the place where he had success before. He started on the fifty-mile drive.

He pulled into the parking lot, put on his disguise, and looked forward to the hunt. After an hour and a half, he saw a ten-year-old girl playing video games and went to talk with her. He did not like girls this old, but she would have to do for now. He told her that her mother had sent him to find her.

David made up a story that when her mother took packages out to the car, her battery was dead. He told the girl her mother had to wait for the man from the garage, and she sent him to find her. The poor little girl had no idea who David was. She believed his story and went out to his car. He only kept her one hour and then discarded her body under a bridge on a remote dirt road.

When the mother came to find her daughter, her nightmare started, just like all the others. David swore to himself that he would stop for a while. He did not want to take a chance on pushing his luck.

The last thing he wanted to do was go to prison. He heard rumors about what happened in prisons to child molesters.

It never occurred to him that any punishment done to him was never enough to pay for all the wrong he had done. He told himself that this had to be the last one for a while. He could feel the heat closing in on him. He had to be careful.

# CHAPTER TWENTY-SIX

Jim was having a hard time concentrating at work. Tom said, "Jim, go home and stay with Maggie. I cannot imagine how difficult losing Sarah is on both of you."

"Tom, I should be helping with these problems at work, but I also want to be with Maggie to help her. I don't know how much time she will need to deal with what has happened. I know she is strong willed, but I wish she would lean on me more. She also needs her own space to learn how to cope with the loss of Sarah."

Jim sat at his desk and remembered Maggie and Sarah's laughter. Every day was a new adventure for the two of them. He used to love watching Sarah's eyes light up when she learned something new. Maggie was a good mother and devoted her energy on her daughter and teaching her what she knew. The future was something the three of them had discussed often. Now, Sarah was gone.

Maggie had retreated to a place where Jim couldn't go. She had closed herself off to family and friends. Even Gwen could not reach her. They had talked about what to do to help Maggie, and decided to step back and let her find a way to deal with the tragedy that now was shaping their lives.

Jim called Maggie two or three times a day while he was at work. Their conversation was strained and he did not know what to say to her anymore. He thought about seeking counseling for the two of them. One of the women he worked with told him about a support group she heard of in her community that met twice a month for parents that lost children to kidnapping and murder.

Jim told her he would talk to Maggie and thanked her for the phone number. He had a business lunch with a new client, and put off calling

Maggie until he returned. He got back to the office, Tom stopped him in the hall with a few questions, and when they were finished, he headed straight to his office to call home.

The phone rang and rang. He left a message for Maggie to call him right back. He supposed she was taking a nap and did not want to be disturbed. He had come home early a few days before and found Maggie asleep in Sarah's bed. The last few weeks had really been hard on her and he knew she did not sleep well at night. She was listless and tired all the time. He missed seeing the sparkle in her eyes.

Jim remembered how Maggie was always busy with Sarah or gardening. Now she did nothing. She would not even take a shower unless he reminded her. She had stopped wearing makeup altogether. He wished he could give her back what someone had taken from them. Nevertheless, Sarah was gone forever. Now life was hard.

He waited for a few minutes and called again. Maggie still did not answer. He got a couple of phone calls so it was twenty minutes before he tried, but no one answered.

Jim went to Tom's office and said, "I am going home to check on Maggie. She is not answering the phone. If she is all right, I will come back to the office in a little while."

"Jim, take all the time you need. I can handle things here."

Jim really appreciated Tom. He was doing the job of two people now. Jim promised he would give him a vacation as soon as things settled some for him and Maggie.

When Jim arrived home, he called for Maggie, and when she didn't answer, he went upstairs to look for her.

Sarah's room was a mess. Maggie had left piles of books on the floor. She told him that she was going to donate some of them to the day care. Jim went through all the rooms, calling her name. He went back downstairs and looked for her. He headed out side and walked all the way around the house. He saw no sign of her.

He hurried to the phone and called Belle, Maggie's mother. "Have you talked to Maggie today?" he asked her.

"No, I was going to call her, but lately she gets irritated so easily and I did not want to bother her. Jim, is something wrong with Maggie?"

"No, I got home and she is not here. I looked everywhere I could think of. I thought you would know if is she had somewhere to go and forgot to lock the house or turn off the lights. I know Maggie has been preoccupied lately. Maybe I will call Gwen and see if she knows anything. I will let you know when I find her."

When Gwen answered, Jim asked her the same thing. "Have you talked to Maggie today?"

"Yes, I talked to her this morning and she said she was going through Sarah's books to donate them to the daycare but she insisted she did not want help so I did not press her. Is something wrong Jim?"

"I cannot find her. I thought you might know if she went somewhere. I wished she had told me. She should know we are all on edge since we lost Sarah."

"Jim you have to be patient. Maggie is dealing with a lot right now."

"I know. It's just that I love her and want to make it better and I can't."

"Jim, she knows you love her. You are Maggie's life now that she has lost Sarah. I hate to watch what the two of you are going through. Let me know as soon as you find her."

"I am going to go through the house once more and then I will call Officer Garret. I will call you later, and thanks for caring Gwen."

Jim walked through the house again, and when he saw no sign of Maggie, he called Officer Garret.

Officer Garret asked Jim what he could do for him. Jim told him that he could not find Maggie. After Officer Garret asked several questions, he told Jim he could be at his house in twenty minutes.

Officer Garret arrived as scheduled. "Mr. Taylor, when did you first call your wife?" he asked.

Jim said, "The first time I called I did not get an answer. I called again about two hours later, but she still didn't answer. Please call me Jim. I feel like I know you after all we have been through."

"Yes, unfortunately, I wish it could have been under different circumstances. Did your wife seem upset this morning when you left? I mean, more than usual?" he asked him. Officer Garret knew what Maggie had to deal with.

"I have to ask these difficult questions, so please do not take offense," he told Jim. "Do you think your wife would harm herself after what has happened? Is it possible she went somewhere to be alone? People have different ways to deal with stress. Would she have left for a few days?"

Jim's answer was quick. "No, my goodness, Maggie would never harm herself. And no, I know she would not have left without telling me. Things between us are strained, but we still talk about important things. If Maggie wanted to get away, she would have told me. I cannot imagine what has happened to her. You cannot be thinking that someone took her too! That is just absurd. I could not live if it all happens again. Please, Officer Garret, we have to find her. I lost my daughter, I cannot lose my wife."

Jim was so upset he had to sit down. His hands started to shake and the nightmare of waiting to hear about Sarah came flooding back. He had to find Maggie. Where was she?

Officer Garret sat down on the sofa beside him. "Jim, I am not telling you that your wife was kidnapped. I was not thinking that. You are right; it's unbelievable that it would happen twice to the same family. There has to be an explanation. Do you have a list of your wife's friends? Maybe someone called her and she left in a hurry."

Jim said, "I remember when I got home that the lights were on and the door was unlocked. Maggie never leaves without making sure she locks the house. It is beginning to look like someone may have been here and she left in a real hurry. I know she has been upset with me, but I cannot imagine that she wouldn't tell me if she was going somewhere."

Officer Garret said, "I must tell you that I am flabbergasted. I guess the first thing to do is check and see if anything is missing. Did you see any sign that someone had been in the house when you arrived?"

Jim thought a minute and said, "No, I did not notice anything missing. I was not expecting Maggie to be gone. I searched the house for her and I saw nothing out of place that I can recall. I can look again."

They stood up and Jim looked through each room slowly to see if anything looked out of place. He noticed nothing out of the ordinary. He went back in the kitchen and saw that the coffee pot was half-full. He knew Maggie usually drank a second cup later in the morning. Her cup was on the counter and he got a picture of her sitting at the kitchen table with her cup and could not contain his emotions.

Maggie was his helpmate. He would not be a complete person without her. He offered to make a new pot of coffee and told Officer Garret he needed it strong. Jim went about preparing the coffee while Officer Garret looked around outside.

He stood in front of the big swing set in the back yard. "What a shame. All the love in the world is here at this home. Why does the bad in life happen to nice people?"

Officer Garret had great respect and admiration for Jim and Maggie Taylor and their courage. He said a special prayer every night for them.

He noticed some footprints at the picnic table in front of the swing set. He bent down to look at them. One set looked small, probably belonged to Maggie. The other set was larger and looked like there had been someone with her. He went back inside and asked Jim if he had been out at the table this morning.

Jim said, "No, I walked to the back yard to yell for Maggie when I got home. I did not get close to the table. I was anxious to keep searching. Why do you ask?"

"I noticed two sets of footprints at the table. I think one of them is your wife's and I need to compare your print with the other set. If it's not yours, then someone may have been with your wife this morning."

They walked out to the swing and as Officer Garret bent to inspect the ground, he asked, "Did anyone else come out here in the last few days? Do you know if your wife was expecting anyone today? Maybe they came out here to sit?" he asked.

Jim said, "No, Maggie did not like coming back here because the swing set we bought for Sarah brought back too many memories. She asked me to take it down two days ago. I hated to get started because it means Sarah is never coming back. No, Maggie would not bring someone back here."

Officer Garret put in a call to the station to tell his men what he needed. The coffee was finished and they sat down at the table.

Jim asked him, "Officer Garret are you married?"

He replied, "I was, to a wonderful woman. She died from breast cancer years ago and I still miss her every day."

Jim's next question made him hesitate with emotion, "Did you have any children?" he asked.

"Yes, we had a son. He died when he was five and a half. I understand your pain to some degree. I lost my wife and son to natural causes. Losing a child the way you lost Sarah is devastating. You and your wife will heal eventually. It takes time."

Jim told him. "I am so sorry. I did not mean to upset you."

Officer Garret replied, "No, I know you didn't. I usually don't talk about my personal life. I hate that the world has so much pain. But we need to find your wife."

When his men arrived, Officer Garret told them what he wanted them to do. He turned to Jim and asked him if the shoes he was wearing were his normal size.

"Yes, they are."

"Would you mind going out to the deck so my men can make a mold of your shoe print?"

In the meantime, another team worked on the prints at the picnic table.

After they were finished Officer Garret said, "Jim, as far as we can tell from the first impressions, the shoes that made the prints beside Maggie's do not match yours. I am not sure what this means. I will call you if I need anything further."

The officers left, and Jim called his parents. When they heard that Maggie was missing, they came right over.

Jim asked his mother to call Maggie's parents. She put the call in to them and they came within a short time. No one wanted to call Gwen and upset her, but thought she needed to know so Jim got her on the phone. Gwen could not contain herself; she cried hysterically. Jim tried to calm her down and handed the phone to Maggie's mother.

After a while, she came back into the kitchen to join the rest and told them that Gwen was not doing well. She and Maggie had been inseparable all these years.

Jim talked with his father and Maggie's father to ask what he should do. How could Maggie be gone? Did she leave him? Would Maggie leave without telling him? They all agreed that Maggie would never do anything like that. She was going through a hard time and had withdrawn from each one of them, but she would not want to hurt them, as she was hurt. She would not just leave. They all agreed that someone had to take Maggie against her will, and maybe they wanted money.

"Yes, maybe after you and Maggie were on the news, someone kidnapped Maggie and they will call and demand money. Why don't you call Officer Garret and ask what we should do," Maggie's father said.

Jim hurried to get the phone and called Officer Garret.

Officer Paul Garret picked up the page and heard Jim on the line. "Have you heard from your wife? Did she come home?" he asked him.

Jim hurriedly told him what they thought happened. "Someone must have seen us on TV and took Maggie for a ransom. Do you think it's possible that is what we are dealing with? It makes more sense than the idea that Maggie just left. Someone else must have forced her to leave. That would explain the footprints outside. What should we do now?" Jim asked.

Officer Garret thought for a second about what Jim was saying. He said, "You may be right. I will send a team to your house right away and we'll have to get a tap on your phone. Hang in there, Jim. We will do all we can to get your wife back safely."

After a short time, the doorbell rang again. The team started setting up their equipment. They showed Jim exactly what to do if the phone rang. They told him to act natural and keep the kidnappers on the phone as long as he could. The equipment was all set. Hours passed and the phone did not ring.

Jim fell asleep on the sofa around 4:00. He woke up around 7:00 when the phone rang. He hurried to answer. It was Gwen asking if Maggie came home.

"No, she did not come home yet." He explained what they were doing and that the police had the phone tapped in case someone called for a ransom.

Gwen was devastated. "How could this happen to poor Maggie? Hasn't she been through enough? Please Jim, keep me informed. I am going crazy. Maggie has been on my mind all night. I love her and I miss her so much."

Jim said, "Gwen I know, I miss her too. I will call you as soon as I can. I promise. Please keep us in your prayers."

Jim offered to make coffee for the men. William, Jim's father came to his side and told him that he would make the coffee. As he stood beside him, he could see the pain in his son's face, and he hugged him and promised him everything would be fine. He sent Jim upstairs to shower and shave.

"You never get used to seeing your children go through pain and suffering," he thought.

William served coffee and the men thanked him. They sat quietly for a couple of hours. Jim offered breakfast and the men declined and asked if there was a diner close by. They ordered breakfast and had it delivered. The next several hours passed with no phone call, Jim was upset. He needed to hear from Maggie.

The men explained that a lot of times the kidnappers made the game longer so when they finally did call, the family members were so anxious that they agreed to the terms no matter how high the price.

"I will pay whatever it takes to get Maggie back. I do not care about money. I just want her back. When do you think they will call?" he asked. The men told him that in these cases it depended on how experienced the criminals were. Some had done it before and they knew the ropes.

The hours dragged by and the fear got stronger. The second shift arrived, introduced themselves, and double-checked the equipment. The hours still passed and no phone calls. For the second night, Jim fell asleep on the sofa. The next morning Jim was impatient and called Officer Garret. He came to the house and they discussed the options.

Jim asked him, "If Maggie had been taken for ransom, shouldn't we hear from them soon? Does this mean that Maggie is no longer alive and they are afraid to call? Would they hurt her?"

Jim was barely hanging on and Officer Garret knew he might break down anytime. He did not want to squelch the hope that his wife would come home to him soon. He did not know what to tell him. So far, they had not found the missing teens. The young children's bodies had turned up in a matter of days. But Maggie's disappearance was throwing him. If they were dealing with the same person, why take Maggie? He really was hoping that they would call for a ransom. At least then, they had a chance of saving her.

"I am sorry Mr. Taylor, we are doing all we can to find your wife and keep her safe"

He thought, if someone took her like the other girls, the whole scenario changed. They had taken Maggie for no reason except their own selfish pleasure. Her life would mean nothing to a serial killer. They did not consider the families of their victims. They saw nothing but what they wanted. Most of the time, the victims did not survive. When they were finished with the women, they killed them and moved on to the next one.

Officer Garret told his men to keep the tap on the line until the next day just in case.

Jim had to put his trust in the law enforcement to find Maggie. "If I give up now, I will never see her again. I lost my daughter and I do not want to lose my wife. Please God, bring Maggie home to me. I need her," he prayed.

# CHAPTER TWENTY-SEVEN

Maggie stirred on the bed. She was so exhausted she slept fitfully for a few hours. When the shed grew dark, the demons gathered around her. In the shadows, she saw the faces of her family. Sarah's face appeared over and over.

In her head, she heard Sarah's voice asking, "Mommy, do you miss me? Why couldn't I stay with you?" Then she would see Jim and her parents. Jim's eyes searched hers for answers. "Where did you go, Maggie? Do you not love me anymore? Maggie, please come home," his shadow seemed to plead. Maggie was barely hanging on.

She spent the rest of the night wondering if she would ever see her family again. Her strength was low, and her body was exhausted. She had to focus on getting through this and returning home. She knew Walter had taken the other three girls. Since she was the fourth one in the shed, she surmised that they had not survived. Would she be his fourth victim?

Maggie found the courage to fight as the sun came up. When he came back today, she would start playing the game the way he wanted. As long as she could keep him believing that, they had a future together she thought he might keep her alive.

Maggie did not want to think about what the other girls had done to him that brought about their deaths. She could not let the thought of what he was capable of enter her mind. She was afraid, more afraid than she had ever been. But she wanted to live. She would do anything Walter wanted. She prayed she would find a way out.

She tried to keep calm when she heard Walter's vehicle approaching. He smiled at her. It was unbelievable how he looked at her as though she were his property.

She thought, "Don't think about it Maggie. Just do as he says."

"Maggie, I brought your breakfast. I put a special treat in for you. I found the most delicious cream doughnuts at the corner store," Walter said.

Maggie sat up in the bed and waited for him to bring the basket of food to her. She silently counted to ten and slowed her breathing.

Walter walked closer and calmly said, "I made you an egg and bacon sandwich and if you eat it all, you can have a doughnut. I could not wait to come and see you today. I am so glad you are here. I want to have you here every day for the rest of my life so we can be with each other. Do you look forward to that, Maggie?"

Maggie concentrated on her plan and said, "I could hardly wait for you to come today. I was imagining what you would bring me to eat. I love the way you make the eggs."

Walter beamed from the praise and as he handed her the sandwich. "After you eat, we can go outside and sit in the sun. The weather is so beautiful; it is a shame to stay inside. I will let you go out every day if you obey. I am not mean, Maggie. All you have to do is listen to me," he told her.

Maggie felt her temper flare. He drugged me, brought me here, tied me up, locked me in, and I have to listen to him or else?

Maggie nodded her head yes. "I promise to listen and I am glad you will let me go out. I want to make you happy. I do not want you to be angry at me."

She could see the wondering in his face. He had not expected her to be so timid. As she ate her sandwich, she felt her insides tremble.

"Maggie do you really think you can outwit a murderer? What choice do I have now," she thought.

Walter got the rope, tied it around her neck, as he led her outside. She sat meekly on the bench and soaked up the heat of the sunlight. Maggie thought of the picture of Jim and Sarah that sat on the coffee table at home, and vowed to go back home sooner or later, no matter what.

Walter talked about the plant where he worked, and how some nights he was so bored. "I used to waste the hours, but now I think about you and how you are waiting for me here. Do you have any idea how happy I am to have found you? I wish I had found you before I wasted all my time on those other girls. There were not as pretty as you are and they were so stupid they did not hear what I told them. It was really their own fault what happened to them."

Maggie turned to him and asked, "What happened to them? Where are they now?" She immediately thought, "Oh, no I made a mistake. He will be angry at me." She felt as though her heart would stop.

Instead Walter said, "I did not want to hurt them, they made me do it and I threw them in the well over there. I hope you don't make me do that to you. I really do love you Maggie. Please don't make me hurt you, okay?"

Maggie panicked and thought, I am sitting here on the bench, and no one knows I am here. He dismisses the other girls as though they were nothing. He is so demented he has convinced himself that it was their fault. But he took them against their will and tied them to a bed. Wouldn't every normal person fight? Concentrate, Maggie. Forget what he did. You have to be strong to survive, she thought. She slowed her breathing and said, "I promise I will not make you do that to me. I do not want to die. I want to live."

"Maggie, I have so much to tell you. I want to read stories to you and plan our future. We have so much to look forward to. It is just you and me out here. The world does not matter, we are here all alone, and no one even knows about this place. Your old life cannot touch you now. I promise I will take care of you and if you want anything let me know and I will bring it for you."

She became nervous and her emotions took over. The tears streamed down her face as she tried to regain her composure.

"What is wrong now?" he asked her.

She quickly recovered and said, "I was thinking of my daughter Sarah, and how I miss her. I can give up everything in my other life, but I miss my daughter and I hate the man that took her. I wish I could hurt him. I could take his life and not feel bad." She spoke her thoughts not realizing what she said until it was too late.

Walter said, "I know how you must feel. I cannot imagine hurting a child. That is the worst kind of a coward. I killed my father but he was a coward. He beat my mother and then he would beat me. I hated him and I stabbed him when I was twelve years old. I do not regret it, and I would do it again."

She shivered in fear. What chance do I have against a cold-blooded killer? I would never be able to kill another human being, she thought. Then she remembered that a few moments ago she said she would kill the man that hurt Sarah. "Could I kill him? Am I capable of taking his life?" she asked herself.

"I wish I knew who killed Sarah?" he said. "I would go and get him for you if you wanted me to. I would do that for you Maggie. I do not want anything to hurt you. I want you to be free to love me," he said.

Suddenly a plan formed in her mind. Is this why I am here? I am to send one killer to kill the other one. What should I say? I want him dead. I really do. Do I send him to find David? Do I want to face him with what he did to my little girl? Could I live with it?

She hesitated for a few minutes and told herself to be careful. If I do this, I can never go back. But he hurt Sarah. He was at the park and took her from me when I went into the woods. Five minutes later, she was gone. He did not think about me, now I will not think about him.

Maggie turned to Walter and said, "You would bring him here to me? Can you get him without someone seeing you?"

"Believe me Maggie, I have taken the other girls, and now I have you and no one has any idea it was me. They have no clues. I did not leave any. I can do it anytime I want. You do not realize how easy it is to grab somebody. One minute they are there, the next minute they are gone. Your family has no idea I have you here. The law would never find us. Do you know who it is? If I do this for you, do you promise to forget about everyone else? You cannot think about your husband ever again."

She sat as still as a mouse. Her mind was in shambles. Hatred built and consumed her reason. She sees David's face and she knew she had to stop him.

"He killed my daughter and probably like Walter, did it before. Men like David Adams and Walter Mills do not deserve any compassion. They are the ones that should lose their right to live," she thought.

Maggie turned to Walter and nodded her head yes. She said, "I know who it is and I want you to get him."

"Tell me his name and where he lives and tomorrow night I will bring him to you. You can decide what to do to him and we will clean him out of your thoughts forever. Then you can be free. You cannot imagine how free it makes you feel. I felt so relieved after I killed my father. I did not look over my shoulder every day waiting for him to come after me. I was free. But I had to kill him. I was glad I did it, and you will be too. We will kill him together. Just think, tied in a bond of blood. Yes, that's right. I never thought of that before. You and me will be bound by our deeds," Walter said.

She cringed at the thought but she would not turn back. If she was to die here, she could avenge the senseless death of her daughter.

She told him that his name was David Adams, and gave him the street and address where he lived. She described him to Walter and said, "I want him dead. Then I will be yours." She committed herself to a deed unthinkable to her a few months ago. However, life has a way of changing you.

They talked about other things for a while. Walter wanted to know about her childhood and if her parents loved her. The love they showed her fascinated him. He never in his whole life felt love from anyone, especially his parents. She asked about his mother and he described how she was an alcoholic and brought the men to the house in front of him.

Maggie began to understand what made a person be so cold. She also knew that some people live under worse conditions and overcome by taking different paths in the road of life. Nothing excused what Walter and David had done. They stole life from too many people. They destroyed the families of each victim. They would continue unless someone stopped them.

She would deal with the consequences later. She shut her mind down and did not pay much attention to what Walter was saying. She noticed he stopped talking and she glanced over at him and she looked in the direction he was pointing. Two bunnies were jumping over each other like leap frog.

Seeing the bunnies rushed her mind back to Sarah. She hated David. She hated Walter. She hated what they had done to her. Yes, life changed you. Tomorrow was another day. How many did she have left?

"I have to get sleep before I go to work. I will bring your dinner later this evening."

She hated to go back inside the damp creepy shed, but she did not argue. What good would it do her? She rose and like a zombie, walked back inside. She had aged in the past weeks. She was no longer the protected Maggie. The lessons she had learned were hard ones. Two men had taken her days away. All she had left was revenge.

# CHAPTER TWENTY-EIGHT

Jim walked out on the back deck. He looked at the flowers Maggie had planted. He remembered digging holes for the rose bushes. She wanted bright colors to brighten their days. Her spirit had been so alive before. Maggie thrived on the pleasure she pulled from the simple things. She could always find something to be happy about every day. Her love for him and Sarah was consuming. She always took every opportunity to let them both know she loved them. Oh how he missed Maggie and Sarah.

As he stood, he felt that Maggie was speaking to him. He tried to listen to what she was saying. He remembered the day she had told him and Gwen that if she left for a while, they had to believe in her and she would come back. Did she know what would happen to her?

"Maggie, honey please let me know you are okay. Please come home," he whispered. "How am I going to live in this house without you?"

The team was in the living room discussing why the kidnappers hadn't called by now. The time limit that Officer Garret had set for the team was running out.

Jim did not want to think about the fact that Maggie may be lost forever. He could not deal with the thought that someone took his daughter and killed her, and now he may lose his wife. The hatred was also building in Jim. No one had the right to steal a child. No one had the right to steal a wife from her husband. If he knew where to start, he would find the man and take his life for what he did to his family.

He heard the phone ring and ran to get it. The men waited and gave him the signal to answer. It was a woman selling insurance. He was so frustrated he hung up. There was dead silence in the room.

"I am sorry I lost my temper."

"Don't apologize to us. We understand fully. No one could go through what you are going through and not become frustrated," one of the men said. The waiting game continued.

At 5:00, Officer Garret arrived and decided to shut the operation down. The men packed the equipment and left.

"I am sorry Jim. I am confident that the kidnappers will make a mistake and we will catch them. I am sorry that we don't have more to go on. Rest assured that my men and I are doing everything we can to find your wife. I will be in touch if I find anything."

After Office Garret left, the quiet closed in on Jim. He wandered from room to room. Everywhere he looked and everything he touched reminded him of Maggie. He saw her cookbooks in the kitchen, her clothes in the closet, and he missed his wife. Jim found Maggie's favorite nightgown and Sarah's favorite pajamas, lay down on the bed, and hugged them while he cried. It was going to be a long night.

# CHAPTER TWENTY-NINE

Maggie fell into a depressed state when Walter left, and her mind felt numb. She stared at the walls, as her sanity and bravery were beginning to fade. How did I think I would be able to win? I have nothing to help me now. I give up. I cannot face the days here in this shed. I quit, she thought. She turned over, curled up, and cried. After a while, she fell into a dazed sleep.

She rose up when she heard the car. Walter brought the basket of food to her. She did not get up.

Walter laid the food out on the bed and she took the plate and slowly began to eat. He went to the table and brought her the mirror and brush.

"Maggie, you forgot what I told you about brushing your hair every day. You have not done that. I want you to make sure you do it fifty times before you go to bed. If you don't take care of yourself, you will be an unpleasant sight. Your hair will only shine if you remember what I told you. You promised you would listen to me. I want you to make sure you stay pretty for me. I hope you understand," he said.

She set the food down and picked up the brush. Mechanically she ran the brush through her hair, and began to count. One, two, three, four, five, six.

He stopped her and told her to eat first. She set the brush down and picked up the plate. She got some food on the fork and raised it to her mouth.

"That's a good girl. Now I have to go to work. I will be back in the morning. The lantern has enough oil for tonight and I will bring some tomorrow. If you are good tonight, I may let you take a short walk tomorrow. You are so pale; the sun will do you good. I will see you in the morning. Sleep well and remember that tomorrow is a big day. We have a killer to catch," he said. He chuckled at the thought. He went out and locked the door.

The shadows came again in the middle of the night. Maggie could almost see Sarah's smiling face. She believed her daughter was in heaven and it gave her comfort. She imagined she saw Jim's face, and he looked so haggard. Not knowing what happened to her must be hurting him.

Maggie willed her thoughts to Jim. "If you can hear me sweetheart, remember I love you. Wait for me and I will come back if I can," she murmured.

In her mind, she saw Gwen's face and she seemed to be angry with her. "Maggie, you have to fight. Do you hear? Fight with all your might. Please come back to us. We all miss you. Maggie, are you listening to me? You have to fight. Don't give up."

Then she saw her mother's and her father's face. They were crying and holding each other. "My poor Maggie. Where is she? I need to know," her mother said.

It made Maggie angry and she got off the bed and paced around the little room. As she paced, her emotions went from being bravery to fright. She really did not know if she had it in her to defeat Walter and David. They had caused her family so much pain. They should pay.

David took her daughter's days from her, and now Walter was taking hers. She pictured Sarah lying in her casket and she made up her mind that she would win. She would avenge her daughter's death at the hand of an ugly and evil man. When she was done with him, she would do her best to rid the world of Walter. He confessed to her that he had brutally killed at least three girls. He deserved to die too.

The morning light came peeking in the window. Maggie felt stronger. She had prayed all night for strength. She knew that even if it cost her own life she would strive to finish this. She wanted to go back to Jim and her family.

Walter came with her breakfast. He chattered while she ate. He promised her she could go outside and take a short walk. After she was done, he hooked her up to the rope. When he was satisfied with the knots, he told her to go out the door.

Walter said, "I should tell you that the last two girls tried to get away. The rope strangled the first one when she tried to run. I shot the second one when she tried to run across the field. So, Maggie, if you think you can get away, remember that I will stop you. I do not want to lose you, but it is your choice. You can enjoy the day or you can make it your last one. If you behave today, you can come out every day for the sunshine. Okay?"

She stopped and tried not to think about how callous and uncaring this man was. It made her hate him more. That hate would keep her strong.

She walked towards the field. Walter was only a few steps behind her and she caught the sound of his humming as they walked. She tried to ignore him and enjoy being outside. When you lose freedom, you appreciate it more. She would never again take it for granted.

After a while, Walter told her to head back inside the shed. He wound the rope and put it back in the corner.

"I have the night off and I want to go home and get some sleep. I will come back around 3:00 and bring you lunch. Then we will map out a plan to get David for you. I want to be outside his house by 10:00 tonight and if all goes well, he will be yours to do with as you please. I have to tell you that I am so proud of you Maggie. You are my kind of girl. You and me are going to get along just fine," he said.

Maggie's blood boiled when she heard him say, "And by the way, I have to remind you to brush your hair. It looks like you have neglected to do as I told you. I saw a box of some things my mother had in her bedroom. It has a lot of necessary stuff that women need to stay pretty for their men. I will bring it tonight. I want you to make an effort. You are looking quite haggard these days. Okay then, I think that is all."

He said good-bye, and told her he would be back later and left. She spent the next few hours convincing herself to be strong and focus on what she had to do.

# CHAPTER THIRTY

Jim rose early the next morning and tried not to think about Maggie too much. When he went in the bathroom, her makeup was there. He went downstairs and the kitchen was full of her things. Her scent was there. He could almost hear her laughter. He went into the family room and got the family picture, and sat it on the table and as he drank his coffee. He studied his wife and daughter's faces and cried. He gave in to the sorrow of the past month. Sarah was gone and now he had no idea if he would ever see Maggie again. He remembered the day they were married. On that day, he had committed his life to his wife and again when Sarah was born. Now what was he to do?

He held the picture close to his heart. Maggie was a beautiful girl. Her hair was long and thick. Sarah had the same blond color and her eyes shone in the picture. If Sarah were still living, she would have looked just like her mother. He thought about the last time he had touched his wife's body. They fit so well together and he missed her so much. He longed to hold them both again. He shook himself and thought that he had to find Maggie, where ever she was. He would search and not stop searching until he found her.

Jim finished his coffee and went to the phone. He called Officer Garret and asked if he could stop by on his way to the office. He told him he would be there in half an hour. He called Tom and told him he was going to the police station and would be a little late.

Jim went into Officer Garret's office. "Thank you for making time to see me. I was hoping you had some news about Maggie for me."

"No, I am sorry to say that the trail is cold. I wish I could tell you something more, but I have my men working round the clock and so far, nothing. I would think that someone knows something. It seems so simple when you see this on TV. If only we caught every criminal and found every victim. The cases of unsolved kidnappings and murders are astronomical. Real life is so different," he said.

Jim said, "I am going to look for Maggie myself. I just cannot stand to do nothing. She is out there and she needs me. I do not know where I will start, but if I stay one more night in my lonely house, I will go crazy. Someone has to know where she is. I am going to make some fliers and tomorrow and Sunday I will spend the days handing them out. It is the least I can do."

Officer Garret looked at him with sadness and said, "Mr. Taylor I would give anything to tell you that we will find your wife. I am trying to figure who took your wife. A child molester takes children. Three teen girls are missing and now Maggie. It does not fit a pattern. That is why we are having such a hard time figuring out what the next step is. If we were dealing with average criminals, it would at least make sense. This pattern is out of the ordinary. If we are dealing with two men, I hate to think that your family has fallen victim to both. It really does not seem likely. But, the facts tell me otherwise. If there are two men, do they work together? If not, how did they both pick Maggie and Sarah? I know that the case has to break soon. I do not want to miss something and then find more victims. I want to stop this as much as you do. I promise you that as soon as I know anything, I will let you know."

Jim thanked him and stood up to leave. He paused and said, "I feel that Maggie is still alive. I know you cannot go on feelings. I hear her voice at night telling me that she is trying to come home. I guess it sounds stupid."

Officer Garret said, "No, it does not sound stupid. You have lived with her all these years, and I do think you may hear her in your mind. I wish I knew where she was so I could go get her for you. Trust in what you think. Keep believing and never stop hoping that she will return. To hope is to keep on going. When there is no hope, we quit. Don't quit on her. Keep hoping." Jim shook his hand and left.

He headed for the office just to have something to do. When he arrived, Tom met him at the door. He hugged him and told him how sorry he was.

"What can I do?" Tom asked him.

"Just keep on praying for Maggie. I was just telling Officer Garret that in my mind I hear Maggie telling me that she is coming home. I don't know what he thought, but I do hear her," Jim said.

Tom got a strange look on his face and said, "Funny you should say that. Gwen said the same thing this morning. She heard Maggie and she told her to fight and come back home. I hope you both are right. She has to be alive."

Jim hugged him and went to his office. After making a few phone calls, he started on the flyer. He cried as he copied the picture of Maggie on all those pages. With each one, he resolved to find her. "Hang on Maggie, I am waiting for you," he said to her picture.

## CHAPTER THIRTY-ONE

Walter prepared a meal for Maggie. He had put a candle in the basket. They would have a candlelight dinner. He could hardly wait. He almost forgot the makeup box and went to his mother's room to look for it. Walter picked up the picture of his mother and said, "Mother, I have my own girl now, so I will not be talking to you as much. I have Maggie to talk to now. So, I will talk to you when I can."

He found the box his mother had kept on her dresser. In it were nail files, polish, and eye shadow, eyeliners, and lipsticks.

Walter glanced at the picture on the dresser and said, "Mother, I hope you don't mind. Maggie will use it more than you will now." He packed the food in the basket and went to his car. Walter was so happy. He knew Maggie was going to be perfect for his life. He would go to work at night and spend every day visiting Maggie in the shed.

Walter did not think too far ahead. He never thought about letting her out to have a normal life. He intended to keep her locked up forever and keep her all to himself.

He unlocked the door and took the basket to the table. Maggie tried to act thrilled when he lit the candle. She started eating and Walter again went on and on about how he loved having her to come and sit with every day. He took for granted that she was content being locked up all day just waiting for him to come and see her.

Maggie was shaking inside wondering what this night would bring if Walter really did go and get David. She tried not to let him see her fear. She concentrated on eating.

When they were finished, Walter told her how he was going to kidnap David. He would park his car outside his house and pretend to have car trouble.  If it went well, David would let him use his phone and once he was inside, he knew he could easily use the chloroform on him.

As soon as Walter left, Maggie went to the table and found the mirror he had given her.  She crawled under the bed and broke it.

Maggie gathered up the pieces and rolled them in a napkin.  She got the biggest one and went to get the makeup box.  She rummaged through it and found the largest nail file.  If she was careful, it should make a perfect sharpening tool.

Walter had no idea that he had helped her by bringing her the box with exactly what she needed.

Maggie would have to hurry before Walter got back.  She had to make sure she did not cut herself and worked as quickly and carefully as she could.  She must hurry.

# CHAPTER THIRTY-TWO

David came home from the office and prepared a steak sandwich with fried onions. He piled the steak high and added the cheese and onions. He added a little mayo and presto, a perfect sandwich. David sat at the bar and poured a glass of red wine, and enjoyed the meal. He decided to spend a few hours on the internet. David discovered a new site where a person could pay for children and have freedom to do whatever they wanted.

David skimmed through the pictures and found a six-year-old blonde girl that looked a lot like Sarah. He missed her so. David hoped someday he could come close to a replacement. He browsed the pictures and savored the young beautiful children. His appetite for them was getting stronger. David was beginning to put his fantasies above everything else. His mind was not always on his job as it used to be. His perfect reputation he had earned was in jeopardy. David's boss warned him about his sloppy performance and told him to get his mind back on what he was paid to do.

David kept thinking if he could have kept Sarah, she would have been the ultimate prize and the appetite for other young girls would disappear. He wouldn't have to sneak around at the mall looking for girls. Sarah would have stayed with him forever. David was so sorry to have to dump her body in the field. It really did break his heart. He would have to look hard to match her beauty. She was what David had been searching for all his life.

David finished eating and conscientiously spent a few hours working on a presentation. His boss would be happy with him tomorrow.

David packed all the posters in the boxes when he was finished. Now, he could get another glass of wine and get down to business. He found the site and skimmed through the ones he had already looked through. He truly was amazed at all the children that were available.

He put in a description of what he was looking for and saw a few that he liked. He knew he could not have Sarah, but some of these looked promising.

David was surprised when he glanced at the clock and saw that he had been browsing for two hours. He decided to take a break and was surprised when he heard the doorbell ring. He had no idea who could be out this late, and thought about not answering it, but he decided to see who it was.

David opened the door and a man he did not recognize asked him if he could use his phone. He glanced past him and he saw a car in the road with the hood up.

The man said, "I hate to bother you, but my car broke down and I forgot to bring my cell phone with me. Could I use your phone to call my garage? I won't take but a minute. I truly would appreciate it."

David hesitated but agreed to let him in. "I sure am glad you were still awake and I promise not to bother you long." David showed Walter where the phone was and turned around to head back the hall.

Walter had the drug soaked cloth in his pocket. He grabbed David from behind and put the cloth over his nose and mouth. Soon David collapsed on the floor.

"Piece of cake. No trouble at all," Walter said.

Walter backed his car in, turned the lights off, and opened the trunk.

Walter grabbed a rug off the floor and wrapped David in it. He made sure he concealed David's body inside the rug and carried him out to the car, and headed to the shed.

Walter thought that Maggie would be pleased. He knew she didn't think he could handle it. He would have to brag a little to her about how easy it had been to capture David. She surely would think he was a real man now

Maggie heard the car pull in and hid the sharpened piece of glass under the bed. She climbed back on the bed and waited for the door to open.

Walter walked inside with the biggest smile on his face.

"Maggie, I have a present for you. Are you ready?"

Maggie did not say a word. She did not move an inch. Did he have David? Did he really get him, she thought.

Maggie held her breath for the next several seconds. Walter came through the door with something wrapped in a rug. He laid it on the floor and bent to unroll it. With each roll, she grew more afraid.

Finally, there he was. It was David Adams. She stared at the body lying on the floor. How could anybody that looked so normal take her daughter to molest her? I will make sure he is guilty and pass sentence when I make sure he is the right man. If he took Sarah then he deserves to die, she thought.

Walter went out and came back with duct tape. He sat David up against the wall and wrapped his arms to his body. He wound the tape from his neck to his ankles.

When he was finished, he came to sit beside Maggie on the bed. "Now, all we have to do is wait. I did not use much of the drug, so it shouldn't take too long," he told her.

Walter said, "Oh, I brought you something else. I will go get it." He went out the door and came back with a small radio. I found this portable radio in my mother's room and I thought you would like to listen to it."

The music played softly and she remembered listening to the same song when Sarah was with her in the car. She used to look in her mirror and watch Sarah sway with the beat in the back seat. Sarah loved music, and she used to talk about wanting to play the violin when she was in fourth grade. Memories are all I have now. And, this man is responsible, she thought. The thought fueled her hatred and she now understood how that hatred could make a person capable of hurting another human being, even killing them to stop this pain. These thoughts frightened Maggie.

They sat listening to the radio for a while. Walter offered her a soda and leaned back on the headrest. Maggie's mind was racing. Her heart was pounding. Would she be able to hurt this man? She wanted to hear from him why he took her daughter.

"What are you going to do Maggie? Are you sure he is the one that took Sarah? He looks like somebody that would take little girls. It was no problem at all for me to capture him. He went down in a matter of seconds. I bet he wouldn't know how to act around women. He must be a sicko to take kids. I will do whatever you want me to do with him. All you have to do is tell me," Walter said.

Listen to you talk about being a sicko, she thought. She answered, "I will wait until I am sure he is the one. I almost know he was the one that killed my beautiful little girl. He had Sarah's yellow hair ribbon in his trunk. She was wearing it the day she disappeared. When I find out for sure, I will let you know."

They waited a little while longer and heard David moan. He roused himself and was startled to see them.

"Maggie, is that you? What are you doing here with this freak? He came in my house. Why are you here? Do you know him?" David asked.

Maggie looked straight at him and said, "David it does not

matter now why I am here. I need you to tell me some things. It depends on your answers as to what happens to you."

David shook his head to clear his mind. "I do not understand. What do you want from me? I demand to know why I am here. Did this creep take you too? I heard you were missing. I was so worried about you Maggie. I was afraid they would find you dead."

Maggie said, "David you have no right to call anyone a creep. I have to ask you a question. Now you can lie to me, but I would advise you to tell me the truth. Do you remember the day you came to my house to take the books to the day care for me? I found Sarah's yellow hair ribbon in your trunk. Sarah was wearing that ribbon the day she disappeared from the park. Did you take Sarah, David?" she asked.

"Maggie, why would I take Sarah? I loved her like she was my own child. How can you ask me such a thing?" David whined.

Maggie went over and sat in the floor in front of him. She said, "I will ask you again. Did you take Sarah and why? I found the ribbon in your trunk. The only way it could have gotten there is if Sarah was in your trunk. You took her body and dumped it in a field. Why did you take her?" Maggie asked him.

David again denied knowing anything. He acted hurt that she would think that about him.

Maggie turned to Walter and asked him if he had a gun. Walter said he had a rifle in his car.

David got a frightened look on his face and asked, "Maggie, what are you doing? You would let him shoot me. Maggie please, you have to listen to me."

Maggie motioned for Walter and told him to go get his gun. Walter went for the door and Maggie said, "David, I told you it was in your best interest to tell the truth."

"Maggie, please I am begging you. You don't want to do this. It is wrong. You can't kill me. Besides, it won't bring Sarah back. She is gone Maggie," David said.

Maggie's anger intensified. "She is gone because of you. She was my only child. Why did you hurt her? She loved to spend time with you. I had no idea that you were so evil. What did you want with her? What is wrong with you? She had a right to live. She did nothing to you. But she was everything to me. I don't care what happens to me now. I will avenge the death of my child. You will tell me the truth before this ends. You can drag it out, or you can end it now," she said.

David turned his head and was silent. Walter came back in with the rifle. Maggie waited for David to answer and when he didn't she turned to Walter and said, "Put the rifle to his head. And when I tell you, pull the trigger."

Walter stepped up to David and did as Maggie told him. He put the rifle on David's forehead. David's eyes began to tear up. He did not know what to do. He believed that Maggie really would have the man kill him.

"Maggie, please don't let him shoot me. I don't want to die."

Maggie turned silent, as the fear inside her stomach is tremendous. This was not the time to lose composure. Maggie's silence and hesitation caused Walter to turn his head.

"Let me know what you want me to do to him, Maggie. I will enjoy every minute of it. A man that takes little girls deserves to be tortured. I will take pleasure in inflicting that torture."

Maggie walked to the other side of the room and took a second to calm down. She had to be collected to go through with this. She stood still for a few minutes and then turned and went back to sit in front of David.

"I do believe that you are sick David. I will get you help if you tell me what you did. I promise that Walter will not hurt you if you just tell me. I need to know what happened to my daughter. Did you touch her David? Did you hurt her?" she asked him.

David said, "No, I told you I loved her. She was the most beautiful girl I ever saw. I wanted to keep her forever. I did not hurt her. I don't know what happened. I put her in a room. She wanted to go home. I had to keep her. She was crying and I thought she would settle down and listen. When I went in to check, she wasn't breathing. I did not hurt her Maggie. I loved her. I had to get rid of her body and I wanted you to find her and bury her in a nice place. I wanted her to stay with me. I did not mean to kill her."

As soon as the words were out of his mouth, he saw the look on her face. The features turned to pure hate. He felt the anger from her. She put her head down and started to cry.

He knew he should have kept his mouth shut. He did not want anyone to think that he could have hurt Sarah. He loved her.

All this time she wanted to think that it was someone she did not know that took Sarah. She thought David was a nice normal loving human being. Why would he take her daughter and throw her away like garbage? She had never been this close to evil. A man like David didn't even know he was evil. He took Sarah just because he wanted her.

"How many times have you done this, David? Have there been others? Have you killed other children?" Maggie asked.

David did not answer.

"I told you to be truthful with me, David. I deserve to know. Please tell me. You have nothing to lose now," she said.

David looked at her and knew he needed her to feel sorry for him. If Maggie felt sorry for him, he may stay alive. He would play on her sympathy.

"I am sick, Maggie. I can't help myself. I have to have these girls. But after I am done, I feel so ashamed that I get rid of them. I can't stop. I need help. I knew if I had Sarah, she would be the last one. I have spent my whole life waiting for her. She was perfect. I would have kept her. I did not want her to die. The others have been nothing to me. Sarah was special. I've tried to find one like her and they are not as special. Please Maggie, you have to let me go. I promise I won't ever do it again," he pleaded.

Maggie had to get away from him. David's confession of killing her daughter was too much to bear. Maggie dropped to the floor and wailed in sorrow. Walter came over to her and tried to touch her arm. She pulled away which made him angry.

Walter went over to David and kicked him.

"Now look what you did. You upset Maggie. I will kill you. I brought you here so she could leave the past behind and the only way to do that is to get rid of you." He grabbed David under his arms and started pulling him towards the door. He dragged him outside. He threw the gun in the car window as he went past.

Maggie could not move. Sarah's face seemed to appear before her and she continued sobbing and wailing in the corner. She couldn't stop. Things were beginning to fall apart. She had a confession from the one that took Sarah. He took her to keep her as his love child.

I am so sorry Sarah. Mommy should have protected you, she thought.

She tried to stand, but when she thought about all the children David had killed, she just collapsed. All the parents and families of each child had to endure torture knowing what happened to their children. Life is worth nothing without our little girls, she thought.

As she lay on the floor, she thought of Jim. She felt as though he was telling her, "Don't give up Maggie. I love you. I need you. I will help you cope with all of it. Please come home."

She prayed softly, "God please give me the strength to hang on and survive this ordeal. I need to go home to Jim."

Maggie sobbed and sobbed. Her strength was running out. Her resolve was leaving. She thought of her mother and she did not want her mother to suffer as she did when she lost Sarah. "My mother does not need to feel this pain," she said with determination.

David's screams snapped her back to reality. Maggie turned and saw the door was open. If she went out Walter would punish her. She crept slowly outside and peeked around the corner. Walter was dragging David to the well.

Walter threw David on the ground and she saw him moving the heavy slab off the top of the well. David was screaming for her.

"Maggie, help me. Maggie, stop him before he kills me. Please, Maggie, I don't want to die. I didn't mean to hurt Sarah. Maggie, you have to hurry." David was squirming and trying to get out of Walter's grip. The duct tape was so tight he couldn't move fast enough.

The last thing Maggie heard was David's scream of terror as Walter picked David up and laid him on top of the ledge of the well. She saw Walter push the body over the side and David was gone. He was in the well with the girls. She did not want this to happen. Or did she?

Her terror and hatred filled her whole being. These two men were capable of cold-blooded murder. Even on each other.

Maggie ran back in the shed and found the weapon she hid under the bed. She would do what she had to do. It was up to her to stop Walter from murdering anyone else.

Walter was coming and she heard him yell. "Maggie, you better be in that shed!"

Maggie hid behind the door and she took the piece of the mirror she sharpened and wrapped her sleeve to keep from cutting her hand. She braced herself and raised her arm. Walter stepped inside. She lunged at his chest with all her might and the broken piece of mirror sliced Walter's heart.

Walter fell down on the floor. Maggie saw the blood pouring out of the wound. She heard Walter gasping for breath and then silence. It was over. She was free. These two men had taken her days from her and now she had taken theirs. A day for a day.

Maggie searched Walter's pockets for his keys. She found them and ran outside. She jumped into the car, backed around, and headed out the lane. She had to get home. Jim would be waiting.

Maggie did not know exactly where she was but she needed to get away from here. As she drove, the tears streamed down her cheeks. Emotions of disbelief and shame of what she had done swept over her and she had a hard time holding on the steering wheel. Her hands shook violently but she kept telling herself to calm down so she could figure out where she was. She recognized the route number at the next intersection and turned left.

She sped down the road and within forty-five minutes, she spotted her house. Maggie was home at last.

# CHAPTER THIRTY-THREE

Maggie pulled in her driveway. It was hard to believe that the last several days were actually over. She jumped out of Walter's car and shivered to think she even had to drive his car home, after all that happened. She was shaking as she walked up the front pathway. She thought she would never see her home again. Now she had made it back. She opened the front door and called for Jim. As she walked to the living room, she passed a mirror on the wall.

Her reflection shocked her. The knots in her hair from the filth were unbelievable. Her eyes were bloodshot and the circles under them were black. She had lost at least ten pounds and it showed in her face. She looked haggard and worn.

Never mind how you look Maggie, just find Jim, she thought. She called for him again and walked out to the garage. His car was gone. She ran to find the phone to call him. She dialed his cell phone but when she heard him answer, she could not speak. Her emotions were running wild.

Jim said "Hello" three times before in a squeaky voice she said, "Jim, its Maggie. I am home. Please can you come home now? I need you. I will explain everything to you when you get here. Hurry."

"Maggie, is it really you? Oh, honey I knew you would come home. I will leave right now. I will be there as fast as my car can go. Oh, Maggie, I love you. Are you all right? Are you hurt? Where were you?" he asked.

"Jim, I am all right now. Please just come home," she said.

"Maggie, hang up the phone and wait right by the door. I am hurrying as fast as I can. Honey, I will be right there."

Maggie went to the kitchen and glanced around at its cheery atmosphere. She was so thankful to be home. She would count her blessings every minute for the rest of her life.

Maggie sat down at the kitchen table and relaxed for the first time in days. She wanted to lie down on the floor and never get up. Even her bones were tired.

Suddenly a thought came to her. How am I going to explain what I have done? I killed David. I sent Walter to get him. Oh, they will take me to jail. I will never be free. I finally get away from Walter and because I was so selfish and wanted so bad to hurt David for taking Sarah, I am going to prison. What am I going to do? How can I explain what I have done?

She paced the kitchen floor and wrung her hands. She could not go to jail. As she paced she found herself talking aloud. "David deserved to die. I did not kill him. Walter did. He put him in the well. Surely, he is dead by now. How far did he fall? Could he survive? He will tell the police that it was my fault. I was the one that told Walter who he was. But I did not kill him. I wanted him dead, but I did not kill him. You are still guilty Maggie. Face it; you are going to have to pay."

She continued talking, "How can you explain why David was taken and thrown in the well? Walter took three girls. He would not take David," she said aloud. Then a thought occurred to her. "What if I told the police that David was jogging past my house when Walter took me? I know David did a lot of running. Would they believe me? David would have to be an innocent bystander in all this."

Maggie's jumbled thoughts made her head throb. Her words grew faster and louder. "David would get the glory for coming to my rescue and dying because he tried to help me. The truth is he was a murderer. Can I let him be a hero? Yes, I will tell the police that David was trying to help me and Walter drugged him too and killed him. I do not know what else to do."

Maggie didn't want Jim to see her like this. She did not have the energy to worry about what she looked like so she sat back down and waited.

Jim rushed into Tom's office and told him that Maggie had come home. "She just called me and I need to go home now. I promise I will fill you in as soon as I make sure she is okay. Will you call Gwen and let her know? Thanks, I have to go."

Jim ran through the office and out the front door. Why did I park so far away, he thought as he ran the few seconds to his car. He didn't stop for anything. If he was caught speeding he would tell them why. He just didn't care. Jim made it home in record time and darted from his car to the front door. He ran in the kitchen and saw Maggie in the chair.

"Oh, Maggie, I thought I would never see you again. Let me look at you," he said as he knelt on the floor in front of her. He laid his head in her lap and he cried.

She grabbed him and held on. They could not stop crying.

Finally, he stood and wiped his tears away. "Maggie, I want to know who did this to you. Where have you been? I thought someone took you for a ransom and we waited and no one ever called and I thought I would find your body like we did Sarah's."

Maggie saw the pure fear in Jim's face.

"Did they hurt you, Maggie? If they hurt you I will kill them," he screamed.

"Jim, I killed the man that took me. I stabbed him. I think he is dead," she said. He was stunned.

Jim looked at her in disbelief. "Maggie, you killed him? I have to call Officer Garret. He will want to talk to you. Don't worry Maggie you are home now. Let me call him and I will get you whatever you need."

Officer Garret was out of the office, but Jim got his pager number and left a message for him to call. Within a few minutes, the call came in and Officer Garret said he would be there in a short time to talk to Maggie.

Jim went back to the kitchen and asked Maggie if she wanted something to eat and coffee.

"You know, I have missed your coffee. Please make me some. I do not want to eat right now. My stomach is still doing cartwheels. It has been a hard week," she said.

Maggie stopped for a minute and gazed at her husband's face. "I love you Jim. I held on to the sound of your voice and it brought me back home. I am sorry for the way I acted about losing Sarah. I felt so bad that I had left you with you thinking I did not love you. Always remember that no matter what happens, I will always love you," she told him.

"Maggie, I never once doubted that you loved me. I felt bad because I couldn't help you enough. I hated the pain I saw on your face after Sarah died."

Jim continued, "Maggie, promise me that you will always let me help you. Don't ever shut me out of anything. I will start on the coffee. There are some blueberry muffins from the church- women. Would you like one?" he asked.

"Yes, I will try one. How long do you think it will be before Officer Garret gets here? I need to clean up, I am such a mess," she said.

"No, Maggie, I want him to see what this man did to you. He may want some evidence so we will wait on him. The coffee is ready. I will get some for you and heat a muffin," he said.

Maggie thanked him and tried to calm her nerves. She did not know how she would explain. She did not want to lie to Officer Garret. "I have to pull myself together before he arrives."

Jim sat with her holding her hand while she drank her coffee. He did not want to let go of her again. Officer Garret entered the room and he too had tears in his eyes.

"Mrs. Taylor I am so glad to see you back home. I need to ask you some questions if you are up to it. I see you are eating, so I will wait until you finish," he said.

Jim offered coffee to him and the muffins. He thanked him and said he never turned down blueberry muffins. They were his favorite. The men talked about how good old home cooking was.

Maggie tried to listen to them, but her thoughts drifted back in time to the shed. She shivered and the men noticed.

"Maggie, are you okay? Do you need a sweater? Are you cold?"

"Will you get my gray sweater out of the hall closet? I am cold," she said.

Jim went to get it and placed it across her shoulders.

Officer Garret told her, "Whenever you are ready, we will go to the sofa so you can be comfortable."

All three went into the living room. Jim sat beside Maggie and reached for her hand.

Officer Garret again told Maggie how lucky she was and how glad he was that she was home and not a statistic. "I want you to start at the beginning and take as much time as you need. I can see by your appearance that the days you were gone were terrible. Try to tell me what happened," he said.

Maggie started with the day she was sitting in the back yard. She left out the part about the yellow hair ribbon. She told how Walter came up behind her and she woke up in the shed.

"There were pictures of three other girls in a photo album. Their names were Shelly, Mary, and Susan. Walter told me he found the first two from articles in the papers. He found me when he was helping with the search for Sarah. He said he killed them and threw their bodies in a well not far from the shed I was held in," she said. She went over everything.

She hesitated to tell them about David, but she did tell the story that he was jogging that day and Walter kidnapped him the same time she was. All four bodies were at the bottom of the well.

Officer Garret asked her many questions. "Do you think you could find the shed again? I would like for you to go with me now if you are up to it," he said.

Maggie turned white. Her hands shook as she said, "I don't want to go back. I can't. I killed Walter when I left. I knew he would never let me go. I had to kill him. His body is in the shed. I never want to see him again. I am afraid," she said.

Officer Garret leaned towards her and asked if she could give them directions to the shed.

"Yes, I think I can. Please don't make me go back," she said.

"Okay Maggie. I did not mean to upset you. I am sure we can find the place Walter held you from your directions. Do you know Walter's last name?" he asked. "Yes, it is Mills. He told me I would be Mrs. Walter Mills. I had to kill him. It was either him or me," she told him.

"And David lives near here? And his last name?" he asked her.

220

"Yes, David Adams. He lives at 648 Chestnut Street, two blocks from here."

He asked, "How did you know David?"

She told him that she baked a lot of bread and cookies when Sarah was alive and the neighborhood stopped and bought it from them. She said, "David used to come twice a week for bread." She tried to keep her voice steady when she spoke of David. Her body was so weak from all she had endured.

"I have all I need for now. I will call my team and we will take care of the bodies. I am sorry Mrs. Taylor for all you have gone through. No one deserves that degrading treatment. You are a very brave woman. I do not know even if I could have survived. I admire your strength. Don't worry about charges against you. You killed Walter in self-defense. I hope you now can rest and that tomorrow is a better day for you."

"We must take one day at a time. You lost your days to a sick man. But now it is time to start healing," he said. He shook Jim's hand and told him to make sure his wife did get some rest.

After Officer Garret left, Maggie broke down and sobbed. She could not control the shaking. She was as cold as ice. Jim wrapped her in a blanket and held her until she settled down. He hated this. He wanted to erase it from her mind.

"Maggie, I want you to put it behind you. God gave you back to me. I will never take you for granted again. Please don't leave me again Maggie. You have to let me help you deal with it all. Sarah's death was hard enough without adding all this sorrow on top of it. I cannot imagine how scared you were. Like Officer Garret, I admire your strength. I heard your voice Maggie. You told me to wait for you to come home. That is what kept me going," he said.

"And I heard your voice Jim. You told me that you loved me. I clung to that and I am home again. I will never be the same Jim. We have to get through the rest of our lives without Sarah. I miss her. We will never have Sarah again. We will take one day at a time and help each other through each one. A day now will be precious to us."

"Maggie, can you make it upstairs? I will fill the tub with warm water and you can soak while I fix you a hot meal." Jim helped Maggie in the tub and told her to quit worrying and relax.

Maggie shut her eyes. Walter and David's face slammed into her mind. She saw the three girls, and then Sarah. She took a second to calm herself and pushed the bad away for now. God would help her to mend in due time. She got her days back and he would help her through each one.

Officer Garret and his team found the shed. It was just like Maggie told them. Walter was on the floor right inside the door. The stench from the bucket he forced the women to use made the shed stink so bad it was difficult to breathe. The men found the rope Walter had used to tie them. The photo album was lying on the floor, and as one man flipped the pages, he saw the pictures with the pasted faces. The scene deeply affected the men. The horrible ordeal of Walter had put these four women through was hard for them to fathom.

They brought in heavy equipment to dig up the well and identify the bodies. They pulled four bodies out of the water, Shelly, and Mary, and Susan, and David. Officer Garret would make a visit to each home and give them the closure and the news that their loved ones were gone.

Officer Garret thought about Maggie and the awful things that would haunt her nights for some time. How could a person experience this type of torture and stay the same. Maggie survived and she had every right to kill her captor. He knew the law would file no charges against her.

The news media caught the story of how Mrs. Taylor lost a child, survived the death of her child, and endured the captivity with a lunatic. The paper hailed David Adams as a hero and an innocent bystander. The incredible story captured headlines in papers all over the country. They all held Maggie and David as heroes.

Officer Garret finished and left his men to process the scene. He wanted to stop at David's house on his way to the station. He needed to tie up all the details in order to write a report. He found the house and went in.

Officer Garret walked from room to room. He had to find information on David's family to notify the next of kin.

Garret heard the computer humming in the den, and when he pulled up the last sites David visited, the trashy filth flashing on the screen horrified him. There were obscene pictures of young girls. Garret sat for the next half hour and looked at what David saw before he met his death. It was so awful he could hardly stand to scan through the many sites.

What was David doing? Was he just an ordinary young man? Maggie did not know this side of him evidently. She did not say a word if she knew, he thought. He skimmed more sites and found a chat room where David was talking to someone who called himself the "Panty Snatcher." As Officer Garret read the words, the awful truth of what David Adams was became very clear to him.

On the site, David was bragging about the many children he had taken and killed. Candy Burns was one of his victims. David described how he disguised himself and went to the mall. He told how he found her sitting at a table eating ice cream. The last few lines were sickening. He talked about how he dumped her body behind a dumpster and how stupid the police were when they could not find any clues as to who had done it. As Garret read further, he could not believe the cold and callous description of how David saw Sarah swinging by herself at the park

In detail, David told how he finally had found his perfect girl. He claimed to have loved Sarah. Then he chatted about locking her in the room and the discovery of her dead body. David even boldly chatted about how he wrapped her in the blanket before he threw her away.

As Officer Garret read, he knew that David had done this for a long time. I don't think he meant to kill Sarah. I remember the autopsy report showing that David did not have a chance to molest Sarah. She died from heart failure before he could hurt her, he thought.

As he leaned back in the chair, he tried to understand. "Was this David Adams the second serial killer we were searching for? Did Maggie know what he did to Sarah? I either have to report this and shame Maggie or I can destroy all this evidence and be thankful that the world is a better place because he is gone," he thought.

Officer Garret knew he could destroy all this proof, and let the story die with David and protect Maggie from going to prison if she deliberately killed David. He was not sure what really happened so he decided to take the computer with him and see what Maggie would tell him. He had one more thing to check, and then he would decide what he would do.

Officer Garret loaded the computer in his car. He headed back to the station, called his team on the radio, and requested DNA samples from each of the victims.

He would test the hair found on Candy's body against David's DNA. If it was a match, David was a child molester and a serial killer.

Officer Garret called Jim and asked how Maggie was doing. Jim told him she had taken a hot bath and she was willing to eat, which was a good sign.

"I need to ask your wife more questions. I would like to stop by in the morning if that's okay." Jim told him they would expect him the next morning.

Jim called Maggie's parents and his parents to tell them the good news. They wanted to come and see for themselves that she was okay and promised not to stay long.

Jim also called Gwen and Tom. Gwen insisted on seeing for herself and Jim agreed that Maggie needed to see her. He sat Maggie down at the table and brought her food to her. She ate a little and looked better than when she first got home. Gwen came in and cried with her. She told Maggie how she too had heard her voice and Maggie told her how her anger towards her kept her fighting.

The reunion showed a strong bond between the two women. It was nice to have a good friend that never gave up on you. The parents arrived and after they were certain that Maggie was safe, they left and said they would call in the morning. They were so grateful that Maggie had come home.

Officer Garret went back to the station. He called for the results of the DNA report on David Adams. The fax machine hummed and he walked to the machine to pick up the paper. He read the results that confirmed his suspicions. The person that murdered Candy Burns and Sarah Taylor was without a doubt David Adams.

Officer Garret hid the paper and did not put it in the file. He was not sure how this case tied together. He knew that David Adams had killed Sarah. But, at what time did David come to the shed?

He went to his car and got David's computer. He logged on and scanned through the last sites David visited. David had logged onto his computer the night before Maggie killed Walter Mills, escaped, and found her way home.

Officer Garret thought to himself, did Maggie lie to me? Walter must have kidnapped David the last night Maggie was in the shed. David could not have been there until the last night.

Officer Garret called Maggie and asked her if he could set up a meeting for the next morning at 11:00. She agreed and told him she would see him then. He jotted down a few notes and closed the office.

He wanted to go home, but he had to make a visit to each of the parents of the three girls found in the well. It was a hard task to tell parents that their daughters would never come home again. At least they knew what happened and would bury the bodies and move on from here.

Maggie went back to sit beside Jim after the phone call from Officer Garret. She snuggled in his arms. She asked him, "Jim, do you believe me about what happened? Do you think I am guilty of murder? I had to kill Walter."

Jim hugged her tighter and said, "Maggie, I have no idea what you went through while you were held by this killer. I do not want to know all the details because I would drive myself crazy every day with knowing I did not protect you. I do not doubt for one second that if you had not had the courage to kill him, he would have eventually killed you. I want you to rest now Maggie. If you can put it away and forgive yourself, I will help you. You defended yourself and there is no guilt in that. I am so grateful that you are home. I take it as a blessing and I do not want you to dwell on it. I want our life back. We have to deal with the loss of Sarah. I know she is in heaven and we will meet her again. Every day for the rest of our lives we will miss her. But she died of natural causes and whoever took her did not harm her. God intervened and now he has brought you back to me. I love you Maggie. I pledge to never take one day for granted ever again."

Maggie wondered what Jim would think if he knew that she lied? I am responsible for David's death. I hope he can forgive me.

"I want you to come to bed and I will hold you all night. I want you beside me. I missed you so much I thought I would die too. I cannot live without you, Maggie. I am so sorry for all that happened to you. I want to make it all better. I cannot change it but I can make tomorrow a new day for you," he said.

She reached for him and kissed him. "I am so lucky to have you. I longed for you each night. I could only imagine what horror was going through your mind while I was gone. Yes, I am back and I want you beside me every night as long as we both are alive. I love you with all my heart. Thank you for loving me," she said to him. They got ready for bed and as he held her tight, she felt secure in his arms.

# CHAPTER THIRTY-FOUR

Maggie asked Jim to go to the store for a few things they needed before Officer Garret arrived. If she had to answer for what she did to David, she did not want Jim to hear it yet. He reluctantly agreed.

Officer Garret took a seat beside her and told her again how glad he was that she was home. "I think you know how dangerous Walter Mills was and how close you came to being his next victim," he said.

"Yes, I did see how dangerous he was. I knew if I didn't kill him, he would kill me. Will I face charges for what I did to him?" she asked.

"No, Mrs. Taylor, you acted in self-defense. There are no charges against you. I made some serious discoveries about David Adams. I have positive proof that he kidnapped and murdered a seven-year old girl named Candy Burns. Did you know about David, Mrs. Taylor?" he asked.

Maggie held her breath. She needed to tell him the truth. She could not live her life running away. Whatever he decided to do with her she would face. She turned to him and started telling the whole story. "Yes, I did know about David. I want to show you something." She took the yellow hair ribbon out of her pocket and handed it to him.

Maggie walked to the back door and Officer Garret followed her. She stood in front of the swing and remembered Sarah sailing high in the wind. Maggie could almost hear Sarah's laughter as she swung as high as she could go into the air. The hatred for David Adams filled her heart when she thought about the fact that she would never see Sarah again.

Maggie continued, "I accidentally found the hair ribbon in David's trunk that day. He had offered to take some of Sarah's books to the day care for me. I was so shocked when I found the ribbon, that I came back here to sit. I heard a noise behind me. The next thing I remembered, I woke up in that shed tied to the bed. Walter told me I had to forget everyone from my past. I decided to play along with him until I could escape."

She stopped to compose herself and said, "I began to think I would never come back home. I was upset about Sarah and I was almost positive that David took her. If I was going to die, I needed to hear the awful truth about my daughter. I was so upset. Walter had told me I needed to be free from Sarah's killer, and he wanted to know who he was. I told him in desperation. He said he would get him and bring him to the shed. I did not think more about it at that time. I really could not imagine that he could bring him there so easily. Walter went to David's house, drugged him, and brought him to the shed. He bound him with tape and I do admit that I threatened David and he finally did admit what he had done to Sarah."

Maggie shuddered as she remembered looking into David's eyes. She said, "I also knew he had killed other children. I broke down then and crawled into a corner. I was devastated and when I looked around both men were gone. I crept outside in time to see Walter throw David in the well. He was still alive but I did not want to see him die that way. I am to blame for David being there. I admit I wanted to kill him. He took Sarah's days from her and I wanted to take his. I wanted his days for her days. She lost hers. In my heart, I was saying A Day for A Day. I am so sorry. I will accept the blame and punishment for what I did. I do not know if I can live with what I have done." Her tears were flowing and her shoulders shook.

Officer Garret sat beside her until she calmed down a little. "Mrs. Taylor, I hate to upset you further, but I need to discuss a few things with you. I was in David's home and I checked his computer and found that David Adams had been a child molester for a long time and there are facts that I cannot tell you which will prove he was far worse than Walter

229

Mills. He harmed several children. I am obligated to follow this as the law orders. I wish I could tell you that this is the end of your nightmare, but I have to report the circumstances of David Adams' death to my superiors. I will do everything I can to protect you. I understand that David's death was not at your own hands, but you did ask Walter to bring him to the shed. I am so sorry because I do believe that the world is a much better place without these two men. I will go now and let you get some rest. I will be in touch as soon as I have any further developments. I am so glad you are safe at home, Mrs. Taylor."

Officer Garret rose to leave as Jim came in the door. Jim hesitated when he saw Maggie's face.

Officer Garret said to Maggie, "I will go now and let you explain to your husband what we have discussed and I will contact you tomorrow."

He shook Jim's hand and squeezed Maggie's hand.

Jim looked at Maggie who was white as a sheet. He quickly went to her side and tenderly pulled her to him.

"Maggie, what happened to frighten you so much? You don't worry now, I am here, and I will take care of you."

Maggie pulled away. "Jim, I have some things to tell you. I did not tell the truth about what happened to David Adams. I did not want you to know about the awful thing I have done. No matter what happens now, remember that I love you and I will understand how disappointed you will be when I tell you what I did."

Jim tried to pull her back into his arms. "Maggie, you only fought to save your own life. You cannot take any blame for killing Walter Mills. He killed the other girls and David and he would have killed you too. How can you feel any guilt? You came back home to me, and that is all I need to know. I will never let anything harm you again. I could not protect Sarah, and now she is gone. But I have you home now and I cannot live without you."

Maggie looked into his eyes, held her hand up to his face, and brushed his cheek lightly. "Jim, you are the most wonderful man in the whole world. I hate to take the love I see in your eyes away, but I must confess something now before you hear it from someone else. I was desperate. I thought Walter would kill me. I wanted to face Sarah's killer before I died. I knew who took her right before Walter drugged me and took me to the shed. David Adams stopped in to check on me about an hour before that. I had the boxes of books I wanted to donate to the daycare sitting in front of the door, and David offered to drop them off at the daycare for me on his way to the bank."

Maggie took a moment to catch her breath then continued, "I went out to open his trunk so he could load the boxes. I moved a blanket that was lying on the floor and when I shook it, a yellow hair ribbon fell onto the ground. I reached down and picked it up. It was the other yellow ribbon Sarah was wearing the day she disappeared."

Maggie felt the same hatred burning in her soul as she did that day she found the ribbon. She turned back to Jim and continued with her confession.

"I was so shocked that I just stood there when David left. I knew he was the one that killed our daughter. I walked to the back yard. The next thing I remember, I was in that awful room. It was a nightmare when I woke up in a shed locked away from everyone. I tried to be strong. I played the game with Walter because I wanted to survive. I hated him and I hated David even more for taking our daughter from us. I did not care much about my own life. I wanted to make him pay for what he did to Sarah. Walter gave me an opportunity to face David with what he did. I told him to bring him to the shed. David Adams ending up in the well

231

was my fault. After he told me the truth about Sarah, I lost control. When I turned around, Walter had him outside. I saw Walter throw David in the well and I did nothing. I was glad to see him die." Maggie stopped and waited for his reaction.

Maggie saw nothing but love in his eyes.

"Maggie, you did not take life from David. I would have loved you even if you did. I only wish now I could erase the painful memory from your mind. David did deserve to die. You may have been the reason he was there that day, but you did not do anything that any other human being would not have done. You need to take each day and let the memory fade until it no longer haunts you. I do not hate you Maggie. I could never hate any part of you. I love you."

He reached out to her and she fell into his arms.

"Jim, I need your strength now to hold onto. Officer Garret has to report what I did to David. I will have to answer for what I did. That means I may have to go to jail. I will do whatever I have to do. Nothing can hurt as much as knowing what David Adams did to our beautiful Sarah."

She walked a few feet away. "I can face this added terror if I know you do not hate me. I just want you to love me. I wanted Sarah's killer dead. I did not have any right to make that happen. I may face charges and I will only be able to handle this with you beside me. I will only say this once and hope I never have to pay for the words I am about to say, but I really did want him dead at that moment. I do not know if God will punish me. I will wait to see what happens."

Jim held her again and they sat wrapped in each other's arms.

Jim rubbed some of the tension from her shoulders. He kissed the back of her neck and reassured her of his devotion. He asked if she was ready for dinner and they went to the kitchen and fixed a meal. Jim bowed his head and asked for God's strength and wisdom. After they cleaned the kitchen, the phone rang and Maggie's parents asked if they could come over and check on her.

After they arrived, Maggie sat them down and told them of the latest twist in the trial the Taylor families had to bear. Her parents hugged both Maggie and Jim, and told them not to worry, because no court in the world would hold her responsible for David's death. The conversation turned to Sarah.

They remembered the good times and held Maggie as she cried again for the loss of her child. Maggie's father attempted to make her feel better by telling her he would hire a friend who was the best lawyer in the world to defend her if she faced charges. They left around 9:00.

Jim and Maggie sat and enjoyed the quiet time and as they got ready for bed, Maggie went upstairs and stopped at Sarah's room. The minute she stepped into the room, she felt it spin.

The loss of their child brought her to her knees, wailing in raw pain. Jim hurried into the room. He wept with her and finally carried her to their bed and as he covered her, he hoped his wife would find peace as she closed her eyes. In the middle of the night, Maggie screamed in agony as the horror of the last few days replayed in her troubled mind. Jim rocked her as he hung on to her. Maggie settled down and finally fell into an exhausted sleep.

Jim watched her for a while as he lay beside her. He vowed to make sure that Officer Garret did everything he could to make sure that Maggie would not have to face the humiliation for the death of either of the monsters that nearly ruined their lives.

CHAPTER THIRTY-FIVE

Officer Garret went to the office earlier than usual. He wanted to gather all the evidence in this difficult case, and make copies of the chat room conversations on David's computer. He wanted to document the guilt of the crimes David Adam's admitted to the buddies in these chat rooms. He double-checked the DNA information taken from the body of Candy Burns. Officer Garret was determined to do everything in his power to show David for what he was. No jury in this county would blame Maggie Taylor for what she did.

Officer Garret started the file on each of the girls found in the well. The evidence included the blood on the rope from Mary. The shotgun that killed Susan matched the gun found in Walter's car. He went over the photos of the horror found in the shed.

Officer Garret wondered if Maggie could ever forget what she had witnessed in that shed. He wanted to be ready to argue in Maggie's behalf if the case went to the next step. In all his years as an officer of the law, he could not remember a time when he had been tempted to hide the truth. He wanted to do what he could for Maggie. She had endured torture from a mad man and now she must answer to the charges of accessory to David Adam's murder.

The phone rang and Officer Garret reached to get it. He heard Maggie's voice on the other end. He could hear the exhaustion in her voice.

He asked her what he could do for her and listened intently.

"Officer Garret," she said, "I hate to bother you so early. I wanted to know if I can come to the station today."

Before he could ask why, she said, "You said I needed to make an official recorded statement, and I want to do it now. I have to put all this right. I cannot go another day without dealing with what I did. I will do whatever you say. I appreciate what you have done for me. I understand that you are obligated to follow the law and I am willing to confess to the my part in the death of David. I am willing to accept punishment for what I have done."

Her voice broke and he calmly thanked her for calling. "Mrs. Taylor, I do need a recorded statement . I have a meeting with the District Attorney at one o'clock this afternoon. If you can come to my office around three o'clock, I will give you all the details on the next step, if he decides to file charges. Can you come in then?"

"Yes," she said, "Three o'clock will be fine. I must spend some time with my mother today, so I'll ask her to lunch. If anything does come up in the meantime, will you call me? I know I am bothering you too much."

Officer Garret assured her it was not a bother and he promised to call her if things changed. Maggie hung up the phone and walked out to the back deck. As she stood there, she glanced at the bare spot between the hedges along the far end of the yard. It took her breath away thinking back to the day when she went into the woods to look at the maroon flowering bush. She had taken her eyes off Sarah for five minutes, and now she must live with the guilt for the rest of her life. David Adams saw Sarah alone and in those few minutes, he took her, and now Maggie would never see her daughter again.

She lowered her head and fell on her knees with the weight of her sorrow. "If only I could go back," she cried. "I would not go wondering around worrying about a bush. I would have stayed with Sarah. I want to go back. I want to have my daughter again. It is my fault Sarah is gone. I will live with this guilt forever."

The ringing of the phone interrupted her thoughts. She struggled to her feet and headed to the kitchen.

"Maggie, honey, how are you doing? You have been on my mind all morning. I do not want to bother you if you were resting."

Maggie said, "Mom, I am so glad you called. I was getting ready to call you. I miss you. Would you have lunch with me? I would love it."

Her mother quickly told her that nothing would make her happier and she asked Maggie what she should bring.

"You know I love your special strawberry shortcake. Can you make that and bring it? Should I call Gwen to join us? I have neglected her these last few weeks. I guess I have scared everyone away. I don't mean to be so moody. I really need to thank Gwen for all she has meant to me all my life. Do you think she would come?"

Maggie's mother shushed her and said, "Maggie, we are not afraid of you. We just don't want to complicate your life any further. I am sure she would love to come. So I will see you around 12:30, okay?"

"I will look forward to it Mom. I want to tell you that I love you and Daddy so much. Thank you for always being there for us. I can't wait to see you."

Maggie wanted to straighten up a little bit before her mother got there, and was on the way to get the vacuum when she remembered she wanted to call Gwen. Gwen was relieved to hear from her, and was concerned about how tired Maggie sounded.

"Maggie, I wanted to call you so many times. How are you doing? Is there anything I can do for you? Please let me help you Maggie. Can I go to the grocery store for you? Maybe I can come and clean for you. Do you need me to cook some food and bring it so you don't have to cook? Anything, just tell me."

Maggie smiled and said, "Gwen, you have always known exactly what to do for me. No, I do not need you to do for me. I was calling to invite you to lunch with my mother and me. Would you come?"

"Maggie, I would love to come. Do you need me to bring something? I will bring whatever you want."

"You know what, I asked my mother to make my favorite strawberry shortcake. Would you make your green-bean casserole? I always looked forward to it. I want to spend the afternoon with my two favorite people in the whole world. And Gwen, I am so sorry I have pushed you away. Can you forgive me? I did not want to hurt you in any way."

Gwen told her sternly, "Listen, Maggie. I do not need an apology from you. I cannot imagine how you survived all you have been through without losing your mind. I really did not want to bother you. I know you needed some time alone. But I will make the casserole and will see you soon."

Maggie told her that her mother was coming at 12:30 and she would see her then.

Maggie headed for the vacuum again and shut her mind off so she could get her cleaning done. She did a few loads of laundry and made sure she did not dwell on the past few weeks. She told herself that any thoughts of Walter or David would not spoil her day. She wanted to have this one last day of freedom.

Jim sat at his desk and thought about Maggie. He did not want to come back to work and leave her but she insisted. He knew she dealt with most things in her own way. But, Jim was concerned about the haunted gaze he saw in Maggie's eyes when she thought he wasn't looking. He wanted to get these few papers finished before he called to see how she was doing.

At the dinner table the night before, she was reaching for the bread across the table when she saw the red marks on her wrists. Maggie grabbed her arm but tried to hide her feelings. Jim went around behind her chair, wrapped his arms around her, and waited until she relaxed.

Maggie held his hand, looked up at him, and smiled. Jim went back to his chair and they finished their dinner. He told her when they were in bed that he would gently love all the hurt away. She cried in his arms and he held her until she fell asleep. This morning when he left she looked a little more rested.

He forced his thoughts back to his paperwork. As soon as he finished, he called home.

"Maggie, sweetheart, how are you doing? I can come home for lunch if you need me to."

She told him that her mother and Gwen were coming to have lunch with her. He talked a few more minutes and was a little shocked when she told him she had an appointment with Officer Garret at 3:00 that afternoon.

"Why didn't you call me? I will make sure I finish early and I will drive you there."

Maggie thanked him and said she would be ready when he got home. She told him to quit worrying about her and get back to work.

"Maggie, I will never stop worrying about you. You are my life," he said.

"And you are mine," she told him

When Gwen and her mother arrived, she greeted them at the door with tears in her eyes. The three cried and hugged each other tightly. Maggie told them to quit making her cry and led them in the kitchen to sit and eat.

They tried to keep the conversation light. Each of them ate a second piece of the strawberry shortcake. Maggie hugged her mother again and told her that if she could package and sell her shortcake she would be a wealthy woman.

"Maggie, I am so wealthy now. I have a wonderful husband, the best son-in-law a mother could ask for an extra special stepdaughter." She hugged Gwen and asked, "You know you are like my own child, don't you?"

Gwen nodded her head and tearfully told her she was so glad she could be a part of the family.

She hugged Maggie again and said, "And you my dear are the greatest gift a mother could ask for." She did not mean to remind Maggie of Sarah, and could see instantly that is where her thoughts went.

Maggie's composure fell apart. Her body shook as she wept. Her mother took her in her arms and consoled her until she quieted.

"I love you, Mom," Maggie told her. "I am so sorry for putting you through the shame of this evil thing I have done. I am not sorry that David is dead. Do you think that God will punish me for what I have done? If I have to go to jail, I do not want you to suffer. Promise me that you will forgive me. I need to know that you understand."

Maggie's mother assured her that she would love her even more. "Whatever pain you have to face, I will be right by your side. I know that you did not mean for this to happen the way that it did. I do not believe in taking the law into your own hands, but the fact that these two evil men are now dead is a blessing."

Gwen came and hugged them both. She said, "Maggie, you did not kill David. Walter was the one that threw him in the well. There is not one single person on this earth that could ever begin to understand what you have endured. I do not blame you in any way. The fact that you wanted to confront David with what he did to Sarah will be understood by any jury." They sat back down to enjoy the rest of their strawberry shortcake.

# CHAPTER THIRTY-SIX

Officer Garret gathered all of the material from David Adam's hard drive and went to find Alex Smith, his best technician. He explained to him what he was looking for. Alex inserted the hard drive from David's computer into his machine. David had used the initials T. B.B.W. to hide files. After a few failed tries, Alex finally typed in "The Big Bad Wolf." David had personal files for each of his young victims.

As they began to open and read David's own words, their blood ran cold. Neither man could read the account without shivering from the cruelness and madness that was inside the soul of David Adams. David recorded pictures from his cell phone and a detailed description of each young girl that he encountered. His inner most evil thoughts and vivid descriptions were twice as chilling as the ones Officer Garret had read on the computer the first night.

They saw David's inexperience as he documented the first girl's story. He gave the details of date and name and description of each attempt to steal his victims. The first girl was a seven-year old Hispanic child named Cassandra. David had taken a picture of her with his phone and downloaded it on the first page of the file.

David wrote how he approached this young girl while she was playing on a small swing set on the side of the store, while her mother shopped inside. The owners had installed the play area to occupy the children for the convenience of the parents.

David hurried up to her and asked her help to find his car. He promised her an ice cream cone if she would help him. She was frightened of him at first, but the more he coaxed her, the more she trusted him. She finally agreed to go with him. David walked with her through all the lines of cars, and was close to his own vehicle when her mother came out of the store. She ran to them and grabbed Cassandra's hand, and threatened to call the police. David did some fast-talking trying to convince her he did not mean her daughter any harm. She finally quit screaming at him and ran back to her own car.

Even though she didn't realize the full danger her daughter had been in, she held on to Cassandra's hand tighter than usual.

David wrote three whole pages venting his anger at not having his chance with Cassandra and all the things he wanted to do. His anger at the mother was so violent. He did not care that he had no right to the evil thoughts of the child; he just hated the mother for protecting her.

The next file was about another young five-year old girl named Maria. The date was one week later and the town was only three miles from where he had stalked the first girl. This time he did succeed. David went into graphic detail of the pleasure he obtained from molesting the young girl. He displayed no remorse when he boasted how he choked the life from her with a piece of rope he found lying in his trunk. Her fate was a quick death at the hand of this demented child molester.

Alex had a hard time hiding his tears and emotions as they read what David had done to this young beautiful child, and noticed the tears in Officer Garret's eyes as he wiped the tears from his cheeks.

They calmed themselves and continued to read. The list was long and detailed his abduction and murder of thirty more children. David's hunting ground extended to four towns and took place over a span of two years.

Officer Garret remembered the report of Candy Burns and as he looked at her picture, he saw that it definitely was a match to the picture on the fax in his folder.

David's own words verified how he disguised his appearance by putting on several layers of clothing to confuse the authorities by presenting a picture of a larger man. His account also told of the many wigs and facial changes he mastered as he scouted for his victims.

The last account was of Sarah Taylor. David's confession of love for this young innocent girl appalled the two men. They read how David became obsessed with her. As Officer Garret read of the last day of her life, he openly cried for the senseless loss of the only daughter of the Taylor family.

He vowed again within himself to present every incriminating fact to the District Attorney. He hoped he could do enough to save Mrs. Taylor from charges in this case.

Officer Garret gathered all his materials and one by one put them in a box. He was ready for his meeting.

At 12:45, he headed for the office of Samuel Bradford, the District Attorney for the county of Clarkstown, Pa. The receptionist told him to have a seat and she would let Mr. Bradford know he had arrived.

Officer Garret shook Mr. Bradford's hand. He accepted the offer of coffee then began to piece together what the case involved so far.

District Attorney Bradford read the official file from the police report of the charges against Mrs. Maggie Taylor. The official charge was accessory to murder in the case of one David Adams.

Mr. Bradford read the official report of the cause of death. The autopsy showed trauma as the cause of death. Officer Garret agreed to the autopsy report.

Next Mr. Bradford read the account of Mrs. Maggie Taylor being responsible for the abduction and reason for David Adams being in the shed with Walter Mills and Mrs. Taylor.

The report told of the pure facts that the party responsible for Walter Mills knowing the identity and location of David Adams was indeed the defendant, Mrs. Taylor.

Officer Garret also agreed with these facts. Next, the report told of the powder burns on the forehead of David Adams. They both agreed that according to the testimony of Mrs. Taylor, Walter Mills had held the gun to David's forehead as a threat.

The report detailed the conditions of the shed. It detailed that Mrs. Taylor was indeed a victim in this shed against her will. Officer Garret agreed again.

Then Mr. Bradford read and recorded the confession of Maggie Taylor herself to be the party responsible for David Adams'sbduction.

This is when Officer Garret opened the file and for the next half hour, presented the rest of the evidence describing the kidnapping of Sarah Taylor and the discovery of her hidden body two weeks later. He described in detail the knowledge of the identity of the person responsible for her death was David Adams. Next, he showed the hidden files retrieved from the computer taken from the home of David Adams.

Mr. Bradford spent a few minutes reading over the documents showing the character of David Adams. He shook his head at each picture he saw. The tears flowed as he read the admission of depravity from the computer files.

Mr. Bradford stood up and walked around his desk to regain his composure as Officer Garret waited. When he sat back in the chair, Officer Garret handed him the folders on the three victims from the shed.

Mr. Bradford read the files on Shelly, Mary, and Susan. He again shook his head when he looked at the horrible conditions inside this prison where Walter Mills forced the girls to stay.

He read the statement from Mrs. Taylor of the five horror-filled days. He was amazed at her strength as he read the account of how she fought to save her own life by playing along with Walter Mills, and how she needed to confront David Adams.

He read where Mrs. Taylor told of her part in the revelation to Walter of who David was, and how she threatened his life to get his confession that he killed her only child.

Mr. Bradford finally finished and closed the files. He cleared his throat and said to Officer Garret, "I first have to say that I have never in my entire career seen such horrific events happen to one person. I do understand that these charges against Mrs. Taylor are legitimate charges. I recommend we take the case before the grand jury. Let them see the circumstances surrounding the charges and we will deal with the next step if they choose to indict."

Officer Garret stood and said, "I do not want to see Mrs. Taylor go through any more pain and humiliation. However, the only way to clear this matter of David Adams is to let the facts speak for themselves. I hope the grand jury will consider the circumstances Mrs. Taylor was going through at the time of his death. I will wait to hear from you when you have the schedule for the grand jury hearing."

Officer Garret shook his hand and headed back to his office. He needed a few minutes before his meeting with Maggie. He hated to tell her that she was not in the clear yet, but he would promise her to do all he could to help.

Officer Garret straightened up the files and added some notes to research David's background and match his addresses with the missing children, and with the dates and locations of their abductions. He wanted to document each child that was hurt at the hand of this man that Walter Mills was responsible for killing, not Maggie Taylor.

Officer Garret called his assistant to his office and showed him the files from David's computer. "I need you to cross-reference each child's name and address in David Adam's files to the records of missing children from each city. I need to know if every case matches the account written by the hand of David Adams. I want to find every piece of evidence against this child molester. We need to prove that Mrs. Taylor is innocent of the charge as an accessory to his death."

The assistant was shocked to hear that the department was going to charge Mrs. Taylor. "After all she has been through, are you telling me that she will face charges for this evil man's death? I will work extra hours just to make sure she has all our help," he told him.

"Thank you, I am sure Mrs. Taylor will be grateful for our help. Let me know the results of your search as soon as you can," Officer Garret said.

After the assistant left, Officer Garret went out for lunch at the diner across the street. It was his favorite place to eat. All the waitresses knew and liked him. Nancy, one of the older waitresses took his order. She made sure his coffee was just the way he liked it.

"I was reading in the paper about Mrs. Taylor and all that happened to her. Is it true that four people died in the well? What a shame about those poor innocent girls killed by this monster. I am glad that this Mrs. Taylor had the courage to end his pathetic life," Nancy said.

"Yes, it is true that this is a sad case. So many lives were lost. What a tragedy. I hope the ordeal for her is over now. Can I see the menu? What do you recommend today?" he asked her.

"I know the cook made some real good homemade chicken pot pie this morning. So far I have heard no complaints," she said.

"Okay, I guess I could handle homemade chicken pot pie."

Officer Garret spotted the paper lying on the counter. He picked it up and scanned the headlines.

Maggie Taylor's ordeal was the top story, giving the details about the shed and the three girls' death. The reporter hailed Maggie as a hero. It tore at your heart when you read how she lost her only child. The story described how she had the strength to survive after being held captive, and brave enough to end the reign of the madman that kidnapped and tortured her for five days.

As Officer Garret read, he hoped that when the story of David Adams came out, the public would stand behind her and find her not guilty for the death of this child killer.

He finished the article and signaled to Nancy that he was ready for the check.

"How was the potpie?"

"It was great. Be sure to give my compliments to the cook."

Officer Garret headed back to the office and waited for Mrs. Taylor to arrive.

Jim and Maggie arrived at the police station at 2:45. They walked into Officer Garret's office and he asked them to sit. He noticed that Maggie's hands were shaking. She still looked tired and the sadness in her eyes touched him.

"Mrs. Taylor, how are you doing?"

Maggie sighed and said, "I have had better days. I need to know what is happening. I want you to be very honest with me. I am willing to take the blame for what I did. Are they going to charge me?"

He waited a few seconds and said, "Mrs. Taylor, I hate to even tell you this. The law has a way of punishing the wrong people sometimes. If I had my way, no charges would ever be filed against you."

He cleared his throat and continued, "But the District Attorney is going to go to the grand jury with a charge of accessory to murder for the death of David Adams. The story will soon hit the press and I am afraid that this nightmare is not quite over for you. It should take about three weeks to get a date to appear before the grand jury. I promise you that I will gather every single piece of evidence against Walter Mills and David

Adams before that time. I want you to tell me anything you can think of about the days when you were held."

He asked her to wait until he had the tape recorder set up. When he was certain it was working he asked, "May I tape this interview? I will let the grand jury hear what happened in your words."

Maggie said, "Yes, that is fine." She started talking, "I thought a lot about what happened to me while I was locked in the shed. I am not sure how I feel about what took place there. I regret taking the life of Walter. I feared for my own life and I believe with all my heart that he would have killed me sooner or later. He wanted a person to be under his control at all times. He convinced himself he could hold me captive forever and we would have a long, happy life together. I do not remember if I told you this before, but Walter killed his father at the age of twelve. It was self-protection for him and his mother. He was an abused child for the first half of his life. After he lost his father, his mother started to drink and bring men home in front of Walter. He really was searching for someone to love him. The first three girls did not listen and when they panicked, he killed them.

I decided to play his game and tried my best to conform to his will. When I showed any sign of denying him complete devotion, he became angry. He told me I had to forget my other life. I could not forget what happened to Sarah. Minutes before Walter drugged me, I found out that David was the one who took Sarah. When I cried from pain of the memories, Walter told me I had to let go of everyone else. He offered to bring David to me so I could learn the truth directly from him. I did not know if I had any days left."

Maggie's voice broke and the tears rolled down her cheeks. Jim smiled at her and reached for her hand.

Maggie continued, "I needed to hear the truth and when he confessed, the hatred consumed my soul. I told Walter to threaten David. I told David I would have Walter kill him. I told him if he told the truth I would get help for him. He told me he was sick and wanted to stop. I pushed at him until he admitted the truth."

Maggie stopped and lowered her head trying to gain her composure. "He told me he took Sarah because he loved her. He claimed he wanted to keep her forever for his own love child. I was devastated. Walter had it in his mind he had to protect me from any more pain. I remember those seconds when I heard David admit to taking Sarah."

Maggie grabbed her chest and they could see the raw stinging pain that gripped her. She could not speak for a few minutes.

Jim turned to her. "Maggie, you don't have to live through it again. I can see how much it hurts you. What can I do?"

She shook her head and said, "I have to do this. I need to get it out. I will be fine."

She looked back at Officer Garret and he nodded his head for her to go on.

"Walter told David he would kill him for hurting me. I crawled to the corner and thought my heart was going to explode it hurt so badly. When I looked up, I saw Walter dragging David out to the well. David was screaming for my help. I should have helped him. I did not think that Walter would actually throw him in that well alive. It was the worst punishment for any human being. At the time, my hatred was so overwhelming. I feared for my own life. I worked on the broken mirror to use as a weapon. When I ran back in the shed, I wanted Walter dead."

Maggie stood and walked a few steps, then returned to her seat. Officer Garret handed her a box of tissues.

"I wanted to go home. I did not want to die. I did not want to spend the rest of my life in a dirty shed with a crazy man who thought I would be his wife and give him children. I waited for him and I lunged at him. I ended his life. I knew it was him or me. Did I want David to die? In many ways I did."

Maggie held Jim's hand for courage and said, "I do not know if I would have hurt him if Walter hadn't thrown him in the well. I realized I was dealing with two cold-blooded killers. They hurt so many people. I cannot imagine what the children and those innocent young girls suffered. I am so sorry for the families left behind. The mothers and fathers lost their own children. If this has to end with me going to jail, I will go. I am glad that the killings have stopped. I would give my life to bring back my child, and all the others. They really are the innocent ones in all of this."

Officer Garret stopped the recorder. "Mrs. Taylor, I do admire your courage and your strength to come here today. In my judgment, you should not have to suffer any more. I cannot give you back your child. I cannot give you back your peace. I wish I could give you an absolute answer as to where this will end. I know that I will do all I can to the best of my ability. As soon as I hear the court date, I will call you. Please Mrs. Taylor, hold on to your family. I lost my wife and child. I learned how to put one foot in front of the other and I will never stop missing them, but now I can think of them with love. That is what I want for you and your husband. Look ahead to tomorrow and be strong. You will get through it."

Maggie stood and hugged him and said, "I appreciate all you have done for us. We will wait to hear from you. Thank you."

Maggie and Jim headed out to the car. Jim stopped her, put his arms around her, and held her.

"I love you Maggie.  I too admire your strength.  I really do want to protect you from any pain.  I will be here with you no matter what."

Maggie kissed him and wiped the tears from his face.  "You are the most wonderful husband a woman could ask for.  I love you too with all of my heart."

CHAPTER THIRTY-SEVEN

The next few days were hard for Maggie. She tried to concentrate on the good things. She sat on the deck and listened to the birds singing as she drank her morning coffee. Jim returned to work and Maggie promised him she would be fine.

The phone rang on the fourth day after their meeting with Officer Garret. It was a reporter wanting to do an interview. She declined.

When the media showed up at the front door, Maggie drew her blinds and stayed inside the house. The phone rang constantly and Maggie stopped answering it. She did not need reminders of the haunting events she lived through. A week passed and the reporters still came.

One day the answering machine picked up a message from Mrs. Burns, Candy's mother. As Maggie listened, she heard the same pain in her voice that she felt in her own heart. She left a number for Maggie to call. The call left Maggie shaken. She wasn't sure she could talk to her but she finally got the courage to return her phone call.

"Mrs. Burns, this is Maggie Taylor. I got your message and I am so glad you called. I am so sorry for the loss of your daughter."

"Mrs. Taylor, I wasn't sure you would talk to me. I am sure that many people wanting to hear your story fill your days. I wanted to thank you for what you did to David Adams. I am glad he is dead and won't ever be able to hurt another child. I read the awful things you have been through every day in the paper. I would love to meet with you. I received a call to do an interview, but I don't want to answer all the questions. I feel a bond with you since we both lost our daughters to the same man."

Maggie sensed the sorrow in her voice as she continued. "My Candy was the light of my life. I live with the daily guilt for leaving her alone in the mall that day. I understand that your Sarah was missing for two weeks before they found her. I am so lost. I thought if we could meet, it might help us both."

Maggie said, "I would love to meet with you. I feel the same guilt. I blame myself for not staying right beside Sarah. Would you like to have lunch tomorrow?"

Mrs. Burns said, "Yes, that would be fine. Why don't we meet at the Robin's Nest Restaurant on Market Street? Would 12:30 be okay?"

"Yes, I will look forward to seeing you."

When Jim came home, Maggie told him about the phone call. "Maggie I think it would be good for you to be with another Mother who knows the pain you are going through." Maggie knew the pain would follow her every day for the rest of her life.

Maggie arrived at the restaurant and spotted Mrs. Burns right away. She had the same look in her eyes that Maggie was feeling. The women ordered lunch and talked for the next hour. It was as if they had known each other before. It felt so good to talk to someone who had experienced the same emptiness. As they discussed the guilt they both felt for not watching their daughters closer, they assured each other that they should not blame themselves to the point of self-destruction, and it helped both women to start to heal.

Maggie mentioned that they should start a support group for other parents that had lost children at the hand of a child molester and murderers. These two women had found a friend after what life had given them to bear.

The next few days Maggie thought a lot about what they had discussed. She told Jim about forming a group and he said it might help her. The thoughts of how she should contact other parents that lost children to wicked and evil people occupied her mind. Maggie was mulling over a few ideas when one day she got a call from the Sondra Show, a national talk show.

The woman told her that her story touched Sondra and she wanted to do the show on abducted children and what signs to watch for so it would not happen to someone else's child. Maggie was flabbergasted.

Maggie really didn't want to talk about the awful things that happened to her, but she thought that telling her story might help the next parent to be more aware of the danger. If it would protect one child, it would be worth telling the world what she knew firsthand. It only took five minutes for David to take Sarah. The warning signs of what he really was had completely escaped Maggie and Jim.

The woman discussed with Maggie all the details and asked her if they sent a ticket for her, would she be willing to come and do an interview.

Maggie said, "I want to tell my story. I would be honored to come and meet with you."

Maggie called Jim and told him what happened. He was thrilled for Maggie to go. He told her if Tom could handle the office for a few days, he would go with her. Two days later the tickets came in the mail. The note said a car would be waiting for them at the airport. The show arranged for the hotel, and they would call in a few days with the details.

They were to leave in two days. Maggie called Gwen and told her. She was tickled pink for Maggie and told her it would be good for her. She jokingly told her that she would call her a star from this day on.

"Gwen, you are completely silly. I will never be a star. I would like to try to tell other parents to watch for the dangers. Maybe it will be good for Jim and me to get away for a few days. I will call you from the hotel the first night." They talked for a while and Gwen told her to get her an autograph.

253

Maggie worried about what she was going to say, and tried to calm her nerves by cleaning and catching up on things she had neglected.

When they arrived in New York City, the car took them to the hotel. The desk clerk gave them the tickets for the shows and vouchers for the best restaurants in town. Maggie enjoyed seeing the city. It took her back to the days when she traveled with her parents. She loved to see all the different parts of the country.

The car was to pick them up at ten the next morning for the interview for the show. Maggie could not sleep for the excitement. She was ready at 8:30 the next morning and Jim ordered breakfast. Maggie couldn't eat much because of all the butterflies in her stomach.

When they arrived at the studio, the manager Maggie had spoken to, met them and escorted them to the guest room. She called room service and ordered sandwiches and coffee for them.

She introduced herself as Amanda Bowers. Maggie was impressed with the compassion Amanda showed for her ordeal with Walter and David. She asked Maggie quite a few questions and when Maggie became emotional, they took a break.

After the break, Amanda said, "Mrs. Taylor, we do have several other people we would like to include in your story." She told them she would be back in a few minutes and left the room.

Maggie turned to Jim and asked, "I wonder who she is talking about? I did not know that anybody else was to be with us."

Amanda returned with several people and introduced them. The first couple was Alan and Ashlee Harris, the parents of Shelly Harris. The second group was Mary's father, Mr. Hollister, and friends of the family. The third group was Susan's parents, Lou and Nancy Halsley and her two roommates, Vanessa Baldwin and Kathy Bailey.

Maggie was grateful to meet them. She only had seen the three girl's pictures in the photo album Walter gave her. She went to each group and cried with them. They talked with each other for a while. The sadness hung over the room.

Walter Mills took so much from this group. Three young girls would not see a future because of his selfishness and cruelty.

After lunch, they were going to meet Sondra. They would tape the hour-long show the next morning.

Amanda escorted them to a larger room and in a few minutes, Sondra came in and talked with them. Amanda introduced her to the families and Sondra was drawn into the story completely. She could not imagine the law wanting to punish Maggie. Everyone in the room felt the same way. One thing they hoped the show would accomplish was to give support to Maggie for the horror she suffered.

Sondra went over the points she wanted to cover for the show. She urged them to show how they felt and asked them to think about what they would tell the rest of the world things they thought could prevent this from happening to others.

Maggie and Jim went back to the hotel room around 3:00. They were going to meet the rest of the group downstairs in the dining hall that evening. Jim saw Maggie's pain remembering the memories of the days that changed her life.

Maggie felt honored to be chosen to speak, but did not see herself as a hero in any way. She still regretted what happened to Walter and was ashamed of the hatred she felt for David.

Jim told her she should take a nap for a while and he would wake her to dress for dinner. Maggie lay down on the soft bed and was asleep in a few minutes. Her body was still tired from all it endured.

Jim woke her after two hours and she took a shower and looked a little refreshed when they went to the dining hall. The group was a little ill at ease at first, but by the time their meal was finished they relaxed and starting to enjoy talking and getting to know each other. Each of them expressed gratitude to Maggie for ending Walter Mill's killing spree.

As Maggie sat amongst them, she wondered why she survived. She glanced at Jim and was thankful that he did not have to bury her as these families did with their loved ones. Somewhere inside herself, she knew she survived for a reason. She could see the shadow of the loss of each child on each mother's face. She knew she would spend every day for the remainder of her life missing Sarah.

After they finished the meal and all decided to walk for a while. It was a warm, breezy evening and they spent the next hour browsing through the sites of New York City. They said good night and looked forward to the taping the next day.

Maggie and Jim called for the car to go to the studio. Maggie was nervous but confident that others hearing about her ordeal may keep the tragedy from happening to someone else. She asked God to lead her thoughts and words. Jim was proud of her for wanting to share her heartfelt feelings with the world.

Amanda escorted them to a room to wait until the show started. She came to get Jim to seat him in the audience and told Maggie she would be back for her soon. Maggie spent the time alone thinking of Sarah. She wished she could go back. She whispered a small prayer to her and tried to settle her nerves.

She was ready when Amanda came for her. The stage was huge. There were hundreds of people in the audience. She sat down in the chair across from Sondra.

When Sondra asked her how she was doing, her first statement was, "I was just thinking how lucky I am to be alive today. I could have been just another name on a file in a folder on a police officer's desk. God brought me here today for a reason. I want to thank you for doing this show. I have always admired your compassion for everyone, no matter how young or old, no matter what status in life, no matter if you are rich or poor, tragedy has a way of touching us all."

Sondra said, "Thank you for being here Mrs. Taylor. I cannot imagine the things you have endured. I must say I admire you. It took courage for you to stay alive. And as I understand, it took a brave person to fight back and end the life of your kidnapper."

Maggie said, "I do not feel brave. I really did not want to hurt another human being. I think I can say that I have seen the face of evil firsthand. After Walter Mills admitted to me he had already killed three young girls, I knew the only way to escape was to stop him. I will never get over what I did. But I appreciate you having me here to tell my story in case it may help someone else."

Sondra asked her to start at the beginning and try to tell the audience what happened.

Maggie told how she was at the park that day with Sarah. She talked about the two horrible weeks that she and Jim waited just to hear news. She went into detail about wanting to sit in the woods every day in the same spot in case Sarah came back. The hopelessness in her voice caused a hush to fall on the audience. She continued and relived the day that Officer Garret came to their house and told them that the police discovered their daughter's body wrapped in a blanket in the woods. She spoke of the funeral and her utter despair after the final act of burying their child. Sondra called for a break and Maggie asked for a glass of water.

When the break was over, Maggie went on with the story of discovering the hair ribbon in David's trunk. She almost lost her composure when she told of waking up in the shed hours later tied to a bed in a dirty, damp shed. As she talked about Walter, she could hear her voice inside her head, but she felt detached. It was as if she was back in the nightmare again. The degradation she felt from Walter Mills was humiliating to hear. The audience listened intently to the awful details of a woman held captive by such a demented man.

When Maggie told of seeing the photo album and the picture of the other girls, Sondra stated that the parents and friends of these young girls would be interviewed after the next break.

The chairs were set up and the whole group gathered around on the stage. One by one, they stated their names. Sondra expressed her sympathy for each family. Each one thanked Maggie for what she did. They were all grateful that Walter Mills could never harm another young girl.

Maggie continued the story, "I wanted to face my daughter's killer. I desperately needed to face him before my life ended. Walter told me about killing his own father at the age of twelve. He told me I had to see David Adams face-to-face, so I could forget the hatred and have nothing of my old life in the way of our happiness."

Maggie openly sobbed when she went over the last few hours in the shed. She spoke of telling Walter to hold the gun to David's head. She told of how they threatened him and how he finally admitted that he took Sarah. Maggie wanted all to know that she offered to get help for David. She emphasized there were no intentions of actually killing him. She told about her loss of control and hearing Walter drag David out the door.

"I crept outside and heard David scream as Walter threw him in the well. At this point, my horror got worse. I knew Walter was completely

258

capable of killing me. I felt as though I would never be free again. There would be no escape. I did not stop to think. I found the mirror and used it as a weapon and Walter's life ended when I stabbed him in the heart."

No one spoke or moved for a few seconds. All eyes were wet with tears.

Sondra finally found her voice and said, "Mrs. Taylor, I can speak for everyone here. Our hearts go out to you. No person should have to go through what you have described. You are in the prayers of each of us. We will be right back."

After the break Sondra said, "Mrs. Taylor, I understand that you want to say something to this audience."

Maggie started by saying, "I was watching a news cast the other day where a family lost a mother and five children in a fire The interview included an eight year old boy. He attended the same school with the one of the boys who died. He spoke of how badly he and the other boys had treated him. He said the boy loved to play ball but none of the boys liked him so they wouldn't let him play. As he wiped his eyes, he told how sorry he was now for treating him that way. Now he was gone, and they could never change what they did. I thought to myself, hopefully this poor young boy learned a lesson about how we treat others. After we are mean to another person, sometimes we do not get a second chance.

Walter talked about how he hated his father. I could see the pain when he told how many times him and his mother went to the hospital. Walter killed his father during one of the worst beatings of his life. This does something to a young boy. His parents did not show him love and he did not know how to act with anyone else. He was just weird to the other kids in school. No one befriended him. No one helped him. He was an outcast in society. I would never excuse what this man did. He had no right to take anyone's life. I also wonder if someone had loved

259

him along the way in his life, if he would have been different. Are we mindful of how we treat other people?"

Maggie continued, "It has been proven that these kind of people search for love in a demented way. They never knew normal. I examined my own character while I was in the shed. I remember stories before of children abducted and murdered. I listened but I forgot it too quickly. Each of those children had parents. A molester like David Adams destroyed each of these homes. I had the pleasure of meeting Mrs. Burns a few days ago. David Adams abducted and murdered her daughter, Candy."

Sondra turned to Mrs. Burns and nodded for her to tell her story. "I was in the mall with my daughter and left her sitting at a table eating ice cream while I went to the pharmacy. There were hundreds of people at the mall that day. When I returned I did not see Candy. The authorities searched everywhere for her. Then two hours later, I viewed the security tapes and I saw a strange man leading my daughter out the door. The police found her body a few hours later. The next time each of us are at the mall, we could be on the lookout for any single man that approaches a child. Even if we are wrong, we could question that man and give that child a chance to tell who he is. These kids do not know how to fear a stranger. Their trust is too quick. If someone had been paying attention that day, they may have saved Candy's life."

Maggie squeezed Mrs. Burns' hand and said, "My husband and I trusted our daughter to go with David Adams to the park alone. Now I wished I'd confronted him with why a single man wants to spend afternoons with my six- year-old daughter. Maybe if I had warned him to stay away from her, she would be alive today. Maybe David would have thought twice about harming anyone's child. We are all too trusting. The world we live in is full of evil people."

Maggie said, "I got a second chance at life. Walter Mills abducted Shelly in a parking lot at a movie theater. Did someone take the time to make sure that a sixteen-year-old girl made it to her car? Walter told me it was easy to take someone. He said one minute they are there, and the next minute they are gone. He told me the police would never find out who did it. He laughed when he told me that there was not a single person that knew where the shed was and that he took me. I think if each one of us becomes more aware, especially with children, maybe we can stop some of the abductions."

She stopped for a minute and added, "Sondra I want to add one last thought. I believe in the power of prayer. If each one of us would pay attention to all the troubles and tragedies that surround us, God would hear. We are all in too much of a hurry. Not one of us count our blessings, as we should. I will from this day forward."

Sondra turned to Maggie, "And I understand that you may be facing charges for what happened with David Adams. They may charge you with accessory to murder. Is that true?"

Maggie said, "Yes, the case should be given to the grand jury within the next three weeks."

Sondra said to her, "Mrs. Taylor, believe me when I tell you that you will be in my prayers and I am sure the audience will join me in that statement. I know this was hard for you to do today. I have to admit you opened my eyes a little and I am sure everyone else will be more aware of what we talked about today. Thank you for coming and telling your story."

After the show ended, the group spent some time together and prepared to leave. Each person made sure they had Sondra's autograph. Maggie was impressed with the compassion of everyone involved with the show. Maggie got each of the other family's addresses and phone numbers and they promised to stay in touch.

On the way back home, Maggie was quiet in the car. Jim asked her if everything was okay.

"I am afraid I may have the worst of this to face. If I am charged for what I did, I will hate being locked up again. It is a terrible feeling not being able to walk outside to see the sun whenever you want. When Walter left me locked in the shed, I dreamed of the day when I could be free again. Now, will I ever be free? I am so sorry for what I put you through, Jim. I wish I could undo the choices I made. I was so shocked to find myself hating someone so much that I wanted to hurt them. I never want to feel that again."

Jim said, "Maggie no one would ever blame you for hating David. He took our daughter. I wanted to kill him myself. If I would have had the chance, I know I would have strangled him with my own hands. No, it is not right, but I understand. You did not hurt David Adams. Walter was guilty, but you are not. We will face this together and I know you will not be guilty of any wrongdoing. I love you Maggie. I want you to remember that. Now, let's stop for dinner at the little cafe we passed before. I am starved and you need to eat so you can get back to the beautiful wife I married. You are just too thin."

Maggie smiled and gently hit him on the arm. "You just want me fat and ugly so no one else will notice me. I know where you are going with this. But beware, Mr. Taylor, I will find me a new husband if you are not careful." It was good to joke with each other again.

# CHAPTER THIRTY-EIGHT

Officer Garret received word from the grand jury that he was to appear before them in the case of Mrs. Maggie Taylor on Friday at 11:00 a.m. He had four days to prepare. He called Mr. Taylor at his office to let him know. He assured him that as soon as he knew the verdict, he would call him immediately. Jim said he would tell Maggie and they would be waiting to hear what the grand jury decided.

Officer Garret said a quick prayer for the Taylor's and went to find his assistant to make sure all the paper work was in order.

When Jim got home, he found Maggie working in the back yard in her flowerbed. She was pulling the weeds as she used to do. He did see a shadow come over her features sometimes, but they talked more about Sarah and even discussed the possibility of having another baby. He told her he was going to change and would help her with the digging. They spent an hour working in the yard, and felt more relaxed than they had for a long time. Healing was starting for them both.

Maggie prepared dinner and they sat down to eat. Jim said, "Maggie, I heard from Officer Garret. He has an appointment to appear before the grand jury on Friday. "

"I will be so glad that this will soon be over. Then I can move on, even if it means being put in prison for what I did."

On Friday morning, Officer Garret entered the grand jury room and took a seat in the front row. The bailiff called him to the podium.

It took almost one hour for him to cover all the material in his files. He did his best to explain all the details, and passed many pictures for the jury to observe. After he was finished, he thanked the members of the grand jury and left. He felt good, and he saw compassion on each of the faces of the men and women in the room as he told all that Maggie suffered at the hands of Walter Mills and David Adams.

The officer of the court told him the grand jury's decision could come as early as Monday.

Officer Garret went back to his office and filed the evidence. He hoped to close this case in a matter of days. The only thing he kept was a small bag. He placed it inside his top drawer and locked it. He wanted to make sure it was safe.

He called Jim and told him that the grand jury would reach a decision by Monday and assured him that as soon as he heard any news, he would call him.

Maggie tried not to think about it all weekend. Jim wanted to have a barbecue on Sunday and invite his parents, Maggie's parents, and Tom and Gwen.

Maggie was worried about spending time with Jill again. When Jill arrived, she hugged Maggie and told her that she missed Sarah, but she thought of her in heaven, and that made her happy. Jill was good therapy for Maggie.

Maggie sensed a peace growing in her heart, and she knew that time would heal. Having a loving family and friends around was definitely just what she needed.

The members of the grand jury room reviewed each case. The first one was Mrs. Maggie Taylor and the charge was for accessory to the murder of David Adams. The foreman asked if anyone had questions before they took a vote.

One of the women raised her hand. "I wanted to be sure about one fact. Is it true that David Adams was thrown in the well by Walter Mills?"

The foreman read the transcript of the police report that confirmed that Walter Mills did indeed throw David Adams into the well.

He asked, "Any other questions? If not, then we will take a vote."

Each juror voted and handed the ballots to the foreman. All twelve of the jurors agreed that the evidence of this case was not against Mrs. Maggie Taylor, but against Walter Mills for the murder of David Adams. Since Walter Mills was no longer alive, they dismissed all charges against Maggie Taylor and officially closed the case.

Monday morning, the rain started coming down around 9:00. Maggie tried to keep herself busy. She was so restless she finally called Gwen and asked her if she would like to go to lunch with her. Gwen said she would love to, so they spent the afternoon eating and shopping. Gwen noticed that Maggie had laughed several times and she hugged her every chance she got all day.

Jim arrived home about 4:30. After they ate the fried chicken Maggie had prepared they went out to the deck to relax and enjoy the evening breeze. A few minutes later, the phone rang.

Jim answered it, and turned to Maggie. "That was Officer Garret. He is going to stop by in a half hour. Whatever the news is, remember that I am right here with you."

Maggie asked, "Did he give any indication what the grand jury decided?"

Jim said, "No, he said he would wait to tell us in person."

Jim walked to Maggie and held her close. He wanted her to know that whatever she needed from him, he was there. Maggie tried not to show her fear, but Jim could feel her hands shake as he held them.

When Officer Garret arrived, Jim asked him if he would like some lemonade, and told him that Maggie was on the back deck. "I will bring your drink. Please have a seat."

When Jim returned Officer Garret said, "I will not drag this out any longer. I did receive official notice today that the grand jury has reached a decision. Mrs. Taylor, they find no reason to charge you of any crime. They have dismissed all the charges against you. From this day on, you are free."

Jim thanked him. Maggie rose to her feet. Her eyes filled with tears as she hugged Officer Garret and thanked him for all he had done for her.

"There is one more thing I have to do," Officer Garret said. "I wanted to give you back something that was taken from you both. I am sure you will be pleased."

He took a small bag out of his pocket. He said, "The officers found these wedding rings on the ground. Your husband told me how upset you were when you told him that Walter took them off your finger and threw them."

Officer Garret walked over to Jim and placed the rings in his hand. "Mr. Taylor, I am sure you would like to place these rings on your wife's hand."

Jim remembered the day he bought the rings. He looked at every set before he chose the ones now in his hands. They suited Maggie perfectly and he was glad to have them back. Jim reached for Maggie's hand. She watched as Jim slipped the rings back on her finger.

It was as though time stood still for just a moment. A new day was here. For Maggie it was a new beginning, and she was relieved to have her freedom. The tragedy of losing Sarah and facing David Adams and Walter Mills had changed Maggie. She would miss her daughter every second of every day until she met her in heaven.

Maggie knew that she would heal a little more each day. She had learned a lesson, she would not take her husband, or her family, or her best friends for granted again. She would embrace each new blessing with a renewed gratitude.

Maggie knew she had to put one foot in front of the other each day, and even though she feared the pain, she knew that God was there with her to help her through.

The next day would be a new start to a new chapter in her life.

## AUTHOR PAGE

Donna Lee Comer was born and raised in Pennsylvania, residing in Red Lion, Pa.

Donna's family and her church play an important part in her life. She has been married for forty years and has four children and six grandchildren. Donna and her husband, Robert, both have ten brothers and sisters. They are surrounded by many loving relatives.

She has read and loved books since grade school. This is her first novel, and she is currently working on her second one.

Made in the USA
Charleston, SC
21 March 2011